FAIRLIGHT BOOKS

LOU GILMOND

The Tale of Senyor Rodriguez

Fairlight Books - Oxford

Fairlight Books
Prama House, 267 Banbury Road
Oxford OX2 7HT

First published 2016 in Great Britain by Fairlight Books

ISBN 978-1-912054-05-3
Copyright © Lou Gilmond 2016

Cover illustration by Rui Ricardo - www.folioart.co.uk
Printed and bound in Great Britain by Clays Ltd

A CIP catalogue record for this book is available from the British Library

Find out more about Fairlight Books at
www.Fairlightbooks.com

To Dennis Hamley
with thanks from all of us

Mallorca, 1964

Chapter I

I can still remember seeing *Ca'n Mola* that first time. It was Isabella who pointed it out. She was standing by her pool with a Bellini in one hand and the sound of the sea was echoing on the wall behind us. Suddenly I saw it, the house of the late Senyor Rodriguez. It was wedged into the hillside a hundred yards further up.

In front of the house was an olive tree with a little stone wall around it, and there looked to be a couple of outbuildings or *casitas* to the side. The estate was surrounded by an orchard of almond trees, from the edge of the cliff, up around both sides of the house and over to the top of the hill.

I closed my eyes and thought of my house back in England, with its pebble-dashed walls and Formica worktops. I thought of my wife in her single bed looking across the room at my empty one. Isabella coughed, so I opened my eyes in case she should see that I had them shut and know at once I was a madman.

'*Allora* ... Do you see it?' She turned to me and smiled.

'Of course. I do apologise.'

'It's easy to miss,' she said.

Isabella was Italian, and so beautiful it was all I could do not to just stare and stare.

'It's the same colour as the hillside isn't it? That's why I didn't see it.'

'Yes, you are right, I suppose.'

We both gazed up at the house in silence for a minute, each of us uncertain what to say, having only just met. It was a *finca* of middling size, not grand enough for a king, but certainly big enough for a knave, such as myself.

Isabella looked at me shyly, as if calculating whether to say what was on her mind.

'How long have you taken it for, Mr Sebastian?'

'Until the end of the summer.'

'And do you know its story?'

I was curious as to what she might mean. Perhaps she knew details of the tragedy that had befallen the late Senyor Rodriguez, the last owner of the farmhouse.

'Miss Ferretti, I know nothing about the place,' I said. I studied her frown while she continued to look up at the *finca*, but then she brightened and turned to me.

'How wonderful, Mr Sebastian. What fun neighbours we shall be. I can't wait to tell Marta of your arrival. It's so early in the season. The rest of the villas are all empty.'

'It does feel deserted, doesn't it?'

I looked out at the sea. You could just see the fishermen's cottages and trawlers jutting out from the bottom of the cliffs, but there wasn't a single pleasure boat yet to be seen going out across the blue from the resorts.

'And you drove straight down from England, Mr Sebastian?'

'Yes. I stopped in Paris overnight,' I lied.

At the mention of Paris, Isabella clapped her hands together like a small child.

'How wonderful. Would you like a Bellini?'

'That's kind, but—'

'Yes, do! And stay... tell me of Paris! Then afterwards we can go up to your *finca*. How wonderful to have a neighbour at last.'

I waited by the pool as she went into the house. When she returned she had pulled a shirt over her camisole and was holding a drink in one hand for me and dragging a chair out

2

with the other.

'I'm so sorry about your magazine,' I said, and we watched it floating in the pool.

When I first arrived I'd walked onto her terrace thinking the house to be shut up like all the rest. I hadn't expected Isabella to be sitting on a chair by the pool with a magazine in her lap. She had been bending over and trailing her fingers in the still blue water. I think I gave her quite a fright. She'd screamed and her magazine had slipped into the pool.

Isabella handed me the Bellini and blew a little air out through her cheeks in a way I found to be quite endearing. It was the first of many habits that I was soon to become obsessed with.

'It's only the *American Vogue*,' she said. 'They don't really understand fashion.'

I looked at the house up on the clifftop again. So that was *Ca'n Mola*. What a find it had been. My entire plan of rescue rested upon that house.

'Is it what you expected?' she asked, following my gaze.

'I don't know. The agent only told me that it was a farmhouse, close to the sea.'

Isabella looked shocked. 'And you took it on the basis of that? You knew nothing else?'

'Only that it's the house of the late Senyor Rodriguez.'

'Ah, yes,' said Isabella, and she looked away from the hillside as if in respect to the dead. 'That is something everyone knows.'

I knew then that there must have been some scandal to the poor chap's demise. The agent in Madrid had been evasive as hell about it, but then it had been one of those 'no questions asked and none shall be answered' situations, and that had suited me down to the ground.

Evidently bored with discussing the house, Isabella tugged me by the sleeve.

'Tell me how Paris is.' She said it as if Paris were a person with whom she was acquainted, rather than a city of a few million people.

So I drank my Bellini and told her of the little café theatres I had been to in the fifth arrondissement full of student intellectuals plotting to overthrow the government. Then I saw that I was entertaining her, so I went on and told her of the beatniks I had met who smoked marijuana all day.

'How wonderful,' she said. 'That isn't the Paris I know at all. I must go back and be more adventurous.' She paused for a short time. 'And your wife?' she asked casually. 'Will she be joining you?'

I reassured Isabella that my wife would come as soon as she was done with her bridge season and then, in order quickly to bring that part of the conversation to a close (but also because my Bellini was finished and another didn't seem to be in the offing), I started to make my excuses and suggest it was time I got on with the final leg of my journey.

So, there it is. That was how I first came to meet Isabella, and on the very same day saw the house of the late Senyor Rodriguez. As we walked down the steps from her terrace to the end of the street I suddenly thought of my wife. Her face was all fuzzy and I couldn't quite catch how it went again. It was as if she was drawn in the invisible ink children use for fun, and her image was fading away in the bright Spanish sunshine. A pang of guilt passed through me, but then I looked at Isabella running her fingers along the bonnet of my Jag...

Oh, what a very real and living thing Isabella seemed in comparison to my wife. Not that I should call her a thing. If she was a thing, she was a delightful thing, a luscious thing, a *covetable* thing. I had only just met her, but already I was taken. I would say she was young, just starting out in life – twenty-one perhaps, or twenty-two – which meant there were at least as many years between us.

She was of average height, with hair that was lighter than you would expect for an Italian – mousy brown, rather than raven. Her accent was wondrously lilting, making our dull English words sound like an aria on her tongue, and her voice was surprisingly deep. If my father were alive he would have been transfixed by her.

What a stroke of luck; the perfect house to hide out in, here on the edge of Europe, with a beautiful young neighbour. I smiled for the first time in I don't know how long. For once, something was going my way.

'Why are you smiling, Mr Sebastian?'

'Oh, I don't know. That holiday feeling I suppose.'

I looked at the long row of villas gazing out to sea with their white walls and swimming pools of turquoise. Isabella's house was the last of them. How she had screamed when I had stalked onto her terrace unannounced.

'*Cosa vuole, Signore*?' she had said, her magazine plunging in for its swim.

I thought at the time that it was all over for me: the police would be called; the game would be up.

'I'm sorry, I'm so very sorry,' I had said, backing away, my hands held up in defence. 'Would you speak English?'

'Are you lost?' she had asked, her voice softening from its hysterical pitch. I nodded and offered up my scrawled directions as a peace offering.

'There is another house, *Signore*, a little further along.'

'I'm sorry I scared you. I thought this was it. I'm very tired from the drive down from England, you see.'

Now that was all over, Isabella and I were the best of friends. In the space of what could only be twenty minutes at the most. It happens that way sometimes. A fright, a nervous relief of laughter, and then friendship.

'Come on,' she said to me, 'or the sun will be setting before we get there.'

It was hard, during that first encounter, to keep up a normal disposition, for at that time I felt like a bottle of champagne that someone has shaken, its cork stealthily rising a quarter of an inch at a time.

The trouble was I'd been scared for too many months. I'm not a very good criminal, I don't have the constitution for it, and it had never been any real intention of mine to become one in the first place. I was born from a theft, that's the trouble. I am half English on my father's side. He sold machine parts across the Americas. I have his nervous temperament and thick, clumsy fingers.

Mother was the daughter of a Venezuelan bandit who my father stole away at great risk to his person and brought back to London. She died when I was young. There is little of her left in me – just my unnaturally dark eyes, too dark for an Englishman, and the hint of a Latin tongue which I can't seem to shake off.

Even though she is long gone, I sometimes still dream of her speaking kind words to me in Spanish. I hear her voice and feel the soft touch of her hand on my cheek. When I waken from a dream like that I always imagine I am back in my little box room in Golders' Green with my mother's dark, dark eyes staring down at me – but then I waken for real and see it is nothing but a couple of chinks in the blackout curtains, with the suburban streetlights beyond, and I hear my wife's gentle snores coming from the other side of the room. Then I remember the second mortgage I have taken without her knowing, the signature of her father which I forged as guarantor, and I contemplate going to the window and throwing myself down onto the tarmac.

'I'm afraid you can't drive it up there.' Isabella shook her head. 'Not a chance. The track gets narrow after the bend.'

That was a problem. It would have been better to have the car out of sight. It was an XK150 Roadster, with the '58 engine. A stupid car to have taken, but I hadn't been able to resist it when I'd seen it sitting there in Madrid with the key in the engine.

Isabella laughed as I pulled my one and only suitcase out of the boot.

'You don't have much with you.'

'No, there isn't much, is there?'

I handed her my hat.

As we strolled up the track the sea was stretched out to the left of us. The sun was by now sitting low in the sky and starting to catch the edges of the water with pink.

'You must come down for drinks sometime, Mr Sebastian, and meet Marta.'

'Is she Italian too?'

'No. She's from... *Beh...* I can't remember. Belgium perhaps?'

'Why didn't you stay in one of the resorts?'

As I asked the question I realised I was being rude. Isabella wouldn't fit in there with the hordes of English and street stalls crammed high with straw donkeys and dolls of Spanish dancing girls.

'Or over in the city?' I said quickly.

Isabella paused to think before she answered, and I saw at once she was hiding something. It takes a liar to know a liar.

'Marta thought it would be nice to be out in the countryside. She's training to be a zoologist.' Then she added, as if it would convince me she was telling the truth, but only told me that she wasn't, 'And the city is so crowded with Americans at the moment, isn't it?'

The path circuited an enormous boulder which jutted out from the cliff, and Isabella started to tell me about the parties she'd been to in the city and the villages around the island.

'Do you know they hang colourful ribbons and dance beneath them? And they serve champagne in water tumblers. It's wonderful.'

As she finished, we came out from behind the boulder to see that the path climbed up between the cliff edge and a low dry stone wall which was capped with shrubbery, and then, a little further on, we saw on our right two ancient stone posts with a dusty driveway between.

The remnants of its rusted iron gates hung open against

the banked up boundary wall. We took the turning, passed through an assortment of mimosa trees and myrtle bushes dotted with tall palms, and then there before us was the *finca*.

The sun was setting, turning the stones on the path around us to the colour of butterscotch, and suddenly I felt a little unsteady.

'Oh! Isn't it charming?' Isabella exclaimed.

After all my rushing about, after all the terror and the panic, here I was at last. I wasn't sure if this was to be the place of my final stand or whether I was going to come up with some brilliant scheme and rise like a phoenix from the ashes. I thought once again of my wife back home. I wondered what she might really be doing. If she had given up the chase by now I guessed that she would be sitting down to tea with the evening papers and Henry, our dog. I hadn't once had the urge to ring her since I'd fled. It would have been too dangerous, but now I felt a yearning to hear her voice and know that she was coping with it all.

'Are you all right, Mr Sebastian?'

'Yes, yes. I think I'm a little tired from the journey.'

'It's probably the Bellini. Are you unaccustomed to drinking in the afternoon?'

I reassured her on that point and told myself, *sotte voce*, to pull it together.

Isabella was right, the *finca* was charming. In the courtyard was a table and chairs beneath a flower-covered pergola, and the building itself had a rustic appeal with its ochre stone walls, dark wooden doors framed in white, and corrugated roof. My wife would definitely have hated every inch of the place.

There was a well in the centre of the courtyard. Isabella went over and peered down it.

'Marta would find this fascinating. So quaint and traditional. Gosh, look at the time. Well, I'd better leave you to it.'

'Won't you come in?' I said, struggling to keep the

disappointment from my voice.

Isabella hesitated. 'In the village, they say it's been left exactly as it was found on the day Senyor Rodriguez died.'

'Yes, I believe that's true. The agent said the same.'

'Why would they do that?'

'Some complication of the will, I understand.'

Isabella frowned and toyed with the chain of the well. 'What sort of complication?'

I shrugged. 'A family squabble over the assets. Nothing's to be touched or sold until it's resolved.'

'How long will it take?'

'The agent thought I'd be clear until the end of the summer. You know how long these legal processes can take, particularly over here. The rent was very reasonable.'

Isabella smiled and came towards me, her hand outstretched.

'Well, do come for supper one evening, Mr Sebastian.'

It's difficult to explain why, but I felt a horror knowing that she was about to leave and that I was to be alone once more.

I looked around. I'm not a cowardly man, but my nerves were in a delicate state after all that had happened. I had a sudden feeling that the late Senyor Rodriguez might be hanging about and watching us. I saw a hint of him amongst the myrtle bushes and then I genuinely thought I caught a vision of him, standing bold as brass beside the *casita*. I shook my head, but the image didn't go away. He, or at least his ghost, was watching us, an old man with stubble and a panama hat. He stood square at his shoulders and his hands were behind his back. He was smartly dressed to my eye, in a colonial suit, and he carried himself with a certain dignity, as does a rogue or a gentleman who has seen the world and largely laughed at it. It was just the Bellini of course.

'Don't you want to see the house?' I said hurriedly.

'Some other time,' replied Isabella, and then she said, 'It is romantic, isn't it? But I don't think I could cope without the modern conveniences.' And with a handshake and a cheery 'Ciao!' she was gone before I knew it.

I looked around nervously to see if the late Senyor Rodriguez really was there, but there was nothing, just the whisper and rustle of palm trees as they swayed in the wind.

I took a deep breath and let myself into the house.

What I found surprised me considerably and I looked around in confusion and delight. It was such a surprise that both Isabella and my vision of the ghost of Rodriguez were chased from my mind.

From the agent's description, I'd been expecting a simple cottage with a few pieces of furniture and a personal item or two, but in fact the house was furnished in a style I'd never had the good fortune to reside in before. Now I understood why the man had rattled on about inventories and dusting for so long.

The place reminded me of one of those stately homes opened to the public where the rooms are cordoned off and one must stretch one's top half over the red rope and crane one's neck just to see properly.

It was a lot to take in, so I resolved to leave my case by the front door and make a thorough investigation, starting from the bottom of the house and working my way to the top. This is what I discovered.

Firstly, there were a number of expensive-looking and tasteful possessions (antique furniture, ancient artefacts, books, objets d'art, and so on).

In the living room there were a lot of books, and they were all arranged by subject matter and then by height. Rodriguez must have been a man of linguistic talent, since the language of the book was of no significance – works of Spanish, English, German, and Italian were all intermingled as though each language was of equal comprehensibility to the next. There were books on art, literature, Egyptology, modern warfare, psychology, astronomy, even applied physics.

Secondly, I discovered that the late Rodriguez had evidently been an avid collector of art. He mostly liked oil paintings with passionate explosions of colour and movement. Nature, the female form, and death (occasionally of the bovine variety) featured heavily.

I wondered if perhaps the books and art were just for show, but then I discovered a study down a little corridor. In it was a desk, on which sat a Royal Aristocrat typewriter with its plastic blue case and white keys. Now, the typewriter's keys were dusty but all around the bookcases were piled high with essays devoted to the enhancement of thinking on the subjects of psychology, art and literature, obviously typed by the late gentleman himself on that very machine. When I realised how mistaken I was, my opinion of Rodriguez rose all the higher for it. He had obviously been a great intellect.

I stopped to look through a shelf devoted to the works of Charles Baudelaire, but I found the poems rather depressing and gave up.

At the top of the house was Rodriguez's bedroom, simply furnished with a bed, a dresser, and some wardrobes still containing his suits of white linen. By the window was a telescope pointing out to sea and on the floor were sketches of the night sky with notes of the elevations and luminescence of certain stars and planets as tracked over many months.

There were clippings, too, from the papers, which had faded yellow where the light from the window had fallen upon them. There was one with a picture of Gagarin's Vostok 1 with what looked to be a set of co-ordinates scrawled in the margin. Poor Rodriguez, all fired up about space and not living to see whether we make it or not.

How excited it made me as I scooped the papers into a pile – to think I would live amongst all this finery and cleverness. It was a world away from my 1930s semi in Tunbridge Wells with the woodblock prints of antelopes and wildebeest on the walls, purchased from Woolworth's at a shilling a pair. Should I ever go back to my wife how surprised she will be when I talk of my telescope through which I gazed at the moon, and of my art collection. Well, mine by rental that is, which definitely still counts as 'mine' as far as I'm concerned.

Back downstairs, I poked around the kitchen and opened the black metal stove to see how it might be fuelled, but it was behind the house that I found the cherry on the cake.

Built into the hillside was a cellar with a collection of wine that made my head swim. *Premier crus* lay happily beside *vins de pays* (it made me think of my bumbling father lying beside his stolen Criollo princess), and all the wine-growing nations of Europe were represented.

Further into the cellar some legs of ham swung about when I knocked my head against them, and there was a shelf lined with six large rounds of cheese with *manchego* stamped on the rind.

There were many other things in the house which I haven't even begun to describe (such as a collection of recordings from symphony orchestras around the world) but I'm sure that's enough already. There seemed no doubt that the late Senyor Rodriguez had been an intellectual giant. He had been an expert in psychology, literature and astronomy, a talented linguist, an accomplished chef, a connoisseur of wine, quite clearly a man of exquisite tastes for the beaux arts, and with a love of classical music.

In short I determined that the late Senyor Rodriguez was everything a man could hope to be and that I, with my pompous boast of a little Latin and some childhood Spanish, was a shadow in comparison. If only I had his talents, his taste, his application to learning and the pursuit of knowledge. In fact, if I had been just half the man that Senyor Rodriguez had been, I wouldn't be in the mess I was in today.

With that thought I carried my suitcase upstairs, lifted some of the late gentleman's clothes from the wardrobe, and made space for my own. Then I made for the cellar from which I took the oldest and dustiest bottle I could find. I spread a red cloth, which I had found in a drawer in the dining room, over the courtyard table and placed the wine along with some roughly cut cheese upon it. The agent had instructed me, quite strictly, that I was not to touch the wine, since the assets of the house must remain frozen until the probate was granted. But there were so many of them! Surely no one would miss a bottle or two?

I wound up Senyor Rodriguez's old-fashioned gramophone, picked a book at random from his shelves, and sat down to my supper as the overture from *Cosi Fan Tutti* floated out to me and thoughts of Isabella filled my head. The book was entitled *First Steps in Astronomy* and by the light of the living room window I began to read. Tomorrow, I thought. Tomorrow I shall start my journey to recovery in a calm and considered fashion, and then I shall show them all.

Chapter II

The next morning I woke in panic and sat up. Somewhere along the way I'd made a terrible mistake. My heart beat nineteen to the dozen and a cold sweat broke out on my forehead even though the room was quite warm. Sunlight was streaming in through a small window onto slatted wardrobes and a white coverlet. It was what was in those wardrobes, those white linen suits, that made me remember.

I was in the bedroom of the late Senyor Rodriguez and my awful mistake was that I'd told my neighbour, Isabella Ferretti, my real name: Thomas Sebastian.

I groaned and lay back on the bed. What an absolute clot. I was supposed to be travelling as Mr Waddington – at least, that was the name I had used to secure the house. When I'd stormed unannounced onto Isabella's terrace she'd been so scared, and I had been so desperately trying to reassure her that I was no villain (which obviously wasn't true), that I clean forgot.

It was too late to change it now. I would just have to make sure the agent and Isabella never met, and I'd also have to think of an excuse why Isabella and her friend, Marta, should not mention my name to anyone. What an annoying complication, particularly when I had wanted everything to be simple and calm so I could have the space to figure a way out of this mess.

Never mind. It wasn't the worse disaster that could have

befallen me. I let out a sigh. From where I was, I could see the blue of the sky and the grey stone corners of one of the *casitas*.

Just think only two days ago I'd been at the end of my tether, wondering what to do. In the space of three months I'd trawled through the Low Countries, through Germany as far as the wall, then down into Austria for a while to shake a particularly persistent tail. Finally, I'd been forced to hide out in the backstreets of Paris for a week, before heading down to Toulouse and from there on to Spain.

It was in Madrid that I'd hit my lowest point. Alone and exhausted, weary that for company I only had bartenders and waitresses, I'd started thinking I should go back to England, turn myself in to the police, and face the music with my wife and her terrible family and all that would entail.

But then there I was, in this smoky bar off the *Calle Segovia*, nursing a Black & White in a hell of depression, when I happened to glance down at a local rag sitting on the table. Right in front of my eyes, between adverts for second hand SEATs and Polaroid cameras, it had read:

'Rustic island farmhouse for rent. Ideal for birdwatchers and holidaymakers wanting to escape the crowds. Uncertain tenure leading to significantly discounted rates. Contact Jose Antonio Gonzalez on Madrid 78493.'

I headed straight over to the back of the bar and dialled the number. Jose Gonzalez himself answered. His nasal tones came rasping out of the bar's old Bakelite handset.

'Señor, you sound like a man of good means. Come in to the office. Let me give you all the particulars.'

He gave me the address, which turned out to be a holiday letting agency in *Calle Segovia* itself and, within a couple of minutes, I was there with a pile of *pesetas* in my pocket. Between the Spanish posters on the windows for trips on the Orient Express and ski holidays in Bulgaria, I saw a solitary man sitting at one of two desks in the shop.

He stood up as I came in and shook my hand vigorously.

'*Señor, Señor*. What a lucky thing that you come in to see me so quickly. There has been much interest in the property.'

He was wearing a checked beige suit with stained armpits.

I saw straight away that this was the sort of situation where the price is set according to a judgement of one's ability to pay. I tried, as I had on the phone, to immediately establish the starting price, but the agent was having none of it.

'Well now, Mr...'

'Mr Waddington.'

'Just so, Mr Waddington. Let me start by explaining the property to you. It is quite sympathetic. Rustic. Would your wife be joining you?'

'Yes, of course.'

'And have you been looking long?'

'Not at all. This is just a passing fancy.'

'I see.'

'If you could give some indication of the cost...?'

Mr Gonzalez wiped his palms on his trousers, then shuffled the papers around on his desk and opened and closed a couple of drawers. 'I have the details here somewhere, Señor. And tell me, Mr Waddington, what is it you do and how come you to be in Madrid?'

'My wife and I are touring. I'm an author, you know.'

This was a line I had used in the past. It always made people accommodating for some reason, and as I genuinely had a desire to write at some point in the future – that is, when I finally have the time for it – to say that I'm an author isn't really a lie. It's just a part of me I haven't reached yet. So not really a lie, more an exaggeration of timelines.

'Interesting, *Señor* Waddington. Are you very much published?'

'In thirty-two countries.'

The agent looked delighted. 'Perfecto. Thirty-two, you say?'

'Yes, thirty-two if you don't count England. It would be thirty-three with England included.'

'*Perfecto, perfecto, Señor*. And you are here to holiday?'

'No, no, Mr Gonzalez. I am here to write.'

'I see.'

'If I were to take the house, my name must be kept strictly confidential, you understand?'

'Indeed?'

'I get a lot of bother from fans.'

At this, Jose Gonzalez smoothed back his hair and straightened his suit as if to present the best memory to my writer's eye.

'I am quite understanding. The property is not large but it has outhouses and many grounds. Were you looking for a large property? What sort of price had you and your wife been considering?'

'Well, I hadn't thought. My wife takes care of these things. What price is it on for?'

After a few more turns, the dance was over and the agent named a price. It took a further ten minutes to beat him down to half that figure, during which time I was forced to be inventive with the truth and, I'm ashamed to say, my wife was somewhat slandered in the process, becoming (as was expedient) fussy, domineering, and a penny pinching tyrant in turn.

Next the agent gave me the extensive rules of the house. I was not to take any of the late gentleman's belongings out of the property – everything was extensively catalogued and the agent would be dropping by on a regular basis to take an inventory. And, most strictly, I was not to touch any of the wine that would be found in the cellar. I agreed to it all of course, trying to hurry him along.

But then Mr Gonzalez went on to explain the situation regarding the house, namely that it was the subject of some legal disagreement of probate and that until the court made some ruling or other, or until the warring factions of the

Rodriguez family came to some agreement, the house could not be sold. It all sounded a bit odd and I have to say the agent was flustered as he told me, so I knew there must be more to it than he said. I wondered if that might create opportunity for my devilment. In any event, the upshot was that I had to be prepared to move out at the shortest notice if required. He went on to hastily explain how the very good price I had managed to secure was in reflection of this situation and that there could be no possible further discounts on account of this or anything else related to the death of Senyor Rodriguez.

'Fine, fine,' I said hurriedly, feeling nervous as to how long I had sat in that open window. Out of the corner of my eye, I could see a *polizia* strolling his beat across the other side of the road.

Then the crunch happened, as I knew it would.

'So, Señor Waddington. If you would be good enough to provide me with your and your wife's passports along with the deposit and I can be completing the administration.'

I took out my wallet, slowly counted out 3,000 *pesetas*, and put them on the desk.

'I'm afraid I don't have the passports. My wife has them in Barcelona.'

The agent frowned. 'That causes some difficulty. Could she join you in Madrid?'

'You want me to ask my wife to come from Barcelona to Madrid, only to go back again for the ferry to the island?'

Knowing my wife as I had painted her, the agent shook his head fearfully.

'Sir. I see this is not possible.'

He flicked through a Rolodex and pulled out a card. 'I can make a telephone call to another agency in Barcelona and arrange for them to see the passports. Are you able to contact your wife?'

Being Tuesday, my wife should be safely tucked away at her Tunbridge Wells WI meeting, at the Church of St Peter and St Paul. Since she'd not heard a jot from me in twelve weeks, I should think she'd be very surprised were I to call and ask her to take our passports to a property agent in Barcelona.

There was only one way to solve it. I stood up, picking up the stack of *pesetas* as I did so.

'I really don't know, Mr Gonzalez,' I said. 'I'd have to telephone her.'

At this the agent panicked. He knew who wore the trousers in my household and rightly guessed my wife would have a very different view on this spur of the moment decision to rent some ruined island farmhouse.

'Now, now,' said the agent, and I'm certain the sweat patches under his arms grew bigger. I suspected it had been a tough winter for holiday and property agents. 'It would be such a shame to disturb her, when there's so much there for her to see in Barcelona ... La Sagrada Familia ... the magic fountains of Montjuic ... Let's sort this out between us men, shall we?'

I sat back down and put the money back on the table. Mr Gonzalez smiled. 'After all,' he said, 'I can be trusting that you are who you say you are, and you can be trusting that *Ca'n Mola* exists just as I have described it.'

So I slid the money over and he filled in his forms.

'Could you please spell your name, *Señor*?'

'W-A-D-D-I-N-G ...'

'W-A-L-L-I-N-G ...'

'No, no ... W-A-D-D-I-N-G ... that's right, W-A-D-D-I-N-G ... T-O-N'

The agent scratched his head when it came to the box requesting passport numbers, and then wrote reams of words instead. Then he asked for a reference and I gave him the name of a Mr Peter Jones of King's Road, London. In return he gave me the paper with directions to the house and we shook hands to seal the deal.

I lingered with some light chit chat while I surreptitiously looked up and down the street to be sure the *polizia* had moved on, and then I hurried out. As soon as darkness fell, I headed out to the suburbs, found the Jag in the garage where I had stowed her, and drove through the night across the *Meseta Central* and over to Barcelona. Feeling relief flooding through my veins, I'd breakfasted by the docks and waited for the lunchtime ferry over to the island.

It was strange to think, as I lay in the bed of the late Senyor Rodriguez looking at that chink of blue sky against the white stone of the *casita*, that that was just the day before. It felt like a lifetime ago. Already I had that feeling one has when one has settled into a holiday house and it has begun to feel like home. I sat up and wondered what my next move should be.

Yes, what to do next? That was the question. I got up and pulled my suitcase out from under the bed and counted the money nestled in its blue lining. There were ten thousand *pesetas* in all. That may sound a lot, but years of inflation meant Franco's *pesetas* didn't go very far.

If I were frugal, I considered, my pot should last until the end of the summer. On that account I would have to be very strict. I'm a mild mannered man, but sometimes the drink can get the worse of me. I sometimes find that once I start, I can't stop. And the double difficulty is that I often can't stop myself from starting.

Here in my island hideaway, I was sure I wouldn't have any of those problems. Even so, I thought to myself, I must be on my guard and be well behaved. This really was my last chance to turn things around.

I do have another idiosyncrasy to struggle with that I really hoped wouldn't bother me here, which is that I suffer terribly from my nerves. It tends to come and go with the least warning. My father-in-law paid ridiculous amounts of money (at my wife's insistence, of course) for the best doctors in Harley Street to examine me. The things they suggested I should do in order to cure the disease were so ridiculous you couldn't scrawl them on a prescription pad: excessively cold baths on a regular basis; complete isolation in a room painted lilac; periodic injections of stimulants through my nose, and so on. It was when they suggested tying me to a bed and wiring me into the mains that I called a halt to the shenanigans.

But the one thing they were all agreed upon, doctors and surgeons alike, was that the nerves were exacerbated by the demon drink, and that I should avoid it at all costs.

But I was sure I wasn't going to have any of that old trouble here where it was so peaceful and quiet. No, I was determined that here, in the home of Senyor Rodriguez, I was going to be a better person.

I would read the late gentleman's books and take on a cultured and intellectual aspect. And I was sure, almost certain, that once in that frame of mind, some sort of solution would come to me; some scheme to win back my reputation or to earn a whole heap of money which would calm the waters and buy my way back to respectability. I was certain it could be done. I just needed to apply my brain to the problem without all the stress and strain I'd been under of late.

With that thought I went downstairs, packed myself a breakfast parcel of *manchego*, picked another book at random from the shelf (*The Handbook of Mechanical Engineering*), and set out for a day wandering about the countryside.

Chapter III

From that evening and for the next twelve days I had no contact with man, woman, or child, other than once when I drove to a faraway village for supplies – tomatoes, fruit, tea, butter, and jam. I feasted on the ham and cheese from the cellar, and managed to bake myself bread following a recipe pinned to the kitchen wall. The larder was well stocked with flour and yeast, and there was plenty of chopped wood behind the house with which to feed the kitchen's little black stove.

One of the rules of my stay (a rule of my own making) was however lazy or lonely I felt, I was never to take the road that worked its way down the side of the cliff to the fishing village at the bottom. From the way Isabella had spoken of *Ca'n Mola*, I felt for sure there was some scandal about the death of Rodriguez and that the house was at the centre of it – murder perhaps. The last thing I wanted was to get swept up in it all and by consequence have the locals start asking their nosy questions about me and where I might have come from.

So I always turned inland when I left the house, and spent my days roaming the empty country lanes. They wound their way through miles upon miles of almond and olive orchards, up to high rocky ground, and I wandered through them until I became quite dusty from the island's chalky earth. Spring lingered yet. Although the almond trees' famous white blossom was gone, they were still smothered in a delicate green leaf and the ground beneath was carpeted with pink and red flowers; I became convinced it was the most beautiful paradise anyone could have had the misfortune to be holed up in.

Often I would find some shady spot in which to sit and read and on other occasions I took pleasure in brushing up on my childhood Spanish as well as learning the local dialect. I had found a manual in the study which converted one language to the other, and I would sit there for hours, practising my verbs on the sheep. As the afternoon sun sank behind the trees they would stream past, heading for the faraway whistle of their shepherd, and the bells around their necks would clang along with my conjugations, '*lavo, lavas, lava*'.

I carried on with this quiet life for nearly two weeks and, by then, I was already beginning to feel like a better man. Often my head was full of Isabella, the way she had laughed so easily and how she had fingered the chain of the well in that half flirtatious way young women do, which means nothing to them, but which acts like magnet upon an older man's eyes and which pushes his wife to the back of his mind.

The morning Isabella returned it was a fine day with a bright, sharp sun. I was taking my breakfast at the table in front of the house and thinking about all that wine in the cellar and what a temptation it was, when I saw her coming up between the myrtle bushes that led from the cliff edge. She was dressed in white shorts and a little pink top and was carrying a watermelon in one hand.

'Hello, Mr Sebastian! See what I've brought you.'

'Miss Ferretti, how lovely to see you. Won't you join me?'

I immediately leapt up and took the fruit from her and then I hurried into the house for another glass for the orange juice. Isabella sat down and, with that most wonderful arrogance that only the young can get away with, helped herself.

'Wow! Isn't it wonderful?' She said after taking a great gulp.

I felt tongue tied after so long with the sheep but fortunately Isabella was full of words.

'You haven't been out and about much, have you?'

'No, I suppose not.'

'Your car's barely moved. Marta and I have been to so many parties at her zoology institute since I last saw you that it's becoming quite boring. Have you been into the city yet? To see the sights?'

'Not yet.'

'Marta says the cathedral is a good example of Gothic architecture.'

'I've been enjoying the peace and quiet, but ... oh, I mean to say, it's very nice to have some company for a change.'

Isabella looked into her glass. 'And have you heard from your wife? Is she to join you soon?'

'My wife? Yes, she's...' Hell. What had I said about my wife? 'I mean ... no.' Hell. I didn't want to be going through some countdown to my wife's arrival every time Isabella and I met. 'No, my wife wrote to say she won't be joining me for several months. She's very upset about leaving the dog.'

It was such an obvious lie that I saw from Isabella's face she didn't quite know where to go next. 'And what is it that you do in England, Mr Sebastian?'

'Property, mostly,' I said, moving to pour some more juice.

Isabella smiled vaguely. 'Property, eh? *Papa's* into property too.'

She said it in such a way, picking up her glass as she did it, that I had a suspicion she had seen through me. I felt I really needed to take control of things.

'You speak very good English, Miss Ferretti.'

'I learned English at school, in Switzerland.'

I wanted to ask her a thousand other questions but I didn't know where to start, so I asked if she would like to walk up to the top of the cliffs. I tried to sound casual, but it came out too gushing.

'You can see down to the next bay, Miss Ferretti, and it's very beautiful.'

Isabella looked at me with a smile as she consented and I resolved to be more composed in future. I carried the remains of breakfast into the kitchen, away from the ants, and then we set off up the track past the house and up towards the cliff edge.

'Is Marta out searching for lizards?' I asked, and Isabella put her arm through mine as if we were old friends.

'Oh! She's found a new species.'

'Really?'

'Yes, everyone's very excited about it. We've had telegrams from London, and yesterday they held a party at the institute in her honour. Apparently it's the most interesting lizard discovery since the miniature gecko find of '59.'

I thought of this Marta beaming and shaking hands with dusty old professors.

'You and Marta must come up for supper one evening,' I said. 'I'll cook you an English roast with all the trimmings.'

'*Si*,' said Isabella, 'But first you must come to Marta and me, and I shall cook the best risotto you have ever tasted. It's my mama's special recipe.'

'I'd be delighted. When…'

'Oh look! Do you see that lizard? If only Marta were here, she could record it in her notebook.'

The lizard was basking on a rock. Sixteen little toes on four little legs splayed out, as if it had been told it could own all the rock it could touch.

'So…' I ventured, trying to think of how to best push for a date to go along with the supper invitation.

'Yes?'

'Umm … oh, nothing. I was just going to say all lizards look pretty much the same to me.'

'*Sciocchezze!* If Marta were here, she wouldn't be happy to hear that.'

'I suppose not.'

'Do you have any children, Mr Sebastian?'

The question caught me off guard and I stumbled for an answer, which caused her to look at me, curiously.

'Heh! You don't seem to be sure.'

'I'm perfectly certain.'

'Certain?'

'Yes, I haven't any.'

Isabella was unconvinced so I struck a pose and asked her if I looked like a family man. What a stupid thing to say. Her answer made me exceedingly nervous. She dug her plimsoll into the sand of the path and said, 'To be honest, Mr Sebastian...'

'Call me Thomas,' I said, stalling in the hope she wouldn't come out with whatever it was she was about to say. 'It really isn't...'

'To be honest, Thomas...'

'Yes?'

'I think perhaps you're a man who's deserted his family.'

My heart leapt into my mouth. How did she know? Had I been traced to the island? Was there gossip in the village?

'Now why would you say that, Isabella?'

'Don't be cross. It's written all over your face, that's all.'

Relieved it was this, I laughed and considered again that I wasn't a very good villain.

Seeing my smile, Isabella was ecstatic.

'Hah! I knew it!' she said.

'You're correct. I did desert my family. That is to say ... I've left my wife and a dachshund called Henry.'

'I'm sorry,' said Isabella.

'Don't be. We were neither of us happy – me and my wife that is. Not Henry and I. Henry and I were perfectly happy.'

Isabella looked out to sea in a wistful way.

'Had you fallen out of love?'

'Not exactly.'

I really hoped at this point she would drop the subject because the bad feelings had suddenly come upon me again. When I'd first fled England I'd felt sick all the time. If it has never happened to a person, they could never understand the horror of being an exile, of being forever hounded from pillar to post, lonely and afraid. After a while the sickness does subside, but it never leaves you entirely. It's always there as a dull and constant ache, from which the horror can spring up once more at a moment's notice on some slight scare. When it happens, I get that tight feeling in my chest and I suddenly feel as if I can't breathe and my head can't seem to hold a thought long enough to cope with the world. I was starting to feel that way now, and I wondered how I could change the subject, but Isabella carried on, not realising the danger we were in.

'I suppose there was an affair?' she said.

'Not really.'

'So you loved her, you didn't have an affair, and yet you left her?'

This was terrible. I didn't know what to say. I couldn't bring up all the trouble with the creditors and that nasty business with the police. What an idiot I was that I hadn't thought of a good cover story before now. I'd had weeks to think of one. I should have been prepared – something good about my wife dying of some terrible terminal illness and how I had come away to grieve. And instead I'd been swotting up on mechanical engineering and Greek architecture and impressionist art and all the other countless topics I had pulled at random from Rodriguez's bookcase.

'We'd started to get on each other's nerves,' I said.

Isabella nodded, as if concerned, so I thought I would carry on along this line and see where it took me.

'It was awful really. I didn't want to go, but my wife insisted. She told me she wanted a bit of space and that I should clear off until she started to miss me.

'How terrible.'

Now Isabella looked at me as if I was some sort of abandoned puppy. This was no good. I didn't want her looking at me like that. I'd taken a real shine to her and, even though I knew there was no chance of romance because of the difference in our ages, I still wanted her to consider me as a romantically plausible man. And no woman wants another's cast offs. I thought I had better change tack.

'Now she's changed her mind,' I said. 'She's written to say she misses me and wants me back.'

Isabella clapped her hands together.

'That's wonderful. Won't you go back to her?'

'Certainly not. I'd had quite enough of her as well.' Now I sounded a tyrant. This was a minefield, this lying business. 'I probably will go back, but not till I'm ready.'

'And when will that be?'

Then an idea blew to me up the cliff edge from the sea, and I jibbed and tacked and set my sail up against it.

'The truth is, Isabella, my wife has been hard to live with of late. It was she who had taken a lover, plus we weren't pulling in the same direction any longer. I need to have a few adventures of my own – get my self-esteem back – then I'm sure I'll be able to go back and live with her till I am old and even greyer than I am now.'

Isabella looked at me. 'I see.'

I hoped that was to be the end of it, but then she said, 'But explain to me how you and your wife pulled in different directions. My parents never do that. They always come with a united position. It makes it so hard not to do whatever it is they think I should do.'

I thought about what I should say in answer to that. The truth was that by the time I was forced to flee the country, I had come to hate my wife.

I thought of that terrible scene when the creditors had ambushed her. I had come home one evening, rather worse for wear, and there they all were – my wife sitting down with a look of fury on her face, Henry in his usual spot wagging his tail but too lazy to get up, and the creditors with their triumphant snarls – all waiting for me. It made me ill to think of it. And I know it had been terribly hard on my wife and really most unfair that she had been forced to go through all the things I'd put her through, but I couldn't seem to find any sympathy for her. I guess that's what happens when you fall out of love with someone.

The thing was she'd never been on my side. There was one occasion, a dinner party, that sprang to mind. It made me flush red thinking about it again. It happened just as the business was starting to go wrong.

What happened was this: My wife came to me and suggested she throw a party for the neighbours; it had been so long since we'd done it that they'd begun to whisper all sorts of things behind our backs. I'd told her things weren't going well with the business – I'd made a few foolish investments which hadn't become the money spinners I'd been promised – and so I told her we couldn't afford a party. Not a chance.

But then she said a neighbour had become friends with a man on the local council, and she wanted to invite him to the party.

I'd told my wife it wasn't going to be of any help because the government have strict rules on who they'll transact with. The real truth was that I'd already inculpated a council man into one of my schemes, which wasn't going quite as planned, and if this council man should have heard wind of it and mentioned it in front of my wife...

Well, I had thought that was the end of it, but I came home a few evenings later to find, guess what, a surprise supper party arranged for me, my neighbours, and their friend from the council. It made me furious.

The government man sat there, telling me to call into his office the next day, while my wife had this half smile of satisfaction sliding onto her face. I couldn't have cared less about the damned government man – all I could focus on was that 'I told you so' smile on my wife's face. It said the next time I should listen to her and do exactly as she wanted because, there, it had been proven that she was cleverer than me and that although I may think she was a dumb-dumb, it was actually me who was the fool and she who should be in charge of things.

Out of nowhere I heard a seagull's raucous call, so at odds with my wife's prim supper party with the hateful neighbours and that damn government man, and I remembered I was standing on the cliff edge with Isabella. I wondered how long I had been thinking about my wife. What question had Isabella asked me?

I looked at her. Whatever it had been, she had long ago stopped waiting for an answer. She was dragging her feet through the sand of the path again, like a child does, and was looking out at some boats, three triangles of white, far, far away.

'Sorry, Isabella ... I lost my train of thought. What were we saying?'

And she prompted me quite sweetly, and without any of that nervousness that people sometimes get on their faces when I lose my thread like that.

'Well ... I wanted to know how you and your wife took each other in opposite ways?'

So I started to tell her about the supper party with the government man (glossing over, of course, the risk of worrisome revelations in front of my wife), but I don't think I got it right because Isabella said, 'I think it's normal for a woman to want to get her own way, no?'

Then I worried that perhaps I'd offended Isabella by seeming to suggest that women shouldn't have a say in the world, in which case I hadn't explained it right at all.

It hadn't been important that my wife hadn't done as I'd wanted; it was that she'd first agreed with me not to do it but then, behind my back, had gone ahead and done it anyhow. We weren't working as a team. If she had said that she really felt strongly about it, I'm sure I would have agreed to the dinner party in the first instance.

I was trying very hard not to go off in my head thinking about it all again, so I said nothing in reply to Isabella's comment, but then suddenly Isabella said, 'Imagine, Thomas, if there were two women in a marriage. They would be forever trying to outmanoeuvre one another.'

We both laughed and I realised she had understood me all along, and then she was back to her usual light and breezy self. I felt that the danger I might get confused in my head had passed, and I was so happy that Isabella and I could get along like this and she didn't seem to mind my odd little ways.

By now we had reached the place where the cliff path ended at the brow of the hill, before splitting into half a dozen little paths through the brush and down the other side. The sun came out at that moment, and the sea glistened as if I had arranged it.

'Wow! *Che vista*! Look how beautiful the beach is!' Isabella pointed down at the neighbouring bay where a long stretch of white could be seen. 'Can we get down to it?'

I knew it wasn't possible and told her so, but I didn't tell her I knew because I'd tried just the day before and nearly broken my neck in the attempt.

It had been one of those silly adventures, the sort you have when out walking and decide for some reason to take a random direction you've never taken before – when you know you're bound to get lost or end up somewhere hopeless, but you do it all the same. I'd seen that white sandy bay, its temptation shining in the sun, and, like Isabella, I thought it must be possible to get to it down the wooded slope.

Progress had been easy at first, but you know how those paths in the brush can be; they twist and divide and then you think you're on a lesser path so you turn back and try another, until you realise they are all just rabbit runs leading nowhere.

The slope became much too steep to continue but I was determined to get down to that bay. It was as if I was fed up with life always being so impossible, and I was going to get down to those sands, whatever it took.

It was foolish. The ground had started to crumble beneath me and I began to slip. It was dark beneath the trees and suddenly I was moving with the loose gravel, tree after tree slipping past while I desperately tried to catch hold of the branches.

On the one hand I was terrified, my heart beating like the clappers, but on the other a mad feeling came upon me. A voice in my head started telling me I should stop trying so hard and let the earth take me with it. It wanted me so badly after all, the voice said. Look at it, pulling and sucking with such eagerness. Let it have you, what use have you been to anyone alive?

I scrambled and slid and tried not to listen to the voice and then... I can't remember what happened next, but finally I was stationary with my arms wrapped around an oak tree and my face pressed up against its crinkled bark.

I don't know how long I stood there, my heart pounding against the tree. All I know is there was an image in my head and the image filled it so completely that no other thought or vision could be given the smallest space. It was of my body slung down on the slope, my neck twisted to an unnatural angle and my leg bent beneath me as one sees a victim in a movie. There were birds in the lower branches of the trees and they were braving their way down, their swivelling eyes focusing on mine.

Somehow, eventually, I did manage to crawl back up the slope. By the time I reached the top the sun had set. There had been no moon that night and the cliff top was in darkness. I'd been so afraid of where the edge might be I was forced to go down onto my hands and knees and carry on like that all the way back to the house.

As Isabella and I stood there in the bright sunlight, I

thought of that distraught and exhausted version of me crawling past in the dark. How strange it was that I should know of and hold this image in my head, whilst Isabella stood beside me with her pleasant thoughts.

I realised, then, that Isabella was looking intently at me.

'Is there something wrong with you, Mr Sebastian?'

'I'm so sorry. I just lose my train of thought sometimes.'

'Ah. There was a priest in the town where I grew up who had the same problem. Sometimes he would hear you, and sometimes he wouldn't.'

'Look! There's a road that comes in from the other direction,' I said, and pointed to a line in the trees on the other side of the bay.

'Oh, but it's so far away. I think it would be too far to walk.'

'Well, I'd be happy to take you and Marta in the car one day.'

'That's a wonderful idea. I'd like that very much,' Isabella replied. 'Let's go when the weather is warmer, shall we?'

Another invitation of indefinite timing. Oh, to be young again, and not care about such things.

'And there's no beach down on this side then?'

Isabella stepped right over to the cliff edge beside us and looked down. It made for a stabbing in my lower regions.

'Be careful, there's quite a drop there.'

I gingerly went towards her. You could hear the waves crashing on the rocks below.

'Jiminy! As my American cousin would say. That sure is a long way down.'

She left out a long whistle, while I waited patiently, afraid to go closer in case there should be some confusion of our paths, but wanting to be close enough to grab hold of her should she slip.

I thought of her parents ganging up on her. Perhaps one at a time wasn't enough to control her.

'It's a terrible way to go. It makes me feel ill to think of it. Do you think he felt anything?' I didn't know what she meant, so I didn't say anything. 'What do you think, Thomas?'

'Come away from the edge and I'll tell you.'

Laughing, she came back to me and, taking my arm again, she turned to walk back the way we had come, back down the hill towards *Ca'n Mola*.

'Well?' she persisted.

'I don't know who you mean.'

Isabella looked at me in surprise. 'You don't know?'

I shook my head.

'That's where he killed himself.'

'Who?'

'Senyor Rodriguez, of course.'

This was most surprising. I couldn't reconcile that with the gentleman I had imagined – whose house I had lived in; whose bed I had slept in; who was so intelligent and worldly and industrious.

'But why on earth would he do such a thing?'

'Oh, Thomas, I don't know. Ask Marta, she knows all about it, the whole sorry tale.'

So we walked back down the hill, and outside *Ca'n Mola*'s gates Isabella gave me two kisses, one on each cheek, and then she left me and disappeared as her path took her around the jutting-out rock.

I weaved my way through the myrtle bushes and went into *Ca'n Mola*. There I stood in the kitchen, staring down at the stone floor.

For the first time I felt bored and lonely. I was like someone from a long-lost tribe who has been given coca cola and clothes and a television set and then suddenly had them taken away again. I had been perfectly fine on my own before, but now suddenly I wasn't.

I knew at once (for it had happened to me before), that I had fallen head over heels in love with Isabella. I was possessed with an obsession to convert every little thought to include her – what she had said, how she had said it, what every bit of her looked like – but I was also consumed with a burning physical desire to have her in my arms and have her whispering that she couldn't help herself and that she felt as I did, to have her bring her lips up to mine, gently at first and then with a ferocious passion.

A sudden loneliness descended upon me and I faltered. I badly wanted a drink.

'What would Rodriguez say?' I thought to myself.

I knew the answer, of course. He would look at me with those eyes that had seen the world and tell me to have a little self-discipline.

So I hunted around in his odds and ends drawer (which of course he had, like every other man on this planet of ours) and found a notepad, a pencil, and a padlock.

I locked the cellar door and put the key in the bottom drawer of Rodriguez's bureau. Then I took the notepad and wrote at the top, 'The Plan for Recovery' and underlined it twice.

I packed into a cloth bag a Thermos bottle filled with tea and some of those wonderful paprika sausages they make here from little black piggies, and set off up a sheep track behind the house.

When the trees grew taller, at the top of a bluff, I turned to look back at the coast. There was Isabella's villa at the end of the row, with its rectangle of bright turquoise and its sun loungers – and there indeed was Isabella, sitting on one of the sunbeds, slumped forward with her elbows on her knees. How she was stooped over. When she had been with me she had been as cheery as anything, but from here she looked as though she had the weight of the world on her shoulders and I wondered why. She got up and the little ant-sized Isabella disappeared into her white-washed home.

I let my eye follow the line of the rest of the villas along the edge of the cliff. The fishing village at the bottom couldn't really be seen, just the stone wall of the harbour and a few of the working boats moored and jutting out into the sea – then

I looked out across the rolling countryside eastwards, with its scraggy, goat-filled woods and tall evergreens.

What a situation had been thrown to me. There was no need to be glum. All I needed to do was to come up with a plan. How hard could it be? With that thought I turned back to the path, and set off with a determination to climb to the highest ground, where the orchards peter out and are replaced by bare rocky outcrops. An idea. That was all that was needed.

Chapter IV

For several days I was hard at it. The padlock remained on the cellar door and my notebook became filled, cover to cover, with extensively scrawled suggestions. They were all splendid, of course, and could have made any man with a modicum of determination rich enough to survive for the few years left to me, but I knew in my heart they were bunkum. Each one required some skill I did not possess, or depended upon an unlikely degree of fortune – and fortune had never come easily to me.

By the third day, I had become quite despondent, so I was immensely cheered to arrive home from wandering the orchards that evening as the sun was setting and discover a note wedged under the door knocker. It read:

> *Dear Thomas,*
> *I called, but you were out. Hasn't the weather been sublime these last couple of days? Marta has invited some professors of biology over to supper this evening at no notice at all, and I have insisted that if I must put up with her tedious friends she shall have to put up with mine (not that you are tedious, of course). Do come. Eight onwards,*
> *Warm regards,*
> *Isabella Ferretti*

What an invitation. And with a definite date and even a

time of arrival confirmed. Immediately I was thrown into a panic of nerves and apprehension. I hurried up to Senyor Rodriguez's bedroom and stood looking at my collection of clothes. None of them, nor any combination of them, were suitable for a supper party. I had the trousers of suits without the jackets, and the jackets without their trousers.

What a mess I had made of the packing but, in the circumstances, it wasn't really surprising. The night before I left, my wife had stumbled upon me in the bedroom hastily filling a suitcase. She had stood by her bed screaming blue murder at me, and I had been standing next to mine, attempting to think what I might need, with the dog howling away the whole time.

Henry had long ago understood the line drawn between our two marital beds, and now he had chosen a side. He sat, crying, at my wife's feet, but I saw that his tail was wagging guiltily and I took it as a secret sign of support for me. I couldn't blame him; he wasn't the only one to figure out which of the two of us was the better bet for a steady meal ticket. Then, of course, I had let her talk me out of it and had put the half-packed suitcase into the cupboard, promising her I would empty it out again in the morning.

Remembering all this, I went downstairs and sat in a misery at Rodriguez's kitchen table. It was over three months since I'd been to a supper party and the thought of going to one filled me with dread, regardless of having nothing to wear. I so wanted to be with Isabella, just to stand next to her and hear the low tones of her laughter and her wonderful voice.

I knew it could only be managed with a little Dutch courage. I would have to drink at the party in any event. To not do so would be unthinkable. There's willpower and then there are Herculean expectations.

It was already past eight, so I hurried over to the dresser and retrieved the key to the padlock, then I pottered out to the cellar in my shorts, unlocked it, and fetched a couple of bottles of claret. One for now, and one to take to the party. I sat in the kitchen taking my medicine like a man. As I did so, a thought struck me.

I had read his books; I had gazed at his artwork for hour upon hour – was it such a terrible step to wear the clothes of a dead man?

Taking the bottle of wine with me, I went upstairs to the bedroom, opened the closet, and leafed through the suits as I had done with the books in Rodriguez's living room. I had never worn a linen suit before.

I had seen plenty in my father's wardrobe in London. They had hung, at the back of the closet, like memories he had tried to forget. They were the suits he had worn when he had travelled the Americas selling the firm's inventions, before he had met Mother and brought her back to Golders Green. What must she have thought of a London shell-shocked by the Zeppelin raids?

I took one of Rodriguez's suits, put it on, and looked in the mirror. It couldn't be danced about – Rodriguez had been something of a portly gentleman.

Before me in the mirror was a tired looking man wearing a suit at least two sizes too large for him. I turned and looked at my side profile. I could perhaps be a man who has lost weight but been too busy to get his suits taken in. I put on a belt and pulled the trousers in tight. Then I hurriedly finished off the rest of the claret and went back down to the kitchen. I opened up the second bottle, just to check it was good, then I set off down the hill, full of nerves.

I have never in my life been good at supper parties. It's difficult to know when to speak and when to stay silent. I always get it wrong and cut some poor fellow off in the middle of a funny story just to say something trifling and dull. Then everyone looks at me and wishes I wasn't there and I wish I wasn't there and swear I never will be again. But then another invitation comes along or my wife persuades me I'll enjoy this particular party because 'such and such will be there and they so desperately want to meet you', and I think this time I will be interesting and talk about this or that thing I read in the papers and I'll try to seem as if I'm up on the world and have a handle on current affairs, but it all goes wrong in the usual way and I come home feeling miserable and full of hatred for myself.

As I came closer to Isabella's I could hear the party was in full swing. The tops of the academics' heads could be seen bouncing about above the railings on the first floor. There was hooting and laughter and it sounded high-brow and fast and clever. I stood still and looked up at the white villa, at the dancing heads, and listened out for Isabella's voice. There, I found it – her soft dark timbre amongst the men's altos. There was another woman's voice too, strong and confident. I guessed this must be Marta.

'No, no. I did throw the dice,' I heard Isabella say.

'But it's really just a deal between the Germans and the French. Germany gets to build on its industrial rebirth and yet support the Gallic farmers,' came a man's voice.

'Well, where did they go then?' said another.

'He's right. But it's a disaster for us. We pay for it but get nothing in return. Who's go is it?'

'Isabella's, but she's lost the dice.'

'I didn't lose them, I threw them. They're there! Under your elbow.'

'But we have to do it this way. It's the only way to keep us from war again.'

'A four and a six. Welcome to Park Lane, Isabella. That'll be thirty-five pounds. Sorry Marta, but what's the point if it allows Germany to become strong again?'

'I agree. We should be telling them what price we will buy their rotten machinery, not having them interfere with our milk. Sorry Marta, do you disagree?'

'No, no, I agree. You're right of course.'

I stood for a while and listened. Then I walked over to the cliff and sat down as close as I dared to the edge. I twisted the cork out of the bottle, and took a swig from it. I knew I wouldn't be able to go in.

I took another long drink. I could still hear them, but the voices had become tangled and I could no longer pick out Isabella's from the rest. I felt as if they had stolen her from me and hidden her in plain sight and I hated them, every man of them, with their clever views and camaraderie and jovial disagreements with Marta.

Amongst the stars I spotted one which moved in a steady arc, but it was just the lights of a plane flying east along the southern edge of the island. Behind it was another, the two of them making their descent to the city, as if in concert.

Perhaps one was a Thomson Airways Caravelle from England, with its twin jet engines. I'd seen the advertisements in the Telegraph. 'Sun and Fun on a Sky Tours Holiday' it had said.

Then I saw the lights of a third plane, behind those of the other two, and it seemed as if the tourists were like an unstoppable invasion of army ants. I thought of them marching their way out of the planes, onto the buses, and then swarming out and onto all the beaches to the west and the east of the city.

It wouldn't be long until that entire coastline would be alive with them, working their way busily up and down the front in search of ice-creams and inflatable mattresses, settling on ledges and rails, sombreros hanging from strings around their sunburnt necks, sending out scouts on water-skis into the sea.

After the wine was finished, I crept to my car and stole away. There was nowhere to go, but I had a yearning to be surrounded by people and most of all I wanted to be in a bar. I wanted the smell of it in my nostrils, to have the convivial chatter around me, and the comfort of a drink in my hand.

So I got into the car and drove into the city. I knew it was a bad thing to do. If I were spotted on the island they could watch the airports and ports forever and my game would be up, but I couldn't take my solitary confinement any longer. I had to live again.

Chapter V

I woke the next morning feeling rotten and horribly confused. To say there were gaps in my recollection of the evening would be an understatement of the greatest degree. I could see from the way the sunlight fell short upon the bedroom floor, rather than long across the slatted wardrobes, that it was quite late, possibly even noon. I groaned. Then I wallowed in misery for a while. Then I groaned again. Lying still was as awful as moving around, so I made the traumatic decision to get up.

The journey down to the kitchen was quite perilous. As I manoeuvred around the banister, a few pieces of the evening's jigsaw were thrown at me. I'm not talking about missing pieces, the ones which are needed to fill in gaps, I'm talking of the pieces one gets after first emptying the box, when one is turning them all over in the hope of finding something to start with. There had been a scene on the Borne. I fear I might have been at the centre of it.

As I sat at the kitchen table the world started spinning in that jarring, repetitive way it does when it's got it in for me. Yes, there had definitely been a scene on the Borne.

I made myself a Bloody Mary (there was no vodka so I had to improvise), took it out to the garden and sat down next to the well. I'd been toying with the intention of pulling up a bucket of water and pouring it over my head, but it seemed like such a ridiculously complicated thing to achieve.

I would be better to put it on hold, just for a minute or two.

A few more oddly-shaped pieces came to me. I was starting to be able to see the picture forming, though was now less inclined to want to. I groaned again, and put my head in my hands.

For some reason, as soon as I arrived in the city I had gone in amongst the crowds and a bizarre notion had come upon me that I could hear the thoughts of the people around me. This was my old trouble returning to me, hastened on, no doubt by those two bottles of claret drunk so quickly in succession.

What an idiot I was. This was exactly the reason I'd decided to become abstemious. I'd never be able to come up with a plan of rescue if I couldn't stick to this one simple rule.

I groaned again for the umpteenth time and allowed the pieces to fall into place. Yes, there had been the scene on the Borne, then there had been bars and a girl and then two girls and then more bars. I remember thinking at the end of the evening that despite the scene on the Borne, the night had turned out to be a great success, full of wild antics, laughter, merriment, and fun.

I knew for a fact this must have been true, because the amount of guilt and misery now sweeping over me was such that I was in danger of being washed away – and as everyone knows the amount of hysterical antics one has at night is always directly correlated with the amount of guilt and misery one experiences the next morning. But it couldn't be ignored; I had been convinced for the entire night that I had been able to read the thoughts of others.

It had actually proved quite useful with the ladies, and had caused one of them to literally fall at my feet. (This was towards the end of the evening, after I think the third bar.)

It had all started as I had come into the crowds of the Borne. I had this feeling that it was the people of the streets who were my true friends (rather than Isabella and those hateful professors) and I wanted to be with them, every one of them. I felt a connection to them, as if they were in my head and speaking their thoughts directly at me.

The idea I could read the crowd's thoughts had come upon me with such a fervour that I'd stood stock still and listened to what those people were thinking as they streamed past me.

'Why does he walk so fast when he knows I have these shoes on?'

'Wo ist das Bar? Der den sie nahm mich mit zu.'

Then it started to become too much and I'd had to put my hands over my ears. This had confused some of those good people who started to turn to me with their kind voices and thoughts, wondering if I needed assistance.

Soon there was a whole lot of them, and their voices were crowding in on me, not just theirs but also those of the others behind them.

'Em pregunto on està pedro?'

'Tomorrow I shall tell her it's over, but not tonight. Tonight I intend to have her one last time.'

'Hello. Are you all right?'

'Is he all right?'

'I don't know. What do you think we should do?'

I began to feel I was being filled up with those voices, such that there was no room for my own sense of self, and I started to moan. Someone was sent to a bar to call for a doctor and suddenly I looked around me and all of those people, every one of them, was wearing a white coat. I pushed at them.

'Get away from me!' I said, angrily.

I couldn't tell which of them was really a doctor, and I was suspicious when one person took control and asked them all to give me some space and to get on with their evening. Soon it was just me and this man, and he was talking to me and saying things that made no sense at all. He wanted me to come with him, and he said that he knew me. I became fearful then that it was a trick and that he was really a policeman in a white coat. So I let him take me to a bench, and I told him I felt much better. Then I asked him for a glass of water.

He called for a waiter at a nearby bar and, when none arrived, he told me to stay where I was and went into the bar. I could see him in the telephone booth through the window. Well, I felt certain then that he was a policeman rather than a doctor, for no doctor would leave his patient in that way just to make a telephone call.

So when a large crowd of Englishmen came by, I slipped myself in amongst them and was carried away to safety.

There was a woman in the group who was darting between the young men, herding them along the street with prods and words of encouragement and she herded me right along with them.

'Keep up now! I don't want to lose anyone.'

She brushed us into the *Via Jose Antonio*, past the *Casa Puigdorfila*, and into a bar. There I detached myself and hid amongst the fronds of a pot plant in the corner.

'Is this the place?' one of the men called out.

'Are we all here? One, two, three, four ... five. All present and correct!' said the woman.

'Is this the place?' the youngest of the lot persisted.

'Of course it is,' the woman said, and she pushed the men aside to get to the bar.

The bar was an old cellar with rough wooden walls and a collection of barrels receding into the dim light.

Before I saw it arranged, the woman had five glasses of beer and was passing them back to the men. They turned to talk to each other, apart from the one who had wanted to know if this was the place. He came over to the woman and annexed her with a tug. I ordered a Black & White and shrunk back into my corner. I was beginning to feel calmer. It was the essence of the bar settling into my veins, like spiritual healing.

'Susan. What's going on?' the young man hissed.

The woman looked surprised. 'Whatever do you mean?'

'What's going on? I demand to know.'

Another of the men approached and he swung an arm over each of their shoulders.

'What are you two up to over here, eh?'

The woman touched the arm on her shoulder in a friendly way.

'It's Richard. He's upset, but I can't get him to tell me why.'

'What is it, old boy? Out with it.'

At this the young man shrugged the arm off his shoulder and leant back against the bar. He jerked his head to flick the hair out of his eyes, but it just fell back again. I stood in my corner just inches from them the whole time.

'It's nothing. Susan doesn't know what she's talking about.'

The woman and the man raised eyebrows at each other. I felt for that poor boy.

'Well, hurry up with whatever it is, because we've thought of a very interesting game, and if you want to be part of it you had better come over.'

That Susan knew I was watching her. She pouted her lips and tossed her hair from her shoulders. 'What's the game?'

'We must all drink with our left hands. Anyone who forgets has to do a forfeit the rest of the group will decide on.'

'What fun,' said Susan, and she glanced across at the rest of the group, huddled in the centre of the room.

'I won't play that.'

'Come on, Dicky. Don't be a bore. You'll like it once we get going.' And the man left to join the rest of the group.

As soon as the man was out of earshot the younger one hissed, '*How could you*?' to Susan.

'Oh, Richard, you heard what he said, don't be a bore.' She glanced over at me, then she left to join the others. After standing to consider for a moment more, the young lad stalked over as well.

I watched them and listened to them for hours. I liked the

look of that Susan. I liked how bossy she was and how the men all wanted to be with her but none had the courage to act. I went to the machine to buy some cigarettes and, when she next came back to the bar, I spoke to her and offered her one.

'Thank you,' she said, and took it.

I didn't say anything then. I just stared at her with a grin and let her make the first move. Because that evening I could hear what she was thinking, so I knew what she wanted.

'Are you from here?' she asked.

'No. Are you?'

'Don't be silly,' she said. 'I'm English.'

She took a long drag from the cigarette and then waved her hand in the direction of the men she was with.

'I have to look after these boys. They're on a tour of Europe. I have to show them around and keep them out of trouble.'

'What do they do?'

'They fence. You know?' and she jabbed at the air with an imaginary foil. 'They're terrible prima donnas. Worse than a bunch of girls.'

'When will you be done with them?'

The girl looked at me, and in her head she considered my proposition and was undecided. She was nervous because she didn't know who I was. But then she thought that was what she had come travelling for. To become intimate with exotic strangers, to find passion and excitement. There had been none of that in Felixstowe.

'I want to take you to an exhibition,' I said. 'A friend of mine, Ramon Casas, has invited me to his opening. I'd rather not go alone.'

She was tempted by that. She looked at the men with a frown. 'Can we take them with us?'

'No. Ramon only likes certain people.'

Susan considered leaving them. She thought about how she wanted to go off with the man. It would be a proper adventure and it sounded as if he was cultured and would teach her things she didn't know. People invited him to parties. And he was handsome in a scrawny sort of way, though his suit was strangely too large for him. But she daren't leave the fencing team. If they got up to no good or landed in the cells for the night she'd be in trouble.

'Could we do it another night?'

I watched her with all these thoughts. How she put up barriers. She could have been wild in Felixstowe if she'd wanted. The barriers had travelled with her. There was little hope for her without my help.

'Perhaps,' I said.

I waited nonchalantly while she asked the barman for a pencil. Then she pulled a paper tissue from the dispenser and scribbled her number on it.

'My landlady will answer, but tell her to go knock on my door and see if I'm there.'

I took it from her and gave her a polite little bow, which amused her.

'Sometimes she says I'm not in when I am, because she doesn't want to walk up the stairs. So if she answers too quickly insist that she goes up.' Then she added, as if it would further her cause, 'I did art at school,' but then I saw she realised that sounded foolish, so she went back to her boys and joined enthusiastically in their games, telling herself resolutely not to look in my direction.

I watched them for a while. They were a busy lot. Back and forth they went to the bar, off to buy cigarettes, away into huddles for arguments which went round in circles until they all agreed upon something so preposterous it had to be the truth.

When Susan was in the midst of it I slipped out. I had left her number on the bar behind me. As I stood outside the bar, trying to remember in which direction the car lay, I felt a hand on my arm and turned to see that Susan was beside me.

'Come and find me later,' she said, and she told me the name of a bar she would be in with a friend once she had taken her charges home to bed. Then she went back into the bar.

As soon as I'd finished my cigarette and started another, I took a stroll down towards the river and then asked for directions to the *Lonja*. Then I wandered over that way, stopping into a few of the bars until it was well after the time I'd arranged to meet Susan.

The 23 Club was what Isabella would have called 'wild'. There was a man dressed in the red and gold of a toreador at the door, and then after going down some dingy stairs I was greeted by the owner, who kept breaking into a flamenco dance at the least opportunity. It was full of tourists. I don't think there was a local in the place, if you didn't count the young boys in search of a *sueca*.

I was trying to fight my way to the bar, and had tapped a woman on the shoulder to ask her to move aside. When she turned to smile at me, I saw it was the girl, Susan, herself.

'Hello there!' she called out and then ducked as the owner began to play castanets over her head. 'There you are. Isn't it funny? Have you been here before?'

I said that I hadn't and asked her who was looking after the fencing team.

'They're all tucked up in bed.'

Another girl arrived with two glasses of Sangria in her hand.

Susan tried to peer through the crowds. 'We were trying to get a booth.'

I caught the owner's eye and, with a quick spin with his cape, the man had it arranged and was pushing his way through the crowd with us following, and getting a recently vacated booth cleaned up for us, all at the same time. It was the suit, I suddenly thought. See how the crowds fall apart for a man in a linen suit. I could see from Susan's expression she was impressed.

'This is Maureen,' said Susan as we sat down. We were joined moments later by a pitcher of Sangria.

'Nice to meet you,' Maureen said. Maureen was older than Susan. She had blonde hair piled up on her head, and scarlet lipstick. Her glass had a sword in it, and she swirled her drink around with it and looked about her with a disappointed expression.

I couldn't think of anything to say, so I looked about me too. There must have been at least two dozen women in the room. I couldn't help but think of Isabella. I resolved that when we did visit the beach, when we did sit down on the sands, I was going to kiss her ... or I'd perhaps move my hand by a few inches in order to take hers in mine, and I'd let it sit there until she smiled at me to tell me it was fine to advance. There were a thousand ways it could be arranged. I knew because I'd gone over every one of them in my head. And all of them, all of them, ended up with me touching her, and with her touching me and begging me not to stop.

But it was the drink making me think like that, with that confidence. In the daytime I knew the courage would be gone, like mist set upon by the sun.

'Did you make it to the gallery?'

I realised Susan was speaking to me. 'What gallery?'

'For your friend? The exhibition?'

'Oh, it wasn't a gallery. It was in his house over in the Arab quarter.'

'Did you make it then?'

'Yes.' I bought some *Ducados* from the waiter and offered one to each of the girls. 'How long are you on the island for?'

'For the summer,' answered Susan. 'Then I'm going to South America. How about you?'

'I haven't decided yet. I'll stay until I get bored.'

Susan nodded. 'How wonderful.'

Maureen looked as if she had swallowed a lemon. I resolved that if she wanted to be that way with me, then I would be that way with her. I ordered another pitcher of Sangria.

I asked Susan where she was from and when she told

me she went into some long description about the town she came from and where it was in England. Then she asked me where I was from.

I considered for a moment. 'Venezuela.'

'Oh. Have you been to Rio?'

'Of course.'

'I want to go there.'

The girls weren't making much progress with the pitcher so I poured myself another glass and topped up theirs.

All the time Susan and I talked Maureen looked glum, but, when Susan went to powder her nose, Maureen changed entirely. She turned and stared at me intently.

'Do you live in the city?'

I told her I had a villa just on the outskirts, a modern sort with white walls and an enormous great pool, and she visibly warmed to me.

'Is it to the east or the west?'

'The east. How about you?'

'Oh, I move around,' she said, and waved her hand in the air. 'I'm mostly over in the hills.'

I wasn't sure what she meant by that, but I didn't question her further; I just let her talk. And as she spoke I wondered what she would be like in bed. At first it was an academic interest. I tried to imagine her in coitus, with her head thrown back. I wondered if she would get on top with wild whooping, or whether she would just lie down and whimper and expect me to do it all. Someone once told me that cooks make the best lovers. So I asked her whether she liked to cook.

'Sometimes. I'm not bad if I make the effort.'

'And what are you like in bed?'

The question surprised both her and me in equal measures. A strange desire had come over me to be bold. First I was telling lies about Ramon Casas being my friend, and now I was being bold with women.

'You're a one,' she protested.

'Tell me,' I persisted

'I'm not bad if I make the effort,' she said, and she wobbled her head to show she was game and not afraid of me.

I lit another cigarette and handed it to her and then lit one for myself.

'Someone once told me that cooks make the best lovers.'

She pulled a blonde curl down from her forehead and twisted it around her finger.

Just for once I wanted to be something other than the pathetic little mouse that I was. Why couldn't I be a real man like Rodriguez? I bet he wouldn't be pining after his neighbour while all this golden fruit was hanging round.

'Will you make love to me, Maureen?'

Maureen looked me up and down and took in the white suit hanging off my shoulders. 'Perhaps,' she said.

I closed my eyes to listen to the swing music and think what it would be like and, when I opened them again, Susan was back and the two of them were having a whispered conversation.

Susan leaned over to me. 'What's your name?'

I thought for a moment, then I leaned back towards them both and shouted loudly over the music so that they both would hear.

'Rodriguez,' I said.

Maureen giggled.

'Don't you have a first name, pet?'

'No,' I said. 'Just call me Rodriguez.'

As all that came back to me, I leant on the wall of the well in a terrible panic of nausea and guilt. The garden started to spin around me – the palms, the myrtle bushes, the *casita*; the palms, the myrtle bushes, the *casita*. All in the right order, but refusing to stay put.

I groaned. I can't begin to explain how angry I was with myself. What a disgrace. I had misappropriated Senyor

Rodriguez's name; I had used it to flirt with women and drunkenly carouse with strangers. I didn't believe for a minute this was how the good gentleman would have behaved.

To get tight like that? To take a woman out for air, and then instead to kiss her and fondle one of her breasts right there in the street? What a disgrace. How ashamed I felt. What a dishonour I had done to Rodriguez.

And the feeling of guilt was made ten times worse by the fact that my head was stuffed full of knives and my own breath was making me feel queasy and wanting to throw up.

For a while I wallowed in self-hatred and guilt. It was a stupid and dangerous thing to have done. I had been openly wandering the main thoroughfares. I didn't know if the man who had been trying to take care of me on the Borne was a policeman or a doctor. Perhaps he had been a thief who had intended to lure me to a back alley and rob me. I would have to be more careful.

I made myself promise, there and then, not to be tempted to drink and go into the city again. The incident would have to serve as a lesson. I would put it behind me and forge ahead with a renewed intensity on working to discover my plan of rescue.

So I spoke to myself in the words of my old Oxford chum, Hugo. He used to force his way into my digs after a night out, just for the pleasure of sitting on my head and lecturing me.

'Thomas, old boy,' he would say. 'Don't be a man at night and a boy in the morning.'

So I agreed with old Hugo and forced myself up from the ground by the well. I became a little recovered after that, but only a little, and I was obliged to remind myself of Hugo's advice several times during the course of the day. I locked the door of the cellar with the padlock again, and this time I threw the key over the edge of the cliff and into the sea.

Later I wearily packed my notepad into my bag. I doubted

today would be my most productive day, but May was nearly upon me. It was the uncertainty that weighed on my mind. Not knowing whether they had all given up and gone back to England, or whether they were still out there asking questions of hoteliers and local police stations, trying to track me down. As frugal as I was, my stash of money was growing noticeably smaller with each week that passed. I had to come up with something soon or I would be lost forever.

Chapter VI

This morning some chickens appeared in the garden. I thought there were five in total but they kept wandering around and swapping places, darting into the bushes, and then popping out again to peck at some new bit of ground; it made them difficult to count. When I first saw them I was curious as to how they'd survived since Rodriguez abandoned them to their fate, but then I saw one of them pecking at an old orange and thought of the natural springs bubbling up in the countryside.

Closing up Rodriguez's book of animal husbandry, I decided they were perfectly capable of looking after themselves, so I had a hunt around and discovered the old nesting boxes in the *casita* and cleaned them out and put fresh straw inside. A few free eggs would be welcome; three days ago I'd received a letter from the agent, asking for rent. It read as follows:

Dear Mr Waddington,

I am trusting that you and your wife found Ca'n Mola without difficulty and that you are having a restful and productive holiday. Can I please ask you now to forward to me the rental instalment for May, as this must have slipped your memory with the excitement of the finding of the property.

The probate of the estate continues slowly. The family members continue to be in disagreement amongst themselves and the settlement of the estate upon my worthy client continues to be challenged.

It is not looking likely to be bothering you and Mrs Waddington for the foreseeable future, but as we know with these things, they can take unexpected turns, particularly since I know that my client has secured for himself the best lawyer in all of Spain and he is full of drive and determination that can only be admired.

So I am reminding you that you may need to leave the property on short notice if this becomes a necessity and the probate is settled in favour of my client (at which point he shall, as earlier explained to you, be selling Ca'n Mola at the first opportunity).

I shall be coming to the estate in the next few weeks in order to arrange the inventory check as is my responsibility to the Rodriguez family, so I expect I shall see you and your wife on this occasion.

Yours with warm felicities,
Jose Antonio Gonzalez
Madrid

PS I have been having some difficulty contacting the reference that you kindly gave me. I find that there is more than one Peter Jones residing at King's Road, London, and indeed I spent some considerable time in a confusing correspondence with a department store there of a likewise name. When I come to be checking the inventory, I hope that you will be able to clarify this so that I can arrange for all the required formalities to be completed since it is now getting to be very late for this.

With a heavy heart, I went up to the bedroom and pulled my suitcase out from under the bed. I had hoped that the southern habit of delay in dealing with such matters might have bought me more time.

There in the suitcase was my pile of very dear and beloved *pesetas* sitting peacefully in their home of blue silk lining. How I hated to disturb them, but the only way to keep the blasted man away was to send money. I counted out three thousand *pesetas*, flicked through the rest, and then pushed the suitcase with its depleted cache back under the bed.

There were just over seven thousand *pesetas* remaining. Enough to pay for June, send another three thousand for August, play dumb about what happened to July, and then stretch out September depending on how eager Gonzalez turned out to be. That left just over a thousand for sundries. Ham, cheese, and now eggs were going to be free, and water could be had from the well (it was a little chalky but fine if left to settle); vegetables and the little *sobrasada* sausages I had grown to love cost next to nothing, which meant the rest of the budget could be spent on cigarettes (the local *Ducados* cost ten *pesetas* a packet) and buying Isabella coffees and ice-cream. And should I persuade her to come to dinner with me occasionally, there would still be enough for that if I were picky about the venue. I wrote a long and carefully worded reply to the agent (adding a charming and perhaps overly-friendly postscript from my wife) and propped it up by the front door for posting.

Then, in case the agent should be true to his word and arrive to take an inventory, I set about tidying the house and making sure any artefacts I might have picked up to evaluate were all back in their correct places.

The act of doing housework reminded me of my wife. It was like a stabbing feeling into my heart, and I wondered what she might be doing. What day was it? Saturday. She would be playing golf with her father at the Royal Ashdown.

Urgh. Now the thought of my father-in-law had forced its way into my peaceful new life.

I could see him, accompanied by my wife, huffing his

way around the West Course, moaning boorishly on as he drags his trolley. She'll be giving him that forgiving smile she always gave – a forgiving smile which she never once gave me. I stood stock still and forgot my housework as the memory of the last time I saw him took hold of me.

He was standing with one hand on his hip, the other clutching a repossession order of our house, his face a violent red colour swelling out like a balloon, and I'd thought he might be going to have a jammer there and then. My father-in-law and I had never really seen eye to eye.

My wife sat, cool as a cucumber, on the chaise longue, and we were all three in that dreadful sunroom her parents had insisted on installing in their Sevenoaks house when they were the rage in the fifties. 'Why don't you get one?' was my mother-in-law's constant refrain.

I'd told my wife over and over not to worry about the repossession order and that I would deal with it, but no, she had taken it to her father, and behind my back no less.

'You're sick,' my father-in-law had finally managed squawk out. 'Sick, I say, sick. And you need to be locked up.'

I remember thinking what a ridiculous over-reaction it was and I'd told him so.

'There's such a thing as optimal gearing,' I'd said in a pointed fashion, and I'd hoped that would be an end to it, but my father-in-law was having none of it.

'Optimal gearing? Are you mad?'

I knew I had him here, because this was something I had taken a great interest in.

'Certainly not,' I'd retorted. (I had been determined on this occasion to stand up for myself). 'Modigliani and Millar have conclusively proved that...'

My father-in-law made a signal that demonstrated his lack of regard for theories of gearing.

'You, sir, are old enough to know better. You are an idiot of the greatest degree.'

As he thundered on I reflected on how he had never

really liked me and had always been against the match. He'd had a thing about my Venezuelan mother and whenever difficulties had arisen and we had been forced to approach him for assistance, the nationality of my mother always seemed to crop up.

'This is not how we do things in England!'

There it was again – this insinuation against my mother. It was ridiculous when one considered I had never once been abroad and was raised boy and man in Golders Green.

At this point I think I made a swift exit. My wife had sat there the entire time, saying nothing, just making her eyes slightly narrower.

But that was all behind me. She would be all right. Her father, the pompous old fool that he was, had connections and power enough to protect her. And I knew that without me she would be more secure and certainly safer.

Still, the memory and the returning feeling of guilt shook me and, feeling my legs failing, I sank down onto one of a pair of Spanish colonial antique chairs in the corner of the sitting room.

I thought of the wine in the cellar and wondered if it would do any real harm to take one of the bottles into the orchards and let that sleepy, joyful calm creep through me.

'Certainly not! I do not want you and I do not need you,' I shouted aloud to those bottles as I leapt to my feet. 'Where is your will power, Thomas Sebastian?'

Five minutes later I was hurrying up and into the high pastures, that tempting dark room full of its dusty black bottles pushed far from my mind, my notebook tucked into my pocket.

Chapter VII

I am officially in love, having now been to the beach with Isabella on four separate occasions. I think I could recite every single word she said to me on each of those four magnificent days together.

The first of the trips was arranged through some engineering on my part – I had taken to sitting on the bluff above my house, not exactly spying, but certainly hoping for inspiration as to how to meet Isabella again. I was afraid to knock on her door, for I was shy and became concerned I might come across as an inappropriate old man.

Finally, one morning, I saw Isabella and another ant figure, who I guessed to be Marta, come out of the villa, hop onto the scooter which is often parked there, and disappear down the road to the village.

I immediately ran down to the back of the house and all the way through it (stopping to check my face was clean and my hair was not looking too wild); then I ran pell-mell down the track to the road with the villas, slowing only when I got to the street. I calmed myself and then walked more slowly along, past Isabella's villa, past the villa of the fat man who had moved in next door, and then past another couple of those white villas which still stood patiently looking out at the horizon.

I found a good place to wait behind a large rock on the cliff edge. From there I was hidden from the eyes of those in the villas (not that I ever saw anyone in them except for the fat man), yet I was able to see large sections of the road winding its way down into the village and the tops of the fishermen's cottages. Part of the quay could also be seen, where the boats were just now coming in from the morning's fishing.

It was such a pretty sight. It would have been a good place to return to with a book, if it hadn't been for the fact it was so close to Isabella's villa I might have looked like a man obsessed.

I watched the fishermen playing with their nets and boats. It grew warm because there was no shade and I was just starting to doze off when the whine of the scooter floated up to me.

Confused for a moment, I jumped up and started casually walking along the road in the direction of the fork to the village.

By the time the scooter appeared over the crest of the cliff, my heart was beating fast. There was just one person on it, and I felt sick to think it might be Marta who wouldn't recognise me. But then I saw Isabella's brown hair curling out behind and my heart leapt a bit.

She passed by me a little way before she was able to stop the bike. I ran back to her and she cut the engine, taking several attempts to manage it.

'Terrible thing,' she said. 'I'm an awful driver. You should have seen me coming up from the village. I nearly killed myself.'

'Where's Marta?'

'Still in the village.'

It was peaceful just with the sound of the sea now that the noise of the scooter had been silenced.

'How will she get back?'

'Oh, she'll walk. She walks everywhere.'

Isabella seemed suddenly shy, and we stood like strangers for a moment or two.

'I'm sorry I missed your dinner party. I didn't see the note until the next morning. It had fallen to the ground.'

'Not to worry. Have you been to the city yet?'

'Not yet. I will go soon though.'

'Where are you off to now?'

'I thought I would wander down to the village.'

'Well, say "Hi" to Marta if you see her. I'm sure you couldn't miss her. She's the only one who doesn't look like she belongs.'

Above us a little bird wheeled across the sky. It made a peep-peep noise I'd not heard before.

'It's getting much warmer now, isn't it?' Isabella said.

'Yes. I thought it was on the turn.'

'Well ... should we go to that beach some time?'

'How about tomorrow?'

'Tomorrow? Yes, tomorrow is fine.' It took her a few kicks to get the scooter going again. 'Don't arrive too early. I'm a real lazy-head these days.'

She wobbled off unsteadily as she waved goodbye and I watched her drive the fifty yards to her villa and get off. Then she gave me another wave and I was forced to turn and follow the road down towards the village. As soon as I had dropped over the brow I fled the lane and pushed through the brush. Then I took a wide circle behind the villas over the fields and made my way back to *Ca'n Mola* with my head full of excited plans for the trip to the beach.

So now we have been four times. As the weather heats up, Isabella sheds her clothes like a bird shedding its winter plumage. She is very keen on sunbathing and has been teaching me how to do it.

Before she began her instructions I must confess I'd held an old-fashioned view about broiling yourself like a lamb chop under the grill. As a Londoner, and then a Tonbridger (if there is such a thing), I'd never had the occasion or the inclination to try to sunbathe before. In my childhood, holidays had been spent with an aunt in the Lake District, and although a desire to escape to a foreign holiday had come upon me in later years, France or Italy perhaps, my wife had made it clear she had no interest in travel and considered the rest of the world to be heathen. It's embarrassing to admit, but when I left England, it was the first time I'd ever been out of the country.

But I knew this sunbathing business was the height of fashion and I didn't want Isabella to think I was fuddy-duddy, so I was determined to give it a try. How annoyed my wife would be to know it. She had, on many occasions, instructed me with a sigh that it was just the thing to be the colour of a walnut. She'd tut and shake her head if she caught a whiff of my disbelief at the sight of her in the garden with our best silvered tray tucked under her chin.

When that first morning arrived, I came down and saw that the inevitable had happened, for nothing can stop a Spanish summer. The mercury had lifted above a pencil line labelled 'hot'. It was a giant of a day, with not a cloud in sight.

I hurried to collect up the things I'd found the day before and then I nervously walked down the hill to Isabella's, tripping over the stick of the parasol as I went.

She came casually out of her gate at the same time as I arrived, wearing a yellow dress with a skirt so short my eyes nearly popped out of my head. Her hair was pulled back with a sweet little orange head band. I didn't quite know where to look (obviously not at her legs) and felt myself reddening, but I don't suppose she noticed, she was so busy laughing at me.

'Thomas, *mio caro*,' she said. 'We're going to the beach, not darkest Peru.'

I was carrying rather a lot. I had a picnic rug, my trunks, and a towel under one arm, an enormous striped parasol on my shoulder which I'd found in *Ca'n Mola*'s cellar, and in my left hand was a bucket with a spade and some books. I was wearing a ridiculous sun hat that had belonged to Senyor Rodriguez, along with a pair of green check shorts I had found in his wardrobe which were far too large for me. They were tied around my waist with a piece of string. I had tried to hide the string in amongst the folds of fabric, but I realised now that an end had come unravelled and was hanging between my legs like a sheep's tail. Inwardly I groaned.

'I wanted to make sure we had everything we might need.'

'Well, I have this,' Isabella said, and held up a small picnic basket. 'Marta has no interest in the beach, but she made us some lunch.'

'Oh, isn't she coming?' I said, obviously feeling delighted at the fact. However pleasant she might be, her company could only ever be unwelcome to me.

'"Lying on a beach all day is not for me, Isabella,"' she said in a lazy voice I assumed was mocking Marta's.

'Not enough lizards?'

'Exactly. *Bravo, bravo.*'

I looked up at the villa, wondering if she might be at home, but Isabella had no interest in enlightening me and I was too shy to ask.

That first time the beach had been fairly empty – just a few families camped out with their parasols and rugs and little brown dogs, their sun-battered SEATs parked on the road behind.

My first initiation to the pleasures of sunbathing was to learn the rules of the placing of the rug. Isabella spent an inordinate amount of time on the task.

The blanket mustn't be on a bit of sand that was too sloped or had too much dried seaweed close by. It had to be spread out to its full capacity without any wrinkles or lumps of sand underneath. And then after all that, we had to move it again because there was another rule that it must be close enough to the water that Isabella felt connected to the sea, but not so near that it might get wet (we had to wait several minutes to determine whether our final spot met with this requirement).

There was more to this sunbathing than I'd realised.

It was funny that it didn't bother me, and how patiently I stood. If I had been with my wife I would have lost my temper long before and thrown the blanket down somewhere awful out of spite.

Then, that first time, Isabella pulled off her very, very short dress to reveal a red swimsuit. I pulled off my shirt and the two of us lay down on the rug with our heads under the parasol. I felt as if I were about to lose my virginity all over again. I would have been hideously awkward about it, but Isabella made everything seem so friendly and natural with her chatter that I was at once at my ease – this despite the fact that the two of us were lying in what, previously, I would have considered to be an embarrassing state of undress.

On the second and third trips she wore a rather daringly-cut swimsuit of a shiny green material and on the fourth she was in a yellow and white paisley bikini. I approved of them all, but for the time being the paisley bikini was my favourite.

'Have you ever been to America?' she said on that fourth visit, when the sun was particularly hot, introducing the topic out of the blue. 'I went there last summer to visit my cousin.'

I couldn't decide whether to lie and pretend that I had. I'm not sure it's the sort of thing you can get away with. She only needed to ask what colour the buses were or what I thought of such and such thing that everyone was raving about and that would be me, caught. So I told her the truth; that I had never been.

'You must go!' she exclaimed. 'Go to New York. It is just like the movies.'

This was no good at all. I was supposed to be trying to impress her. I tried to move the conversation onto sea birds, pointing out a few that were wheeling away above us (I had been swotting up from Rodriguez's botany books in preparation for meeting Marta), but Isabella barely registered my comments and carried on talking about America.

'We drove up to this festival in Newport. Have you ever heard of it? It's quite famous. They have all types of music there – American folk music and the music of their country people. But my cousin says it's about more than the music. It's about the young people and their hopes for the future of America. I'm going back again this year. I'm decided upon that.'

'When is it?'

'July.'

I struggled to think who might have been playing. Dylan someone? Had there been some article about someone called Dylan? Or was I getting confused with a rabbit from a children's show I had seen in France?

'Well ... who was the best then?' was all I could think of.

'Oh, it had to be Baez. I could close my eyes and die in that voice of hers. She's even better than Connie Francis – and that is something for an Italian to say.'

'I've not heard of Baez. Baez who?'

'Baez who? Joan Baez, of course. Really, Thomas, where have you been? I'll bring you a record.' Then she added as an afterthought, 'You do have a record player, don't you?'

'Of course.' I thought of Senyor Rodriguez's old wind-up machine. How Isabella would laugh if she saw it.

After a while we began talking of the Profumo scandal, which was still continuing to rumble on even then in 1964.

'I don't understand why he lied in the first place,' Isabella was saying, referring of course to Profumo. She pointed at her magazine. 'Look here. It says that he'd openly been about with her, and everyone in the party knew he was trying to put her as his lover in a flat.'

I shifted my head under the parasol, trying to line the edge of its shadow with the orchard tan line of my neck. Then I closed my eyes and let her voice sink into me and the sand about me.

'You don't understand what it is to be British, Isabella.'

She turned over to face me.

'So, explain it to me, Mr Sebastian. Tell me what is going on in that British head of yours.'

That was a question which was extremely difficult to answer since invariably when I was at the beach with Isabella there was very little going on in my head other than an overwhelming awe at the fact that I was lying half naked beside a scantily clad Isabella and a desire to jump on top of her.

'It's about the neighbours, you see Isabella. Profumo couldn't care less what his party thought – they were probably all at it too – but he'd be in agony as to what the neighbours might think.'

'Because of his wife, do you mean?'

'To some extent,' I said, and thought of my wife probably even now trying to ignore the whispers behind gloved hands at the WI meeting. 'It's the neighbours themselves really. I mean … Whatever would they say if they found out the chap next door was swanning about in a Bentley with some seventeen-year-old girl? However would he be able to face the wives at the bridge club?'

'The neighbours? You can't be serious, Thomas. What about the connection with the Russian, Ivanov?'

'The Russian? Profumo wouldn't give a damn about that. No, it was the neighbours I tell you. He was embarrassed and ashamed they would think him a silly fool over the girl.'

Isabella rolled back over and stretched out her long limbs and pointed her toes.

'And the church, what would they think at his church?'

At that l laughed out loud. 'He wouldn't care about that, Isabella.'

'Even if he were Catholic?'

'In England? Certainly not. There are Catholics and then there are English Catholics, you know. The two are very different.'

How easy it was to be confident of one's views when one talks to someone so young and fresh into the world.

'How funny you English are,' she said, and got back to the serious business of sunbathing.

And it was a serious business. I had the hang of it now and could lie in a meditative state, listening to the wash of the waves and the distant murmur of the nearby families. I watched with pleasure as my porridge-coloured skin turned to a golden bronze, finally giving credit after all these years to my mother's heritage. It made me feel more connected to her. My chest was slick and glistening from the oil and I had on a pair of sunglasses I'd found in one of Rodriguez's drawers. It was my opinion I was starting to look like a cross between James Bond, 007, licenced to kill, and a Latin gladiator.

'Be a darling and pass me some more sun oil, would you?' I said.

Isabella turned and grabbed it from where it was holding down the edge of the rug and replaced the weight of it with a shoe. Then she lay back down with her magazine held above her head.

I thought again of the wind-up record player back at *Ca'n Mola*. Perhaps I should make a joke of it if she and Marta came for supper. Something I had to find a way of arranging. I couldn't wait to meet Marta. It was essential we become the best of friends so as to ensure there was no barrier to Isabella and I spending as much times as possible together. 'Isabella?'

'Mmm?'

'Do you think we should arrange a supper? You, me, and Marta?'

'Why?'

'Well. We've been neighbours for a month, and I've never even introduced myself.'

Isabella turned her head and stared at me with a blank expression. 'That's because she's always off with her stupid lizards.'

'Still, I wouldn't want her to think I was being rude.'

I can't say that Isabella looked too enthusiastic at the prospect, but she said, 'I suppose you are right. Let me speak to her.'

Then I felt uneasy, because she obviously wasn't as keen on the plan as I had hoped, but the arrangement had to be made so there was no going back.

Chapter VIII

The next day I received another of those frightful missives from the agent and I was forced to send another three thousand of my beloved *pesetas* to him. This one read:

Dear Mr Waddington etc etc,

I hope that you and your wife are well and enjoying all the amenities that Ca'n Mola has to offer.

I write, firstly, to be reminding you that your rental instalment for the month is overdue again. I do not like to be put into a position of having to remind you of your obligations in regard to the agreement. I am finding this most unfair to me, but this is the second time that the rent has been arriving late and I feel obliged to remind you that this is most unacceptable. I have still been as yet unable to contact your references and without suitable replacements from you I am having to make my own enquiries.

I have been delayed in my attempt to come to the estate to complete my inventory check but I shall be doing so in the very near future.

Please give my regards to your wife,
Yours with warm felicities,
Jose Antonio Gonzalez
Madrid

He was such an annoying and persistent man, and I considered the tone of his letters to be disrespectful. At first his letter got me down considerably. I still hadn't been able to arrange that supper with Isabella, and I was no further forward in achieving a plan of recovery, despite hours and hours of racking my brains. I was really beginning to feel full of despair again, but then something happened which led, finally, to me having an idea. The more I thought about it, the more I realised this was THE IDEA. As soon as I realised I had it, I became beside myself with excitement and desire to put it into action. It was such an excellent idea, so perfect for my situation and so *doable*.

Before that, I'd been eyeing the padlock on the cellar door with my fingers itching to take a crowbar to it, and the days (other than those spent with Isabella) had been slithering by in a dust of boredom. For two weeks not a drop of alcohol had passed my lips. I felt I should have been awarded a medal for bravery.

In any event, it occurred to me, when I received the letter, that I should search through all the cupboards and drawers of the house to see if there were any extraneous cash lying around.

I felt a bit guilty at the thought of taking Rodriguez's money, but since living in his house and sleeping in his bed and reading all his books and using all his possessions, I felt as if a bond had grown up between us.

How wonderful it would have been if he were alive and I had truly been his guest and his friend. I imagined us greeting each other in his sitting room as we both came down for our evening aperitif. He might say again how pleased he was that I had come to stay with him. Of late I had been studying his art books in the hope of understanding some of the large modernist canvases that hung there. For what is a man, I considered, if he can't understand the simplest thing as a painting?

I imagined the two of us standing side by side in front of

the fireplace, gazing up at the Ramon Casas.

'It's a deliberate movement away from the idealism of the Romantics, wouldn't you say?'

'I think you could be right.'

'But so in keeping with the *modernisme* thinking.'

'*El meu volgut*, Thomas,' he would say, 'How good it is you stay with me.'

'No, no, Senyor Rodriguez, the honour is all mine. I hope I'm not disturbing your studies.'

'*Mai*! It is good. Very helpful to me.'

Would I have the courage to ask him about Isabella?

'Senyor Rodriguez,' I imaged myself saying to him. 'Do you think anything could happen between a child such as Isabella, and a man such as me?'

At that, Rodriguez would chuckle. 'Hardly a child, my friend. She is a woman, and you are a man. What does the rest matter?'

I imagined him as a larger than life character. About my height but broader and stronger, not a ten stone weakling like me. He always wore his white suit, and, when he was spruced up for the evening, I'm guessing he looked very dashing in it, with his greying hair swept up off his face and curling down to his shoulders. His cheeks were chubby and both they and his nose were tinted red from drink. On the bridge of this nose sat a pair of wire spectacles, and often, when he was saying something part serious and part outrageous, I imagined him bending forward and winking at me over the top of them.

To feel bad about taking the money was nonsense of course. It could do Rodriguez no good where he was and with Franco the inflation was out of control, so it was better spent than left lying around.

It should also be taken into account the fact that the family were fighting over quite a large estate (*Ca'n Mola* being just one of a number of holiday retreats), or so Isabella had told me, and that the whole affair was possibly worth millions of *pesetas*. Would they be concerned about a handful of notes distributed about *Ca'n Mola*? Of course not. Even after they'd stopped squabbling and finally agreed the settlement, there would be much to be done, what with the selling of the art collections and the much larger Barcelona estate that the agent had mentioned. They may not even get around to thinking of the little summer house over here for some time, and even then would they care about the petty cash lying within it? Of course not. By then Rodriguez's relatives would be so rich, they would probably say to themselves, 'Hah! I'm not going over there to search through that old man's things. I'll pay for someone to clean out the house and bring back the antiques and artwork, and whatever else they find, good luck to them'.

After all that reasoning, I felt comfortable with my actions and it was a small step from there to the concept that the money was mine and belonged in my suitcase. There wasn't much in any event, three hundred and fifty-four *pesetas* in all. I'd put the notes into the case and dropped the *centimos* into a dish by the front door.

This of course wasn't the IDEA – but it was the search of the house which had led to the IDEA. For in my ransacking of the drawers, and my browsing of the shelves for any hollowed out books, I found in the study some manuscripts, obviously typed on that dusty blue Royal Aristocrat.

They were a whole series of novels that appeared to be written by Rodriguez himself; each was in a different stage of completion, one looking like a complete work and others with just a few chapters or plot outlines.

I was particularly drawn to them because I'd been getting so bored with my dog dry days, and I thought if I were to read one more book on the history of contemporary art or how to build a transistor radio, I might throw *myself* off the cliff. So I'd been quite excited at the thought of some fiction, and written by the great Senyor Rodriguez himself, no less.

I chose the one which seemed closest to completion and

started reading that very afternoon. It was strange to see Rodriguez's close-looped handwriting in the margins, suggesting this improvement or that; I felt closer to him for it. How terrible! To think that the gentleman who had made those markings would never again be able to put pen to paper and leave in ink the contents of that great brain of his.

Once I started on the book, I have to say I was gripped. What a splendid story it was. I was entirely consumed by it and barely noticed the evening and the next day go by – I was so desperate to get to the end.

It was about an old priest called Father Gomez and it was as if the world of the priest leapt off the pages of the manuscript and straight into my brain. I started reading faster and faster. I had to find out what fate had in store for Father Gomez. He was a very believable character – a good man like myself, whom outside circumstances had troubled to a terrible degree. It was very easy to empathise with him, and I guessed this was what made the book so truly excellent.

But then it was all very unsatisfactory, for just as the story was winding up and obviously reaching its crescendo, it stopped abruptly. There were a few handwritten notes on ways the story might end, but none of them clear or concrete and I have to say it was most upsetting.

I went into the study and rifled around but there definitely weren't any other pages I could find. The truth was that poor old Rodriguez had killed himself before he had finished it. I picked up one or two of the other manuscripts, but they were in even earlier stages, some of them barely started at all.

It wasn't until later, several days after finding the manuscript, that the IDEA came to me. It was so good it didn't even need to go into the notebook. I knew straight away that this was the one. I was on the beach with Isabella and the two of us were working on an enormous sandcastle when suddenly the idea came to me. I stopped patting the top of the bucket and looked up. 'Isabella?'

'Yes, Thomas?'

'Do you know anything about publishing?'

She was just linking the channel she had made from the sea to our moat and her arms were covered in sand up to the elbows.

'Publishing?'

'Yes, do you know how to go about publishing a book?'

She smiled broadly. 'Why? Have you written one?'

'No,' I said hurriedly. 'A friend of mine has. He's coming to the island and I have to meet him for dinner.'

'A friend?' she said in surprise. I tried not to take this comment the wrong way.

'Yes, a friend,' I said bristling a little despite myself.

Realising she had been rude, Isabella blushed and set about her work again. 'He needs to get an agent. London is the best place. Or New York. I could write and ask my cousin for a recommendation, if you like?'

'No, no. I'm sure he knows what he's doing.' I patted the top of the bucket again and it lifted clear off, the last in a long line of turrets. 'Thanks anyway.'

I resolved there and then that I would go into the city that evening and find myself (or should I say Rodriguez) an agent. It was dangerous, but such a gamble had to be made if the scheme were to be carried out. I would slip in after dark and park the Jag in the shadows by the port. Luckily the Spanish work late into the evening, when most English men are at home with their slippers and pipe, so I thought I would be sure to find an agency open. It was an IDEA all right, and the best so far by a country mile.

Chapter IX

I found a literary agent, a chap from the mainland called Salvatore Matro, without much difficulty. He was described to me as the best agent in the whole of the city, but I had a sneaking suspicion it might be because he was the only agent in the city.

I found him to be an exuberant and intelligent man, and I liked him from the off. He wore red trousers, a green smoking jacket, and a Lebanese scarf, and when he was excited he would leap to his feet, throw the end of the scarf (which would always keep dropping down) over his shoulder, and start to pace about his office.

I had found him by the simple method of asking at the *correos* if they knew any literary agents and then walking over to the address on San Nicolas Street. His office – if you were generous enough to grant such a tiny space such an official title – was in the attic of an old merchant's house. The words 'Salvatore Matro: Agent to Celebrity' were engraved in Spanish on the glass of the door. He ushered me in; we had a few moments discussion, during which he established I had something to show him, then within five minutes he was reading and pacing.

'I like it!' he declared. Then he told me to go away and not come back for another two hours, because he was a fast reader, he said, and would have it finished by then. I went over to the Borne and sat upon a bench watching the tourists promenading with their ice-creams. All around me the bars were full of the early evening crowd, spilling out onto the streets with their holiday cocktails and pre-dinner gins and tonic. I became desperately thirsty, and the only way I restrained myself was by sitting on my hands and telling my feet they had been nailed to the paving stones. Finally, the two hours were up.

When I returned to the office I had to let myself in. There had been no answer to my knock because Salvatore Matro was still reading and pacing, a cigarette hanging from his yellowing fingers, but I could see that he was on the last few pages.

The man's ability to pace was a skill in itself since the room could only have been eight feet square, and into it were crowded a desk, two chairs, one of which I sat on, and a filing cabinet whose doors were wedged open and which were overspilling with typed manuscripts. Every shade of manila could be seen hanging out of the drawers, from crisp bleached white to the colour of cream that's been left out in the sun.

'It's good,' he said, finally, and he clutched the manuscript to his chest so that some of the pages became bent. 'Where did you say you came from?'

'My parents travelled.'

'To the Americas?'

'That's where they came from. They travelled to the Arctic, where I was raised. They were scientists.'

Salvatore took another good look at me. 'What did they study?'

'Penguins,' I said. It is always better to lie with brevity.

'Fascinating,' said Salvatore Matro, and he picked up a small gold box from his desk and offered me an American cigarette. I took one, lit it, and sucked on it greedily. Salvatore waited patiently for me to finish.

'But tell me, Rodriguez,' for that was the name I had given him, 'Why doesn't the washerwoman help the little girl when Father Gomez asks her to?'

I had expected this question and was prepared for it.

'It's symbolic of the Franco state.'

'Mmm. Dangerous. But not obvious.'

'Will it be a problem?'

Salvatore thought, standing stock still while he did so. 'The language is more the issue. Catalan ... well ... you know how it is.'

I hoped against hope he wouldn't ask me to convert it to Spanish. That would take months and I might not even be able to do it. And I doubly hoped he wouldn't try to speak to me in Catalan, for then the game would be up. As it was, my heavily worked upon Spanish, though just about holding up, was confusing him by its accent.

'Ah! Perhaps you could...' Then Salvatore shook his head. 'No, it wouldn't be the same. It would lose the nascent beauty of the original.'

He came and squeezed himself into the space behind his desk and stubbed out his cigarette. 'Things are loosening up. Maybe the timing is right. Is this why you waited and came to me now?'

I shrugged my shoulders, not wanting to take credit for the timing of Rodriguez's death.

Salvatore smiled in a beneficent way at my modesty. 'I think I know a publisher who might be brave enough.'

'Here on the island?'

'In Barcelona.'

'Can't we find a publisher here?'

'Here?' Salvatore looked at me as if I was mad. 'What would be the point of that? No, Barcelona is the only way.'

'The problem is my nerves,' I said.

'Don't worry about that, Rodriguez. I'll take care of that.'

He opened the box of American cigarettes again and turned it open to me.

'Good,' I said, and took one. There was also a bottle of whiskey on his desk; my eyes kept drifting to it.

'But what about the ending, Rodriguez?'

'The ending?'

'Yes. It's not really finished, is it?'

'Oh, that,' I blustered. 'There's not much needed to end it. Just a few chapters.'

'Yes, but how does it end?'

I looked around the office in hope of inspiration, at the cabinet spilling over with manuscripts.

'There are several endings. I just need to choose the one I prefer.'

Salvatore seemed satisfied by that.

'Well, Rodriguez,' he said. 'You just get this book finished and I will take care of the rest. How long do you think it will take?'

'Not long – a few weeks, perhaps. Once I've figured out which ending to use, it's just a matter of typing it up.'

'Fantastic, Rodriguez. Let's have a drink to celebrate.'

And I knew I should have said something as he searched in his drawers for another glass, and I know I could have said something as he poured out one glass and then started on the next, but it would have seemed churlish. This was such an important project; it was essential Salvatore was on my side and that he should feel the two of us were partners in this venture. So I took the glass of Dublin whiskey, my gaze still fixed to the label which read 'Not a drop is sold till it's seven years old' and took a swig.

Then Salvatore leapt to his feet, told me how excited he was by the project, and insisted he was going to take me to dinner at a restaurant called Luigi's, so I quickly drained my glass and followed him to an Italian place two doors down.

He ordered wine and all the food, and then told me how he had tired of the mainland and come to the island instead.

'It's all pulp,' he said, 'that's all they want. And paper! Who would want to read a paper backed book? I told them they'd never get any of my clients published straight to paper. But they were all as bad as each other. The agents, the writers. They were all happy in paperback. What about you,

Rodriguez? Would you be happy to see your book encased only in paper? Hah! I'll publish the books myself is what I told them! But I didn't, of course...'

I groaned inwardly. Had I managed to find the only agent in town who had no interest in making money? It was money I wanted and Salvatore had better know this from the off or I determined we would part ways there and then.

'I couldn't care less if they published in toilet tissue,' I said. 'So long as they pay me.'

I thought perhaps Salvatore was going to throw down some money and storm off, but he fingered his wallet, which sat on the table, and gazed into the distance.

'Very well. You make yourself perfectly clear, Rodriguez. A little fluidity in life would not go amiss for me either, right now.'

'Well, there are bills to be paid...' I started. Then to make him feel better, I made up some nonsense about a child over in Madrid whose mother was particularly demanding in a financial sense.

'As a matter of fact,' I said, 'her spending habits are wildly out of control, but I can't bring her over here because she wouldn't take to the island and I very much doubt the island would take to her.'

Salvatore nodded gravely, and I thought perhaps by his face he was trying to tell me that he had been in a similar situation himself at one time.

'You shall make money Rodriguez. I have no doubt of that. And I shall be part of it. The translation rights alone will be enough to appease your *Madrilena* until she is old. Perhaps even until the child is old.'

At this I couldn't help my heart leaping and I wondered if perhaps I could play this game a little longer than I'd initially planned. My first thought had been to take any advance I could, but what if there was more to come? What if there were to be a whole series of payments? I hadn't considered that.

The major difficulty was that I was not Rodriguez, and eventually that would out. Would anyone on the island be able to connect Senyor Rodriguez (up and coming writer) with Senyor Rodriguez (lately deceased)? It was a common enough name. The only connection, of course, was *Ca'n Mola*. Damn it. Perhaps I should have taken the novel and tried to publish it in my own name. But then ... how would I have explained the fact it was written in Catalan?

I resolved immediately that I must keep my address a secret from Salvatore. After our lunch I would go back to the *correos* and purchase a mail box in the name of Rodriguez and tell Salvatore to correspond with me there.

Salvatore continued to look glum, but then the owner of the restaurant, a fat Italian in chef whites, came out from the kitchen and Salvatore threw his scarf over his shoulder and (seeming to resign himself to all that was to come, hardback or paper) got up to enthusiastically hug the man like a brother; the subject of paperbacks was forgotten.

I was introduced to Luigi as Salvatore's greatest find.

'Rodriguez is a literary genius,' Salvatore said excitedly, patting me on the chest with the arm that wasn't already laced up with Luigi's.

Luigi became more excited then than Salvatore and arranged for a ridiculous pile of profiteroles to be brought to the table with sparkling sticks, so that the whole restaurant turned to look at us even more than they were already and I became embarrassed and tried to remind Salvatore of his promise that I would be kept discreetly anonymous.

'Yes, yes,' said Salvatore, 'but this is Luigi's. That doesn't count here.'

So then I was subjected to the waiters coming over to shake my hand and congratulate me and again I was forced to remind Salvatore that we hadn't even secured a publishing deal yet, and that perhaps we should keep things on the lowdown until everything was sorted. Salvatore agreed by putting his finger to his lips and shushing and waving Luigi and all the waiters away in a dramatic fashion.

'Quite right, Rodriguez,' Salvatore said. 'Let's not tempt fate.'

So we started upon the pile of profiteroles. He ate very few and instead talked with great excitement about which publishing houses he would approach and why, and meanwhile I steadily ate all the soft glossy brown rounds until my stomach was fit to burst and my heart was full of happiness; my head was undoubtedly the biggest of the lot, and amongst it all I somehow forgot that it wasn't me who had written the book, it was really the late Rodriguez. When I remembered that I felt slightly ashamed – but needs must when the devil drives and all that.

At the end of the meal, we arranged that I would return to see Salvatore in a week, by which time he would have been over to Barcelona to see the publishing houses and would have some better idea of who we should allow to publish my book.

'The only thing I'm not sure about is the title,' he said as we parted. 'It's a little dull isn't it?'

At this I smarted, for the title was my only true handiwork in the project. (After days of anguishing I had finally settled upon *The Tale of Father Gomez* and had spent a good hour one day, when the sun had been shining, sitting in Rodriguez's dusty study typing up a front page with it all spelt correctly.)

'We can change it if you want,' I said, somewhat sulkily.

'No, no, not if you don't want to. Let's call it a working title for now.'

So the book remained *The Tale of Father Gomez*, which I was pleased about. Then I felt at least I had some true claim to ownership since it was now already a collaborative work between Rodriguez and me.

Salvatore and I shook hands; he threw his scarf over his shoulder one final time, and made me promise to finish the book as quickly as I could. Then we parted ways – he back to his office, and me to a bar to celebrate.

Chapter X

This writing business isn't as easy as one would think. Each day I tried for hours, but every word had to be fought for and soon even my diction stopped making sense. Sometimes I would sit in Rodriguez's study and look over what I'd written, and realise I had begun to mix up my languages. There'd be one half of an English expression married unhappily to another of Catalan and yet another of Spanish, such that I didn't see how anyone could make any sense of it. My contribution to the book held so little similarity to Rodriguez's elegant prose that it must have been apparent my ending was a complete work of fiction.

As the summer progressed, a few of my old habits crept in. I didn't see that I could be blamed. It was hard, sitting day after day on my own in the heat, trying to be creative, with the pressure of it all on my shoulders.

Each day the temperature rose and nudged the little maximum line of the thermometer up yet another mark, and I knew another day of summer was gone, with the book no closer to being finished and my rescue no nearer.

Outside, the crisp greens and yellows disappeared and instead everything became dusty and bleached. In the afternoons, it seemed as if the very air of the garden lifted off the ground to hover at shoulder height, creating a haze in which all the brightness and colour merged together in one great confusion of heat.

Pretty soon I only went to the orchards first thing in the morning because for the rest of the day it became impossibly hot; afternoons I shut myself away in the study.

I tried so hard to keep off the booze, at least until the sun was touching the top of the *casitas*, but I didn't always succeed. (The padlock on the cellar had suffered an unfortunate accident.) On and on I struggled, trying with this ending and then with that one. Whether it was because I was a beginner to this writing game or whether it was because there was something fundamentally flawed with Rodriguez's story arc, I couldn't for the life of me find a satisfactory ending for Father Gomez.

Then, each evening, five o'clock would approach and I'd hear Rodriguez's clock in the hall sound out its chimes. I'd say to myself, 'I haven't made much progress. Let's try and work on until at least six.' But then would come the voices of all those dear friends of mine in the cellar. 'Apertif, Thomas!' they would call. 'Apertif!'

My productivity would start to wane, and before I knew where I was my fingers would be off the typewriter keys, my legs would be marching over to the back door, and there I'd be, standing in the dim light of the cellar, caressing the racks.

And I have something worse to confess. I picked up a nasty habit of going into the city at night and having a few drinks in the bars there. I'm a weak man, that's my difficulty If only I hadn't taken that glass of whiskey from Salvatore.

Often I would shout at myself, 'Thomas! Where is your willpower?' and look at those bottles in the cellar and tell them, 'I don't want you! I don't need you!' but they would always come back with something clever, something I hadn't thought of. After all, they would say, you are the one under the cosh. There'll be plenty of time for sobriety and getting your act together once the money situation is resolved.

The added trouble was that I was full of frustration and desire, and it wasn't sitting well on me. As I made my lonely supper each evening, all I could think of was of Isabella and

Marta getting on their scooter to head off to some party or other. I had to find a way to become friends with them both, so that we might spend our evenings together.

So, on my bad days I would be tempted into taking a little wine with my supper to chase away the blues, and then of course a spirit or two. Then often I would sit on the sofa and take a little more wine and think about Isabella. And I would start to think of how I might manage my return to England once I had the funds released from the book and how she might want to come with me.

The more I drank, the fancier my schemes of returning triumphant became, and I would begin to write lengthy notes to myself in order to suggest this or that strategy, with scrawled details as to how it might be achieved. I would pin the notes up where I might see them in the morning, so that these very excellent thoughts might not get forgotten. This was often the way my bad evenings went.

Sometimes I would manage a day or two off the booze and I would be full of congratulations for myself and think how I had finally cracked it, what with the chanting and the willpower and the like. These were the good days.

But after the good days there always seemed to be some reason why a little drink was much deserved or else very much needed. Often I would think to myself, 'Now I've been so very good recently and I have completed so many pages of writing that I deserve a little treat'. Or something trivial would happen which would upset me and remind me how hopeless it all was, and then I would think what terrible luck I have, and how I couldn't go on without a little support, and that any man of merit would feel the same.

Either way, on these days after the good days, I'd tell myself I would only drink a moderate amount. Be moderate and temperate, that was the thing. I would just have half a bottle. I might even make a mark on the bottle and say, 'There, I shall drink only to the mark'.

But the glasses always seemed to slip away so quickly that

often I wouldn't even have finished my supper before the mark was reached, and I'd consider it would be a shame not to have a little wine with the cheese, (for eating cheese without wine is like making love to a woman without touching her).

So I'd turn the bottle around so I couldn't see the mark; I'd tell myself how ridiculous I was being and that I was a grown man, perfectly capable of having a few drinks and controlling myself.

I don't know why it always went so badly wrong from there. Usually another bottle would seem appropriate, or perhaps a little spirit, for that would only be a short and a short could be nursed over many hours, by which time the wine inside me would be gone, so really by drinking a spirit I would only be keeping things in a state of constantness and not slipping down that slippery slope.

On those sorts of days, before I knew where I was, I would once again be sitting on the sofa writing notes to my more sober self for the morning, and ranting and raving about whatever had got me worked up into a temper that evening.

Sometimes, when I was in one of those moods, something odd would happen. I would start to think about that suit.

I have no idea why. It had something to do with the white linen. Perhaps it was a connection to my father, to whom I had been such a disappointment, and his colonial past – a badge of empire, or passage to a club to which I had never belonged.

You see, a man in a linen suit is a man in charge of himself and his situation. That time in the city, Susan and her friend Maureen and the barmen – all of them had treated me in a way that was different from how I was accustomed to being treated. I had become a man of substance when I was wearing the white suit, like Rodriguez himself.

The first evening that this realisation came upon me I felt a sudden excitement at the thought of putting it on again and becoming that other, more confident, man.

I had been cross with myself for my behaviour the last

time, and I'd made a promise not to go to the city again, but really... would it really hurt? So long as I was careful and didn't spend too much; I could just sit quietly in a bar and nurse a Black & White or two – that wouldn't make such a noticeable hole in my stock pile of *pesetas*. That was how my thinking went.

I know it sounds odd, but that evening I felt the suit began calling to me. It was calling my name and telling me not to be such a coward. I tried for an age to ignore it, but the more I drank, the more I could hear it. I was forced to skulk upstairs feeling guilty and embarrassed – as if there was anyone to see. I pulled it out of the closet.

It's difficult to explain what the sight of that white linen did to me. I touched the soft fabric and held it to my cheek. Then I laid it carefully down on the bed while I undressed. As soon as I had it on, I felt a change in my demeanour.

My height, I'm convinced, increased by at least an inch, and my shoulders became squarer. I'd put on a little weight since I'd last worn it, what with all the *manchego* and *sobresadas*, and I now nearly filled it out. With my newly acquired tan one might even say I could pass for a modern-day conquistador, a rugged version of handsome.

'*Buenos Tardes*,' I said to the mirror.

In my cups, I fancied that the late Senyor Rodriguez stood behind me with an approving look, his hand clamped to my shoulder.

'*Molt Bona*, Thomas. At last, you look like a real man.'

I tried to explain to Rodriguez that I hadn't the funds to go out, but he just shook his head in disbelief.

'What is money for, but to live?' he growled.

So I went to the suitcase under the bed and took out a few notes, barely anything at all.

'Take a little more, Thomas,' Rodriguez said, looking over my shoulder. 'You don't have to spend it all, do you?'

He was right, of course. So I did take a little more, and then I hurried downstairs and out of the house before I could change my mind.

Isabella and Marta's villa was all shut up and in darkness, but I guessed they were in bed because the scooter was parked neatly by my car, its front wheel turned towards the sea.

I was afraid they might hear the car, so I let the Jag roll along a bit before starting the engine.

I couldn't possibly name all the bars I visited on that first night out – definitely the 23 Club and then Miami's, and then later a place called Tito's, down on the front.

As I strolled down the Borne with my hands in the pockets of Rodriguez's trousers, I thought of who I might be in my white suit – the Governor General of some far flung British territory; Rodriguez, the Viceroy of... of... somewhere exotic where the very air is wet from the heat.

I felt as if the city was healing me, that something oozed out of those stone walls and settled into me, calming me, and correcting the balance of the chemicals that flew through my arteries and into my heart and head, causing me to panic or take the seed of some crazy thought and nurture it like a demon until it possessed me from the inside out.

I came out at the waterfront beside the cathedral, or the *Seu* as they call it around here, and stood for a moment in front of its majestic walls, looking at the lights dotted around the bay. In one of Rodriguez's books I had read of Rusinol who had said of the cathedral that it looked as if it had been 'erected with one single blow of the hammer, in one single moment of creation, and of one solid block'. I thought about what that must feel like, to be created into a form which will never change, that is so sure of itself and its rightness. Perhaps that was how Rodriguez had felt, I considered, as I continued over to Tito's.

It was there that I bumped into Susan and much jollity was shared when it happened.

'Why didn't you call me?' she said with a pout after she

had stopped laughing.

'I lost your number,' and to be fair this was true.

So I kissed her on the cheek and she didn't seem to care, and even suggested we go over to Miami's because she thought that Tito's was dead that night, and although I had just come from there I agreed and went with her.

That, of course, was the first of many nights venturing out into the City after dark. I met with Susan on many occasions but always by accident, for my heart belonged to Isabella. Susan and I never made plans to meet, but she was always careful to tell me in which bar she might be found were I to come on such and such a night.

Each morning after a long night out, I would remind myself that I hadn't the money to be drinking in the city and entertaining girls, but by the evening my resolve would weaken once more. I'd feel the need to talk to someone other than myself, and I'd think it wasn't healthy sitting alone night after night.

It's funny how inventive the drink can be, because of course all I really wanted was to be in a bar, surrounded by the smell of it; to be close to my fellow congregation, all of us praying to our god.

Susan wasn't Isabella, but I was in such a fervour of desire by this time I felt drawn to the company of women. She was a lovely girl and, although I say it myself, she had begun to idolise me. I had taken to talking to her in a very knowledgeable way about all sorts of things – all the cleverness I had picked up from Rodriguez's books, and she lapped it up. I'm ashamed to admit I saw her as a testing ground for my conversations with Isabella, but it didn't really work as Isabella would always yawn loudly if I so much as started on a fact. In any event, so long as Isabella never found out about Susan, I wasn't doing anyone any harm. It was all very proper and British with Susan as she was a bit of a prude if truth be told. I just had to be sure to keep the spending under control and not lose the run of myself, as I have in the past, for the amount of *pesetas* in the suitcase was becoming alarmingly low.

Chapter XI

Towards the end of July I received another letter from the agent. It came on a day I would have preferred not to receive it, as my head was split open from a particularly wild night of carousing with Susan the previous evening. What fun that girl was, and such a bad influence.

I ripped the letter open angrily. Why was I constantly disturbed by this ridiculous man? It read:

Dear Mr Waddington,

Further to my last correspondence, I had by now been expecting to receive your rental instalment for the month of July and I am exceedingly upset to inform you that I have still not received it.

I am expecting that this is an oversight on your part, but this is become a serious matter as the August payment is also now due. Perhaps my note has crossed over with your sending of the funds to me. If this is the case, please ignore the above with my heartfelt apologies.

Otherwise I find that the relatives of the late Rodriguez are more increasingly nervous of this situation and are pressing down on top of me. I have attempted to reassure them that you are an English gentleman, and that there is therefore no cause for them to be at all concerned, but nonetheless, they are becoming more and more unsettled and will look to

remedy the situation if it continues in this way.
  Please give my regards to your wife,

  Yours with warm felicities,
  Jose Antonio Gonzalez
  Madrid

After that it was hard to maintain my positive frame of mind, and it took all my courage to go upstairs and look into the suitcase under the bed. My heart beat fast to see so few notes nestling within the blue silk lining. Where had they all gone?

With a heavy heart, I took them out and counted them. One thousand, eight hundred *pesetas*. Not even enough to pay for the August rent, which meant my plan of attack for the agent had gone awry. I sat glumly down on my haunches before looking underneath where the suitcase had sat. Then I searched the pockets of the white linen trousers, where I found a few *reales*, but no more *pesetas*. If I hadn't had the prospect of the book I would have been very scared indeed by now. At my last meeting with Salvatore he had told me with delight that a publisher had been found. The book had been sold and was due for delivery at the end of the month.

I could hardly believe it when he told me. His face had been crumpled up with delight and he had joyously lit a cigarette for himself, then another for me, then he'd poured us both a glass of whiskey to celebrate.

'Imagine, Rodriguez,' he had said to me over his desk in an excited fashion. 'Imagine what a comeback this will be. They'll be calling me back to Madrid. How in demand I shall be as an agent.'

Then he swallowed a mouthful of the Jameson's and hurried on to say, 'And you too of course, Rodriguez.'

Then he pressed me on how the final chapters were going.

'Good, good,' I'd said, and tried to leave it at that. Fortunately he was a trusting sort and didn't push me any further.

The terrifying truth was that I was no closer to having an ending, but there were still three weeks to go and I was sure with a little concentration I would get there.

Not today, though. Today I was due to see Isabella, and of course that always came before work. The two of us had decided to try out a new beach. Our old one had suddenly become horribly busy with the August holiday crowd, and nowadays it was hard to find a spot to ourselves without some child plopping beside us and showering us with his sandy fun.

I'd also found some snorkelling equipment in the cellar of *Ca'n Mola* and I was desperate to try it out. It came with a spear gun, a mask, and a little rubber snorkel. Via messages passed between us all, Marta was kind enough to inform me that a particular cove just west of our usual beach was likely to be the best for my squid-fishing adventure. The narrowness of the bay would act as a funnel for the sea life, Marta had confidently reassured Isabella. The warm waters over the submerged rocks would be certain to be crystal clear and make for good hunting.

For once I had arranged to bring the picnic. I splashed out, even though I shouldn't have, on fresh *ensaimades* stuffed with pumpkin; I'd made egg and tomato sandwiches from my very own chickens' eggs, and brought fresh figs from the garden, and some wild strawberries I had found growing in the orchards.

I was stuffing the picnic into the car's locker when Isabella came out of her house and over to me. I was still feeling terribly hungover, and wore Rodriguez's sunglasses. I so hoped Isabella wouldn't notice, but things were in such a bad state I guess it was unavoidable.

'Goodness, Thomas. Did you fall into a bottle of gin last night?' she said, after giving me her usual kisses on each cheek.

Then I felt terribly embarrassed. 'I'm so sorry,' I said, and I muttered a disgraceful lie. 'I met up with that old friend. The writer, you know?'

Isabella raised an eyebrow, so I stumbled on. 'His agent's found him a publisher. He was desperate to celebrate. I couldn't really say no. I'm so sorry. I'm in a bit of a state.'

Isabella smiled in a knowing way and I wasn't sure whether the smile meant she knew that boys would be boys, or whether she knew I was lying.

'I don't know why you don't come to one of the institute parties with Marta and me one evening. I keep inviting you.' Then she finished off by saying, 'And we wouldn't mind if your friend came too.'

I wasn't sure what she meant, because she said the word 'friend' in a most pointed way. Did she think I'd spent the evening with another woman? Was she jealous? I hoped that was the case.

'Mmm, of course. I'd love to come,' I said hurriedly, though it was impossible. It was all due to that stupid mistake I had made on the first day we'd met, when I'd told her my real name. There was no way I could go to a party and have her introduce me to a host of people. Imagine it! Imagine one of them turning politely to me and saying, 'Thomas Sebastian? *The* Thomas Sebastian? The one who is wanted by Interpol and the British taxman? The one whose wife is desperately searching for him all over Europe?'

In any event, I decided it best to seem to acquiesce; I could tell Isabella herself was in an off mood that day. I didn't think it was my fault, but to be honest I wasn't in a state to be capable of making any sort of judgement. All I knew was that women can have days when nothing around them is right and everyone else is a monster of the first degree. Certainly my wife had had plenty of those sorts of days and I had a sneaking suspicion that Isabella was having one too. How close we had become.

The beach turned out to be a rocky little affair, wedged at

the bottom of a natural cove, between two cliff faces. We'd found the place without difficulty, parked as far down as we could, and then walked the rest of the way, following a steep path down to the beach. We found, when we got there, that we had the place to ourselves.

'Isn't it a relief after the other beach has become so crowded?' Isabella said, but there was no reply from me because the walk down over the rocks was taking my breath from me, and Isabella was already giving me those looks out of the corner of her eye which suggested she saw how laboured my breathing was, but was too polite to mention it. I really hoped she understood that it was because of the heat, not because I was old and out of shape. I had put on a few pounds, I must confess. Rodriguez's shorts now fitted me rather well.

'So do you know how to do it?'

'Sorry, Isabella?'

'Do you know how to do it?' Isabella pulled the snorkel out of my bucket and waved it at me.

I had to confess that I didn't, so Isabella put the mask on and the snorkel in her mouth and demonstrated, pretending to swim in the air. Then she handed them to me.

'Don't get burnt, Thomas.'

As I wedged the stick of the parasol between two rocks for her, I promised I wouldn't.

'Is that ok?'

'Yes, *basta, basta*! Go and do your snorkelling thing. Bring me back a squid.'

'Yes, yes. No hurry is there?'

I lay down on the rocks beside Isabella and looked at the dark waters. Going in might cure me or finally polish me off. 'So where is Marta today?'

'Mmm?'

'Where is Marta today?'

'On the north side, somewhere near Alcudia. She left at five this morning.'

I wondered with a horror whether I had passed her on the road as I came back from the city.

'And when is she due back?'

'Around five this evening.'

'I'm beginning to think she doesn't exist and you've made her up.'

Isabella already had her nose in a magazine, and she didn't look up, but laughed and said, 'Wouldn't that be exciting?'

I brooded and looked down at my green shorts. I wanted Isabella to talk to me. 'Isabella?'

'Mmm?'

'Why don't you ever swim?'

'Because I don't know how, Thomas, *mio caro.*'

'I see.'

There were waves lapping gently on the rock by our toes.

'Do you want me to teach you?'

'Not now, Thomas.'

Eventually it grew so hot that I was forced to dip into the water and quickly pull myself out again just to cool off, and then I managed to persuade Isabella we should start into the picnic basket, even though it was still only eleven.

'Are you feeling better?' she asked after we had eaten.

'Yes, thank you.' Actually I was gagging for a Bloody Mary, but there was not much that could be done about that. I should have packed some wine in the basket. Was it too far to drive back for it? Isabella would have thought I was mad. In any event, it wouldn't be worth the cost of the missed time with Isabella.

'So your friend found himself an agent?'

'Yes. He's doing very well. They're very excited about the book.'

'Did you know your late Mr Rodriguez was a great supporter of the arts?'

'Was he really?'

'Yes, Marta said so. Lots of young artists lived with him. They used to quite turn the village upside down when they were on a rampage, she was told.'

We both looked at a seagull that was trying to brave its way over to the remains of our lunch.

'Goodness, it's hot, isn't, Thomas?'

'And where are they now, I wonder?'

'Yes, it's sad, isn't it?'

'Yes. Why did he do it, do you think?'

A shadow passed over Isabella's face.

'Let's not talk about it, Thomas.'

'No, of course not.'

After that I tried to read a book, but it was too hot, so I gave up and took one of Isabella's gossip rags instead, but I found it all a bit racy. What with the heat and the hangover, and the lounging around, the brain does click onto certain things. Today, Isabella was wearing a brand new white costume and very little else. It was all I could do not to stare at the soft rounds of her breasts poking out of the top and lick my lips when I spied the beads of sweat forming between them.

What a torture it is to be an Englishman. Because you know we are hopeless when it comes to these things unless we have plenty of gins and tonic or a Scotch or two inside us. I promise you I thought Isabella could lie there naked, with her legs wide apart and moan, 'Take me, Thomas!' and I'd probably answer, 'Well now, Isabella, are you sure, because I wouldn't want to misunderstand, and would you please clarify whether you mean now, this minute, or whether you are suggesting an agenda for later this evening, or perhaps even later this year when the weather has turned again?'

There had to be an opportunity for drink to be involved – a little Dutch courage for me and for Isabella. I had to arrange that supper with Marta. Nothing would move forward between us without it.

'Isabella…'

'Yes?'

'I'm sorry I've not come to one of your institute parties. It's just … I'm not great with crowds.'

She didn't even look at me. 'That's a shame.'

'Why don't we have that supper one night?'

'Who do you mean?'

'You, me, and Marta, .'

Again Isabella didn't put her magazine down. 'If that's what you want. It won't be as much fun as you think, you know.'

I suddenly wanted to tell Isabella I had fallen in love with her, but instead I asked her about Marta and how the two of them had met.

'In finishing school,' she said. Then almost straight away she went on to say, 'I was very unhappy,' and she suddenly looked intensely sad, as she had when I'd seen her from the hill top, sitting beside her pool.

Oh dear. What did one say to that? I didn't want her be sad. I had planned that today I would reach across and take her hand and tell her how I felt about her and ask whether there was any hope for us. Things weren't going according to the notes I had scribbled drunkenly down last night before I went to bed. And now here we were dredging up her unhappy moments. It was all my fault for being such bad company.

'Look!' I said, and pointed up at the sky. 'I think that could be a purple heron. How unusual to see one this far north. They mainly stay in Africa, you know.'

'Really?'

'Yes, honestly. We're very lucky to see it.'

Isabella pulled down her magazine, scrunched up her eyes, and peered at the speck in the sky.

'Well, I feel very privileged,' she said.

We sat for a moment in silence and then I gave in. 'I'm sorry you weren't happy in school. Was it the other girls? Did they bully you?'

'A little.'

'And are you happy here? On the island, I mean?' I asked.

Isabella seemed to consider the question. 'I'm happier, but

I wouldn't say that I'm happy.'

Then it all came out. I don't know whether it was because she was out of sorts or because I was in such an obviously dreadful state and it was to take my mind off it (that was the sort of sweet thing Isabella would do without even making a fuss), but she went on and told me her sad story in all its terrible detail.

When she was nineteen she had been seduced by a scoundrel who had pretended he was a count and turned out to be nothing of the sort. She had been spending the summer with friends of her family in a house on the shore of Lake Maggiore when she had been unfortunate enough to be introduced to him.

It seemed the more she talked, the more she wanted to talk, until she couldn't seem to stop, and it all came flooding out: how the seduction had taken place; how it had hurt a little, but how she had been so enthralled with the devil, and so convinced he would marry her, she would have done anything he asked.

She said it was only after she realised she had been taken for a fool that she had discovered he had used the same words on her as he had used on Maria Velotti a year earlier. 'Exactly! Exactly the same words,' she exclaimed, 'sentence for sentence all exactly the same.' She told me this with the amazement of it still lingering in her voice.

A message had been sent to the man to see what his intentions were. Fortunately the man was wealthy. His intentions turned out to be generous, if not honourable. A compromise was reached and Isabella was sent to school in Geneva, where she was to learn to ski, speak perfect English and French, and a little German. The journey to the school was interrupted by a short stay in Zermatt where everything was handled with ruthless efficiency and the problem taken from her.

'Right now he must be learning to speak,' she said. 'His first word will probably be "mama". Isn't that ironic?'

I didn't know what to say, so I didn't say anything.

'I wonder what language it will be in,' Isabella continued. 'I suppose it is the same in so many. Mamma, Maman...' Then she frowned. 'I hope it isn't German. Mutter. No, I hope it is a romance language like mine, and not German, or English for that matter.'

I wanted to take her in my arms and hold her, but it was as if I were glued to that rock.

'Marta was my saviour,' Isabella said. 'She told me that nothing in the world really mattered except that I should live in the moment and that there were always good things to be found in the moment.'

I imaged Marta sitting cross-legged on a bed in a flannel nightgown while Isabella, dressed in Parisian silk, lay on her side. Isabella's hand was tucked under her head and a tear rolled down her cheek as she looked up at her friend and confessed her troubles.

'Like *ensaimades*,' I managed to stutter out.

Isabella looked at me with a confused expression. 'Sorry?'

'Good things in the moment. Like *ensaimades*.'

'Yes, exactly.' And then she laughed and the bright and breezy Isabella returned.

'Do you know, Thomas, you are now one of only nine people who know my secret. I hope you won't tell anyone.'

I promised her faithfully that I never would and then I tried to figure out who the nine people were. I think she guessed it because she went on to say, counting on her fingers as she did, 'Mama, Papa, me, him of course, you, the doctor in Zermatt, his nurse, my head teacher (she had to be told in case there were any complications), and of course they had to tell Marta.'

'Why did they have to tell Marta?'

'Marta was the school nurse.'

'Marta was the school nurse?' I said, not being able to hold back the surprise from my voice.

'Yes, didn't I say? Oh, I see what you mean. Did you think

Marta was one of the students?'

'It was just that you said you were here with a friend, so I thought...'

Isabella looked a little bashful. 'She is my friend, but she's also my ... my ... travelling companion.'

How old fashioned, I thought, but then I shouldn't have been terribly surprised. She was Italian after all. So Marta was a chaperone. Paid for, no doubt, by the parents – or perhaps even by the scoundrel, if he were still on the hook for such things.

'Marta was supporting herself with the nursing while she studied. Her real passion has always been zoology.'

'So she became a professor?'

'A professor? Nothing so grand. She has a job helping a professor with his field research. She has to count lizards.'

'Count lizards?'

'Yes.'

'How many are there?'

'Oh, dozens. You'd be surprised.'

'And you came with her because...'

'They all thought the peace and quiet would do me good. You see, at first I didn't seem to care too much. It was as though it had never really happened, as if it was just a dream or something. I went over and had that wonderful summer with my cousin at the Newport festival. We just slept on the beach and sang and laughed – but then at Christmas I couldn't seem to get him out of my head, the baby that is. I just started going over and over thinking about him and wondering what he was doing until it drove me crazy and then I ... I ... It didn't work, obviously.'

I put my hand on hers. 'You don't need to say it.'

She moved her thumb and gently touched the top of my hand with it.

'Marta was planning to come here anyway because of this job she's taken. It seemed to make sense to everyone that I should go with her, and have some time to rest.'

'What about you?'

'How do you mean?'

'Well, what did you want?'

Isabella frowned and took her hand away. 'I wanted to go to America to stay with my cousin again, but nobody thought that was a good idea.'

She laughed as if she could see in her head exactly the fun she'd have had. So I was obliged to change my vision of Marta and think that she might not add to things in the way I had hoped.

'Are you going to snorkel then?'

'I suppose I ought to.'

With my skin feeling as if the touch of her thumb on it were still there, I put the flippers on and inched, on my bottom, over the rocks to the sea, with the mask in my hand. Just before I jumped in I looked back at Isabella, but she was already lying back out, her magazine held above her head again.

I jumped in, and the air in my shorts ballooned out. How well they fitted me. All the sitting around and writing and reading had quite changed the shape of me. I was starting to be as heavy as Rodriguez must have been, for I'd noticed that his suits were also a much better fit.

I dipped my head in the water, flailed around a bit, and then pushed off over to the left side of the cove. Kill, was the answer to what the water might do to me, rather than cure. I suddenly thought I might be ill, but Isabella had asked for a squid, so I would just have to get on with it. What an idiot I was. Why couldn't I have gone to bed at a decent hour last night? I knew this date was in the diary. Resolved to the matter, I pulled the mask down from the top of my head and headed away from where Isabella lay on the rocks. I wasn't sure if I trusted myself at that moment; a little of my stomach came back into the pipe, so I had to pull it out of my mouth and swill it around. It would be best to put some distance between Isabella and me, I thought, in case I should embarrass myself.

If you've ever snorkelled, which I'm sure you have, you'll already know what I discovered that day, and that was that there's a weird little hole in time and space that you fall into. Isabella's warning not to let my shoulder burn was ringing in my ears, but I was such a swarthy colour these days I didn't think it likely.

It's strange to watch a world you can never be part of. There they all are, the little fishes and the big ones, with their own rules and pecking orders. There are the nervous ones hiding amongst the weeds, loners patrolling in a haughty fashion, lazy ones half submerged and dozing their life away.

They live in another dimension, don't they? We only have to cope with left and right, backwards and forwards, and that's hard enough. Imagine if we had to add up and down to it all the time.

I could hear the throb of a motor far off, over the sucking of the sand; a boat must have come into the bay, and then I saw the squid. I counted quickly – two, three, four, five, six. I fumbled to bring the long nose of the spear up but there was no need for a rush, the six of them hung below me, their skirts fluttering in the waves, their great silver eyes looking up at me in ignorance of their fate.

I tried to pick one. How should I do this? How should I play God and decide who was to live and who to die? If there had only been one of them.

I gripped the gun tightly. After all the fuss I'd made trying to figure out how the damn thing worked I would look such a fool if I returned to Isabella empty handed. Would I have to lie to her and say there were no squid to be seen? That would be no good because it might look as if I were contradicting Marta about this being the best place to come, and that would mean the two of us not getting off to the great start I'd planned. And I had intended to offer the squid to the girls for their supper in order to thank Marta for the picnics she had made for us and get into her good books.

How I hated myself. What a useless, hopeless excuse of a man. See? After all the terrible things I had done, I hadn't the courage to finish off a luminescent piece of rubber with eyes.

I was just about to lower the gun, when suddenly I was startled by a vision of Rodriguez floating in the waters to the right of me. I closed my eyes in the hope the vision would clear and turn out to be just a large fish or a dash of surf, but when I opened them again, there he still was. The white skirts of his suit were fluttering about in the currents like the skirts of the squid. 'Go on,' he mouthed at me.

I was so surprised at the vision of Rodriguez, hovering a foot or so beneath the surface, that I totally forgot my squeamishness at killing the squid.

The spear shot forward, its dark rope wobbling behind.

'Now dive down,' he barked.

The water roared in my ears as the pressure rose.

Rodriguez's face zoomed up close to me as he dived with me. He still had his wire spectacles balanced on his nose, even though he was underwater.

'Go on,' he mouthed aggressively. 'Finish it!'

A cloud of black ink rose up from the fish and enveloped us. The white of Rodriguez's suit, topped by his determined face, came and went in the billowing darkness.

I took the knife from my hip and quickly put the creature out of its misery. Poor thing, it was only once it was speared it had realised the danger and put up a fight with its oily black smoke.

Rodriguez was gone. I looked around for him, taking clumsy swings at the water to twist and turn to find him, but he was nowhere to be seen.

I surfaced and pulled the goggles from my face, taking deep panicked breaths of the air and choking as the waves rocked into my mouth.

It was the most intense vision I had ever experienced. I'd not had this type of trouble since coming to the island. The thought of it scared me and I knew it was the result of partying too hard night after night. The best thing to do was to ignore it, for the worry of it was only worsening the issue.

I looked back to the rocks. What a relief to see the real flesh and blood of Isabella snoozing there.

She propped herself up on her elbows. The she saw me and raised a hand and waved, so I tried to lift up the squid and show it off to her. What a hero I felt trying to swim towards her with the squid slippery in my arms whilst being careful not to drop the spear gun or get pushed by the waves onto the rocks.

Isabella sat and patiently watched me flailing around in the water, then she came down to take the fish and help haul me out.

'Oh! *Bravo, bravo!*' she said. 'It's a monster.'

We put the squid in the bucket and then I lay next to her and let my costume dry in the sun.

'Was it hard to catch?'

I thought nervously of the vision of Rodriguez shouting at me to finish it. 'A little. I had to be quick once they saw me.'

A lizard came and sat on a rock beside us. I watched it for a while and when I looked back at Isabella, I found her looking very glum again. 'They're sort of sweet,' she said. 'But I can't think why anyone would want to study them all summer.'

'I don't know how you could,' I agreed. 'One looks pretty much like the next, if you ask me.'

'Not according to Marta.'

Isabella looked very fed up then. She must have been brooding when I was in the water. Much as I hated to do so, as I knew she would make herself unhappy again, I felt I was expected to ask the question.

'Is everything all right between you and Marta?'

'No, not at all. She's used to be fun when we were in Switzerland, but here she's being such a bore. She only ever wants to go to parties at the institute and if I meet anyone there who happens to be interesting, she's immediately by my side like glue. Once this very nice man invited me out to his villa in Deia and before I could stop her she started speaking for me and saying I couldn't go. It was all so embarrassing and I felt like a child again. For goodness sake, I'm twenty-two, Thomas!'

'Indeed,' I hurried to agree, trying to look as if twenty-two were a respectfully ancient age to reach.

'And I know she is reporting to my parents. Twice I've caught her writing a letter that she covered up when I came in the room. I'm fed up with it and on top of it all my cousin keeps writing to me and asking me why I haven't come over for the summer as I said I would last year. And of course I can't tell him because that would involve divulging the *first scandal* and also the *second scandal* and after everyone's worked so hard to keep it all a secret for me, I just can't, can I?'

Then she paused to take a deep breath, but she wasn't through.

'I so wanted to go to that festival again. We had such a wonderful time last year. My cousin told me that Bob Dylan played and brought the house down, well there wasn't a house, it was outdoors, but you know what I mean, and I missed it. And if only I hadn't been tricked by that horrible man, none of this would have happened. Perhaps I should have just gone straight over to America and had the baby there and stayed there. I don't think it matters so much there…'

Then she was in tears and burying her head in her hands.

'Now, now,' I said, and nervously patted her on the head, which turned out to be the right thing to do because she looked up at me in surprise and started to laugh.

'Thomas, *mio caro*, you are funny. I'm not a dog, you know.'

I blushed red. 'Sorry. My wife always said I was hopeless with this sort of stuff.'

Isabella wiped away her tears. 'Let's organise that supper.'

My heart leapt for joy. 'Really?'

'Yes. It will have to wait a week or two. Marta and I are going over to see the other island.'

The thought of two weeks without Isabella hurt. 'More lizards? Sounds awful.'

'No, a school friend of mine will be there. I can't wait to catch up on everyone's news. Some of the girls are preparing to leave this year. In the proper way, that is. But supper shall be arranged I promise, as soon as we are back.'

'Are you sure? We don't have to, you know.'

'Well ... I just wasn't sure how Marta would feel about you.'

'That's why you've been keeping me away from her?'

'A little...'

Suddenly Isabella looked bashful. 'There are these rules, you see, that my parents set. About being alone with men.'

'But Marta knows we go to the beach together, doesn't she?'

'Yes, of course, but ... oh, never mind. Let's do supper next weekend, shall we? I'm fed up with tip toeing around Marta. Do you like risotto?'

'Yes, I love risotto. Let's do it, but what is it that Marta thinks?'

But Isabella wouldn't tell me, and I was forced to drop the subject. What could it be? Then I suddenly realised with a groan; I must be an acceptable companion because I'm so horribly old. So horribly old that Marta would never believe Isabella would be tempted to do something inappropriate with me.

As Isabella chatted on about risotto and what desert she would make me, all I could think of was how hideously and horribly old I was, and that there was no hope for us. It was all so awful. I wanted a drink in my hand.

I didn't have long to wait. Isabella needed to be back at the villa because the girls had another 'death by dullness' institute do as Isabella had started to call them, so she didn't want the squid after all. We packed up and picked our way back up the path to the car.

As we said our goodbyes outside the girls' villa, Isabella peered at the squid in the bucket.

'What a funny thing. There's something quite hideous about them, isn't there?'

I peered at the pinky-white creature slopping around in the water when I tipped the bucket to one side.

'Do you know how to cook it?' I asked.

'Yes. Either quickly or slowly. Nothing in between.'

I thought of Rodriguez and wondered if he were stuck down there in those cold waters, without any friends, lost on his way to whatever place he was supposed to have gone to.

When I got up to *Ca'n Mola*, I stood by the gates in the front of the estate and looked at the squid. I had no idea what to do with it. I so hoped that Marta and I would become friendly so that Isabella and I could see even more of each other. And you never knew, if Isabella had a little wine with dinner, we might become closer; that is how it usually works of course, and then something might happen.

I went over to the cliffs and threw the fish over the edge. The splash, if it made one when it hit the water, was lost to me.

Chapter XII

'See how the artist has refused to be confined to a momentary concept of beauty?'

'Is it supposed to be ugly?'

'Do you find it ugly?'

'I find it ... unsettling.'

'Good. That's what the artist is trying to achieve.'

Susan screwed her eyes together in an effort of concentration and we moved on to the next canvas. I could see she was tempted to step back, away from the painting, so I took her hand and pulled her right up to it.

'It's black, isn't it?'

'Exactly.'

She thought hard about what that might mean. I knew the answer because I had read it in one of Rodriguez's books.

'There are a lot of colours beneath the black.'

'Very good, Susan.'

The gallery was nearly empty because it was shortly due to close for the night. The only other visitors (apart from Susan and I) were a couple of English ladies who seemed to have come in order to have a discussion about a dog. They were going through the exhibition in the opposite direction to us, which meant that we kept meeting them in the central hall as we moved from one set of rooms to the next.

Apparently the dog had become epileptic. The episodes of fitting were so traumatic to the dog that the owner was considering having him put to sleep, but the trouble was the next day the dog would be right as rain again and didn't seem to be in any worse state of humour from the attack. Now that didn't take long to explain, but you would be surprised by how long this took the two ladies to discuss – and not even with a decision made by the end.

Eventually the topic of the dog did run its course and they left, which I was very pleased about. I've always considered an art gallery to be like a swimming pool or a newspaper, in that it's a pleasure best enjoyed alone.

When the two ladies were gone the curator slowly got up, closed the great gallery doors behind them, and locked them with a key which hung from his waist. I had visited this particular gallery on a number of occasions at this time of the evening, and I knew that he just wanted to be sure no late entrants would arrive and that he would wait patiently, without interrupting, until I was ready to leave.

We stood in the main hall and Susan gazed up at an Antoni Tapies which hung there. When she found that I had come up behind her, she put her hand behind her back so that our fingers would touch. 'Have you really met him?' she whispered.

There's nothing worse than when you tell a little white lie and someone insists on repeating it and enquiring after it.

Sometimes, particularly after I've had a drink or two with Susan, I have got into a habit whereby I avoid having to talk about the initial lie by introducing another; just another little one in order to have something to move on to. Because to move on to the truth would make that first lie stand out like a beacon in my head such that I feared Susan would see it flashing away there in my eyes as I tried to change the subject.

Of course, if one has a very inquisitive partner this can snowball to a whole series of lies. This is something I had to be careful about with Susan because she was (I had discovered) quite intelligent. Because of that, the last time

I had bumped into her and spent the evening drinking with her, I had been forced to arrive at telling her a whole series of nonsense. Like how I knew lots of artists and in fact had a few staying with me at my villa; that I provided them with a safe harbour in which to paint, and that I didn't ask them for money because I wanted to support them; that one or two of them were very good and I was expecting great things from them ... oh, and some other nonsense like that, like I had an enormous villa with a swimming pool shaped like a shark and several servants who always grumbled when they had to work overtime to arrange my parties. I don't know why I said all those things. I think it was because I thought they would make Susan happy.

The painting by Antoni Tapies was truly outstanding and I have to confess I had developed a genuine passion for his work even from that very first day when I had seen a print of his in one of Rodriguez's books. When I'd found this painting by Tapies in the gallery here in the city – well, I can't explain how excited I was by it and how it moved me to see the great white canvas and to be able (when the curator was occupied in one of the other rooms) to reach out and touch its distended surface and feel the objects beneath the paint.

'What is Tapies like?' Susan asked, and I thought perhaps it was time we went over to the restaurant where she might drink some more wine and become amenable to my advances.

'Like all artists,' I said.

The curator had never once bothered me before, but the presence of Susan had given him the false belief that I was a sociable sort, and, rather than sit back in his chair as was his usual habit, he came over to talk to us. The key to the front door of the gallery swung back and forth on a chain at his hip, back and forth in time with his limp as he made his way over.

'We're very lucky to have it,' he said in a wheezing voice. 'Most of his work goes to Paris and London.'

Susan nodded as if she agreed; it could have been that she understood the work or it could have been that she was just pretending to like it. I didn't care which it was, but now that the curator was here beside us I had a sudden desire to understand if the painting moved him as much as it moved me. After all, he was lucky enough to be able to sit at his desk there looking at it all day.

'Susan,' I said. 'See how the artist has taken things that are part of nature and used them along with the paint?'

Susan opened her mouth to say something, but then, intimidated by the presence of the curator, closed it again.

'See how the reality of the substance is there, mixed in with the colours?'

'Yes, I see that.'

I turned to the curator.

'It's brave, isn't it?' I said, timidly.

The curator refused to reply, but he didn't deny my statement.

Then, after a silence of a minute or two during which we all stared at the canvas, he lowered his head and his hand reached down, automatically, as if it was doing so of its own accord, and touched his stiffened leg.

'As I said, we are lucky to have it,' he said.

Then suddenly Susan appeared to have thought of something to say and I realised too late the mistake I had made by letting the three of us stand there together.

'My friend has met the artist on several occasions,' she said.

Oh, damn it. The curator looked at me with the slightest suggestion of a raised eyebrow.

'Susan, look at the time,' I said, and took her by the elbow with the aim of saying we must be off, but she suddenly became as unpliable as Venus de Milo.

'He's a patron of artists, you know. He has several staying at his villa over in the east.'

The curator's face lit up. 'Here on the island?'

On and on she went. 'Yes. It's wonderful, isn't it? Do you know he creates a space in which they can express themselves away from the everyday commerciality of life?'

'May I ask who they are? Are they displayed yet?'

'No,' I said testily. 'They are young, only just starting out.'

'But we could do an exhibition for them.'

'That's a great idea. Rodriguez darling, you should definitely do it. I'd help. We could print up leaflets from my office.'

'No,' I said firmly. 'They wouldn't want it. I've promised them solitude.'

'Nonsense,' said the curator. 'Every artist wants to be seen. They are just being coy.'

'Well, perhaps that is true,' I said, thinking it might be better to acquiesce if only to allow a speedier exit from the gallery.

At this the curator puffed out a big breath so that it raised the few remaining hairs off his forehead.

'Excellent, excellent. Come and speak to me when you are ready and we will look at my diary and find a good date.'

Then he asked for the name of my beautiful young lady friend, causing Susan to literally expand with joy at the thought that not only was she now the girlfriend of a patron of the arts but a beautiful one to boot. But the worse of it was to come.

I was trying to get out of there as fast as possible, but the old man insisted on shaking our hands and giving me a card, whilst he started repeating over and over, 'It's wonderful to meet you, Senyor Rodriguez!'

That he should pick up on Susan's referring to me as Rodriguez filled me with panic. I wanted the ground to open up and take me right down to Hades where I belonged.

I had to quickly promise him that I would speak to the artists who didn't even exist and find out whether they would be interested in displaying in his silly little gallery. It was the only way I could finish the conversation and get out of there, and it was all Susan's fault. And now it would be difficult for me to go back to look at the paintings again, because that curator would be forever pestering me about those damned artists and calling me Senyor Rodriguez.

Susan looked crestfallen when she saw how annoyed I was for giving out details of my personal life (I mean Rodriguez's personal life), but I had to admit I was a little to blame. So I took her by the hand and kissed her on the cheek, feeling guilty for being angry with her when really she was just being sweet. It was me who had caused the problem with my lies.

Then I took Susan along to a restaurant behind the glassworks which I had become fond of recently, but she hesitated at the doorway and I could see she wasn't happy.

'What's wrong?' I asked, but she said nothing and actually looked as though she might burst into tears. 'Aren't you hungry?'

'Yes, but...'

'What? What's the matter?'

Then I saw she was peering into the restaurant as if it was some sort of Stygian hell hole, and it was only then I realised that her dress was quite nice, probably borrowed from a friend, and her hair was so perfectly in place she must have gone to a salon, and all in all she had evidently been expecting I would be rustling up something fancier than this after our visit to the gallery.

'I'm sorry,' I said. 'I'm being an idiot. You're dressed up. Let's head over to the Borne.'

As we walked away I tried to make up for my ill manners by making up some nonsense that one of the waiters there was a friend of mine who painted in his spare time and who was always looking for models and how I thought I would introduce them, but then that made her even more upset and she wanted to go back, so I realised it had been a stupid thing to say. So with gritted teeth I promised we would return there some other time and we headed over to the *Almudaina*, which I knew for a fact I couldn't afford.

There we had a lovely meal, though I took control of matters right from the off and ordered for both of us because I could see there were truffles on the menu and I didn't want to take the chance Susan might lose the run of herself. I was obliged to borrow some money from her to settle the bill, at which point I made up some story about how I had forgotten my wallet and only had my running around cash out for the evening. She bought the lie (yes, another, I'm ashamed to admit – I really was going good guns that evening) hook, line, and sinker, and even leant another fifty *pesetas* to me so we could go over to Miami's for a digestive.

Towards the end of the evening I realised I had made quite a fatal error. She let me kiss her, there was no problem in that, in fact we did quite a lot of kissing on a bench out on the terrace, which was full of people, but everyone there was so tight nobody noticed or cared. But then when I tried to suggest, for the second evening in a row, that we go back to her rooms, she became all funny again and said she was surprised that was what I wanted and wouldn't it be better to wait until another evening when she could come out to my villa and things wouldn't be rushed and last minute. And I realised that what I had done was take a sweet and up-for-it Felixstowe girl and turn her into some sort of monster who now believed she was a raving beauty being pursued by a rich old man who wanted her for his muse.

So then I was subjected to the torture of having to walk her home while she wound me up nonstop, and then after some more furious kissing, left me on the doorstep of her landlady's house in a state of pointed disappointment.

I went back to Miami's and returned to the bench Susan and I had been sitting on. There I ordered more wine and continued with my evening until the rest of Susan's fifty *pesetas* were gone.

Chapter XIII

Finally, the day of Isabella's supper party arrived. I was filled with trepidation as to how it might go and whether the introduction of her chaperone might change things. My head was filled with a thousand images of Isabella and I coming closer together, both physically and in a friendly way, and how Marta would be bowled over by my character and warmth.

I carefully chose my outfit. I wore the bottom half of the linen suit, a blue striped shirt of my own, and put a pullover of Rodriguez's over my shoulders. There were great holes in the sleeves so if the evening turned chilly I couldn't put it on – it would have to stay clamped to my back, in that terribly pretentious European way. I was quite determined to keep things under control, so I had abstained all of that day and the one before, and took just a tiny nip from the brandy in the bureau before I went out. I set off down the hill, fretting about how I would go about saying hello to Marta and plotting how I might try and kiss Isabella if she gave me even the slightest encouragement.

Isabella was waiting for me on the upper terrace of her villa. She leant over the balustrade and waved to me.

'At last! Come on up.'

I let myself into the house, which was in darkness downstairs, and mounted the spiral staircase up to the sitting room. My shoes echoed on the white tiles and I was unsettled by the fact that my entrance must be head first, revealing my face before my body could follow.

Isabella stood by the sliding doors of the upper terrace and she called me to come over and out to them. I could see Marta sitting at their terrace table, her back to me. She turned to look at me through the glass as I came towards the door but she didn't get up; she just stretched out her hand so I was forced to go over to her like a courtier being granted an audience. I didn't like it and whether it was because of that, or whether it was because of those thousand little signs that you pick up when you first meet a person, I knew at once that I didn't like Marta and I knew for a fact I never would.

'Well, here he is,' Isabella said. 'The one and only Thomas Sebastian. Would you like a drink? We have some bootleg gin from the other island. It will put hairs on your chest, they say. Mamma mia, it could even put hairs on my chest, I think.'

'Do stop prattling, Isabella,' Marta interrupted, and finally she got up and walked over to the drinks trolley which had been pulled out onto the terrace. 'I think she's nervous of our meeting, Mr Sebastian.'

Marta made me a gin and tonic and I took it, even though I hadn't yet agreed it was what I wanted.

'So what is it you do, Mr Sebastian? Isabella couldn't seem to tell me.'

'A few things,' I replied. 'Investment, mostly.'

'And you're here on holiday?'

I looked into my gin and took a big swig of it. 'That's right. Bit of the old Spanish sun. Get a bit of colour, you know.'

Marta was short and top heavy. Her breasts were swathed in a striped sweater and her hair was cut short in today's fashionable elfin way, though there was little of the elf about her. She was wearing some little round sunglasses that were trendy with the kids and, as it was a long time since she had been a kid, I thought they looked foolish on her.

'Well, it's good to meet you at last,' Marta said, and

touched me on the arm (which of course annoyed me, but made me think I really must give her a chance). After all, I had only just met her, and if Isabella liked her she must have some good points.

Isabella went over to the table and patted the back of a chair. 'Come and sit down, Thomas. You're late and the rice will be ruined if I don't serve it soon.'

Marta and I were now left alone with each other and an awkward silence fell between us. I looked out into the dark emptiness of the night while I tried to think of something to say.

'I hear you found a lizard,' I eventually dredged up.

'A new species, Mr Sebastian. Of the genus *pedioplanis*.'

'Do you get to name it?'

Isabella came out of the house with the risotto between oven mitts. 'Oh, do you?' she said, and I got up to clear some space on the table.

'I know,' I said, hoping to score points with both of them. 'Call it *pedioplanis Isabella*.'

Marta blushed red. 'Well ... That's exactly what I did name it.'

Isabella wouldn't catch my eye at that moment, and gave a forced laugh. 'Did you? Why didn't you tell me? What a funny joke.'

There was an awkward silence, so I filled it. 'Hurry up with that risotto, Isabella. I swear I could eat a horse.'

It was very pleasant on the girls' terrace. You could hear the sea crashing on the rocks below and the air smelt of salt and of the wine in the rice.

'Delicious, Isabella.'

'Yes, indeed,' Marta agreed, and then she turned to me. 'That's some car down there, Mr Sebastian. How long have you had her?'

'Not long. I bought her from a friend in Paris.'

'You bought her?' interrupted Isabella. 'I thought you had borrowed it?'

'Well, yes…' I stuttered. 'I have her on loan to try her out, you know. See if I want to buy her.'

Marta waved her hand over the distinction. 'But I think the car must be worth a lot of money, am I right?'

Isabella looked at me as if reassessing. 'Is that right, Thomas?'

Marta snorted. 'Isabella, you have been driving about in it for weeks. Didn't you see it was a British Jaguar, and a pretty fast one at that?'

'I didn't look.' Isabella retorted abruptly.

'There's no reason to know,' I said. 'The marque fell off the back. It's somewhere in the Pyrenees, is my guess.'

The truth was I had unscrewed it along with the model badge and thrown them into a river before I had come to the island. I had also taken a little paint to the 'L' in the plate and converted it to an 'E', and the 'F' to a 'P'. After all, it was not strictly true that the car was borrowed from a friend. In fact, it wasn't true at all.

Marta pointed her fork at me. 'I expect you could write and get another.'

'Yes, I hadn't thought of that.'

I can't tell you how disappointed I felt. I had spent so long thinking about how the three of us would spend time together, how we would dine every night from now on in one another's houses, how we would laugh together and get all sorts of private jokes going. But I just didn't like this woman. I would try to, I promised myself that, but … oh, just to look at her made me feel queasy. She was sitting beside me, with Isabella opposite the two of us, and she was breathing heavily through her nose while she ate and the sound of it was putting me off my supper.

In between mouthfuls she would purse her lips as she thought of something she wanted to say and then out it would come, some new statement of so little interest to anyone it would make a Cistercian monk call out for her to stop. And she had this terrible habit of using the word 'um' to hold the conversation and not let you get a word in edgeways during each of her diatribes.

What could Isabella have seen in the woman? Honestly I can't tell you what I hated most. Whether it was the flesh which fell around the edges of her watch, or whether it was how, after her supper was finished, she kept touching and rubbing herself, her neck and her chest, and rubbing with her hands on her legs. How it unsettled me.

Later on, when they were discussing the sights of the city and advising me what I should go to see, Marta went to get her handbag to retrieve a pamphlet on the *Palace D'Almudaina* which had only recently been opened up. Afterwards, when she was done, she just threw the bag onto the floor so that everything spilled out. There was a whole heap of things (and I didn't want to look too closely for a man never wants to know the contents of a woman's handbag), but the things just sat there on the floor as though she couldn't care less whether anyone were to slip on them or crush them, and for the rest of the evening as we took a drink after dinner I could barely concentrate on what was being said because of those things on the floor.

'The nature of today's landscape is due to the work of the Archduke Salvator in the nineteenth century,' Marta droned on, and I saw that Isabella looked bored and frustrated. She had twice tried to say something but Marta had cut across her and continued on. 'Did you know, Mr Sebastian, that at one time the islanders nearly stripped the place bare in order to burn the wood for charcoal?'

'Oh, Marta, Thomas doesn't want to hear about that. He's not an academic.'

We sat in silence for a minute, with Marta swilling her wine and frowning. Then she said, 'And how are you finding the house?'

Goodness.

'I find it has a lot of character.'

'And it doesn't bother you, about what happened?'

I looked at Isabella, but she looked down at the table.

'I don't really know what happened.'

Marta looked at me in surprise. 'You don't know?'

I hated to be at a disadvantage to Marta and have her crowing over me, but I knew Isabella didn't like to hear about the scandal of Rodriguez's demise. So I was forced to pretend I had no interest in asking, even though I was desperate to know the full details of why he might have done it. Marta, on the other hand, had obviously no clue that the subject was upsetting to Isabella or else she didn't care.

'Mr Sebastian, how can the agent not have told you?'

I glanced at Isabella, whose gaze was fixed firmly to the table. 'I don't suppose it's important. I mean, it's all in the past.'

Marta looked disgruntled at having her superior knowledge reduced in this way. 'It may not be important to you, Mr Sebastian, but when Rodriguez killed himself it was a terrible loss to the world of art.'

I still couldn't marry this with the gentleman I knew. Why would someone with all that talent and taste and money do such a thing?

Isabella started to pull together our dishes to hide her discomfort, but I saw it plainly. I knew her so well now – better than Marta, I thought with satisfaction.

'Let's not go into it all, Marta,' I said.

Marta glanced at Isabella with raised eyebrows. 'Oh, I see. You don't want to hear about it, Isabella. Is that it?'

'Not really,' was the reply.

At this, Marta made a harrumphing noise. 'Isabella, my dear, there are certain things in life you are going to have to get used to hearing about again.'

How awful, I thought, that Marta should try to surreptitiously chastise Isabella in this way. There she was, hinting about something horrible in Isabella's past, right in front me. Marta had not even considered I would know about the baby and what Isabella had tried to do afterwards. It felt as though there was now a different secret – one which only Isabella and I knew.

'You're right of course, Marta,' said Isabella, and I hated the thought of her giving in this way to anyone. 'And actually Thomas is desperate to hear about it. I know that for a fact.' Then she smiled at me and it was too sweet to resist. I smiled back in a way that showed I understood what was in her head and Marta's eyes darted from Isabella's face to mine and then back again to Isabella's.

'I must just learn not to be squeamish,' Isabella continued, and then she forced out a laugh and, all the time, Marta was watching us.

'Go on then, Marta,' I prompted. 'Tell me about Rodriguez.'

Marta hesitated because her mind was on other matters. I saw at once she was assessing how close Isabella and I had come. Seeing the calculations going on behind the woman's eyes, I knew it had been a mistake to reveal it. She turned cold eyes on me.

'Rodriguez was told the woman he loved had married another, and that evening he took his own life.'

'How do you know this?'

'Everyone in the village knows it.' I thought Marta was trying to imply I was an idiot for the fact that I did not.

'And why would one suicide make the papers?'

'His family are well known. He comes from a long line of industrialists. Plus ... it's believed his relatives may have assisted him with his suicide...' She raised her eyebrows as she said this, as if she were the narrator in some horror waxworks show.

'Now that's just ridiculous gossip from the worst of the rags,' Isabella protested, and she got up to take away the plates.

'No, it's not. I have it direct from the *notario*'s son down in the village.'

'Why? What did he say?' Isabella stood and waited with her hands full of plates, despite herself.

'Ah! So you do want to know?'

'*Basta*, Marta! Just tell Thomas.'

I waited patiently for them to finish and for Marta to continue.

'You can dismiss it if you like, but this is what I've been told. The night before Rodriguez's death, his family came over to the island specifically to tell him his Russian lover had married an American football star. When the *notario* was called to the house the next morning, he found rat poison on the kitchen counter, a loaded shot gun in the hall, and all the knives had been sharpened.'

Isabella made an exasperated noise of disbelief and went away into the house.

'And tell me again, how did he do it?' I asked as soon as Isabella was safely inside.

'He threw himself off the cliffs. Terrible timing. The whole village had arrived at the top as part of their annual *Festa*. They have a procession, you see, once a year, that starts at the village and goes up the cliff path. They carry their statues of the Virgin and sing hymns – it's a wonderful sight I expect. Have you seen any of the local *Festas*? I'd definitely recommend going to see one. I think I have a list of them here somewhere...'

I politely declined the list, and urged her to continue before Isabella got back.

'Well, there they all were, milling around and saying their prayers to bring good luck to the fishermen, when Rodriguez came out of his house and threw himself over. Apparently the mothers tried to hide it from the children, but you know what small boys are. They were all running to the edge to take a closer look, wanting to see the body and scaring their mothers half to death.'

'What a terrible thing.'

'Yes, but it's a pretty little spot isn't it? I have to confess I might have taken something rural like that, but I do like the modern conveniences. Do you have running water?'

'No, but there's a well.'

'And tell me again what it is you do?'

'I sold a property business. My plan is to travel, enjoy myself for a while, and figure out what to do next.'

'And your wife is back in England?'

'That's right. She has her bridge club and the dog, you know. She'll be out soon.'

Isabella returned at this moment with bowls of pudding. Whatever it was, it was delicious.

'Did you make this, Isabella?'

She just gave me a smile in return and I saw Marta once again glance at her and then back at me. 'And what was your father's business?'

Really, Marta was just like a man in many respects. I half expected her to put her foot on her knee, but she didn't. She took one of the *Ducados* that I offered and Isabella took one too.

'He sold farming equipment in the Americas. It was there that he met my mother.'

'And where do your parents live now, Thomas?'

I explained that they were dead, and that my father had accidentally killed my mother by running her over with a steam roller (steam engines being his passion up until that moment). I explained how father had intended to put the machine in reverse but his great clumsy fingers had hit the wrong button, sending it forward, catching Mama's dress at first and then, in a horrible slow motion, the rest of her. Neither Isabella nor Marta knew what to say about that, so I changed the subject.

'Tell me more about those dastardly relations of Rodriguez.'

'Well, their money came from cotton, during the industrial revolution of Spain.'

'And what did Rodriguez do?'

'Not much. I understand his elder brother ran the firm – ran it into the ground, from all accounts. But Rodriguez lived as playboy for a long time. He skied, played polo. Clever though – a master at chess.'

Isabella blew the smoke from her cigarette out into blackness. 'Must we talk about a man who killed himself?'

I begged to be allowed one more question, and asked after the girl.

'She had an awkward beauty,' replied Marta. 'She was slim, petite, but with a very huge nose. He fell in love with her immediately. That's how he was, you see, so the *notario*'s son told me. Impulsive you could say. He stopped the playboy lifestyle overnight and became a patron to the arts. He set up communes for painters and sculptors in the hills near Begur on the mainland.'

'So then how did he come to be here on the island?'

'This was just his summer house. He had a great mansion in Barcelona,'

'I'd heard that.'

'Yes, and another where his art collection is kept in Begur. It's supposed to be worth a fortune now. That's what the family's after, they say.'

'Really,' snorted Isabella. 'What nonsense. Please don't say another thing about it.'

I wanted to ask Marta more, but Isabella stretched her arms above her head and yawned loudly and I realised that time was running out.

I clapped my hands, rubbed them together and jumped to my feet. 'Let's get this party started shall we. Another gin, girls?'

Marta started to protest that it was getting late, at which Isabella immediately held out her glass to me.

'Splendid idea, Thomas.'

I went over to the drinks trolley and made three strong gins.

Marta took hers with a frown, but Isabella took one with

a flourish of her hand and giggled. 'Really, Thomas, you might get the pair of us tipsy.'

'That's my plan,' I said with what I hoped was a rogue-like smile. 'Now, what have we got here?'

Their record collection seemed to be eighty per cent Beatles, a bunch of 45s (the Animals, the Kinks, the Rolling Stones), a whole host of older stuff, and then some American rhythm and blues which I assumed Isabella had brought over from her time there last summer. I plumped for the Beatles and held out my hand to Isabella to dance.

Once more I saw Marta not bother to hide the frown on her face.

'When did you say your wife will be joining you?' she called out to me.

'Oh, any day now,' I replied, and winked at Isabella which made her giggle.

There was more dancing and drinking after that. I was forced to do a couple of numbers with Marta for politeness' sake and then the two girls danced together.

I noticed that the girls had slowed down on the drinking and every time I got up to refresh our glasses I found theirs still to be full.

'What sort of party is this? Come on, girls,' I said, realising as I did so that I was being overly merry and was perhaps steaming ahead of the rest.

'Isabella is not used to drinking, Mr Sebastian,' Marta said, and Isabella made a face at me behind her back.

Eventually Marta's persistent monologue about how late it was killed the party mood, and when Isabella herself suggested perhaps it really was getting late, I instantly declared it was time I was off.

'Let me see you out,' Marta said, getting up and collecting glasses.

What an old horror she was, I thought, but fortunately Isabella leapt to her feet and pulled the glasses out of Marta's hands.

'Don't be silly, Marta. You've lizards to count in the morning,' and she and I giggled while Marta looked stony faced. Then, before she could argue, Isabella had run down the stairs, and I had grabbed Marta's hand, shaken it to say goodnight, and followed behind Isabella.

When I got down there Isabella had the sliding doors open and was standing beside them, laughing giddily. Unfortunately, in the dark, I missed the bottom stair and came crashing down onto the kitchen tiles. It was an easy thing to have done in the dim light and I blame the slipperiness of the white flooring.

'Are you all right?' Isabella said, helping me up.

'Of course, of course,' I said, and, knowing this was my chance, I took hold of Isabella and tried to kiss her. I thought for a moment she was going to succumb, but then she tried to wriggle free of my arms.

'Thomas, don't.'

'Why not?'

'Because you're drunk.'

'Only a little.'

There was an awkward moment where I wasn't sure if she wanted me to persuade her, but knowing everything that had happened I couldn't take the chance.

So instead I tried to laugh it off as a bit of drunken silliness and apologised very formally for my out of place and inappropriate behaviour in trying to kiss goodnight to the most beautiful girl on the island, and this made Isabella laugh and everything fell all right between us again.

Chapter XIV

Looking back, I could see that my greatest mistake with Isabella was not to have acted sooner. She and I had now fallen into that horrible state of friendship, and, once a girl has got it into her head that a man is a friend rather than a romantic prospect, it can be dammed difficult to reverse.

What a woefully inadequate Englishman I was. Why couldn't I have the effrontery of the Italians? Or the machismo of the Spanish? How angry it made me. I didn't have that trouble with Susan.

When Isabella had said, after her risotto supper party, 'Because you're drunk,' did that mean that if I wasn't drunk...?

Oh, it was hopeless. I hadn't seen her for a week as she had gone off with Marta to the north of the island so that Marta could look at more lizards and Isabella could sit around being bored (her words, not mine).

All I could do was to focus on our next meeting, which was to be a return supper at *Ca'n Mola*, and on that occasion try to walk that tightrope between drunk enough to act, yet sober enough to appear attractive.

In the meantime, it was my intention to finish things with Susan. When I was with her all I could think about was Isabella, and I felt guilty about all the lying it involved.

We'd arranged to meet for a drink and a spot of dinner so that was the time to do it, before it went any further, but when I went to the pot I found there were only six hundred *pesetas* left. I reeled at the sight of them. Six hundred *pesetas*! How had this disaster befallen me? And I still hadn't paid Susan back the fifty *pesetas* I'd borrowed from her.

I took out two hundred for dinner (it would have to be tapas), fifty for drinks, another fifty for petrol, and another fifty to give back to Susan. Then I had a rethink. Fifty *pesetas* went back into the pot. As I was going to tell Susan I was leaving the island, I could ask for her address and send the money later when I had the funds from the book. I'm not such a cad I would steal from a woman, but as it happened the evening turned into such a disaster I never did get her address.

The drive into the city was pleasant and there was a hot breeze blowing in across the harbour. I parked up on the outskirts and completed the rest of the way on foot. I was still nervous about the car. It was too recognisable. If only I'd taken a different one.

When I got to Miami's, Susan was already there at a table out front in the plaza. She leapt up to kiss me on the mouth as if we were lovers and I instantly regretted coming. It was a hopeless situation. I knew she wanted to go back to my villa with the pool and the retinue of staff ready to wait on her hand and foot, but I couldn't do that any more than I could magic a carriage out of a pumpkin and take her to visit the Queen.

I did have a soft spot for her. I liked how intense she was about everything, but, as I sat there, I felt nothing but guilt (other than my obvious carnal desire) – a guilt that I was sitting with Susan when it should have been Isabella; a guilt that I couldn't afford to take Susan to the *Almudaina* for a second time; and a guilt that I was going to have to tell her another whole heap of lies about my leaving the island so as to get rid of her nicely.

The square was quite busy that evening and the tourists milled about us with their sluggish confusion.

'Roddy darling, I was wondering, do you know the

Whytes?'

Susan looked very with it that evening. Her dress had a sweet little collar to it and her hair had been cut into a bob so sharp it appeared as if your fingertips would come slicing off if you tried to run your fingers through it.

'No, should I?'

'I don't know, darling. They have a big villa over in the east near you, so I thought you might.'

'Is it Samuel and Deidre?'

'No. It's Freddy and Alison.'

'Oh. Let's think. Is she slender with blonde hair?'

'Yes.'

'And is he tall with a bit of a stomach?'

'Yes! That's them. I knew you'd know them!'

Fortunately the waiter came over, so I ordered a round of Sangrias and promptly changed the subject. I had to find a way into the fact I was leaving the island. When the drinks arrived, Susan giggled.

'You're a terrible influence, Rodriguez. I had such a head the morning after we last met.' And then she bent across and kissed me, as if to remind me of all the furious kissing we had done on the bench up on the terrace above us and of the unfinished business that lay between us.

I felt my guilt receding and kissed her back. Then she sat back in her chair and smiled at me in a coquettish fashion.

'Do you still have the builders in?'

'Afraid so. They've taken up the marble flooring.'

'Really, what for?'

'They want to send it to Italy to be reconditioned. I've told them it's a ridiculous suggestion.'

'It is! I'm sure there must be somewhere on the island that could do it.'

'That's exactly what I said. Look here Susan, I've something to—'

'I'll ask the Whytes when I see them. They've miles of marble.'

131

Susan took a pocketbook out of her bag and made a note. Then she snapped it closed and, all in one movement, bent over and kissed me again. I was slightly embarrassed as we were sitting right in the bustle out on the Borne, but I enjoyed it all the same.

'What about your place?' I whispered, but Susan shook her head with a mock sorry face.

'My landlady's a dragon. We shall just have to wait,' and then she came and kissed me again, as if to make her point about the waiting.

I racked my brains for what to do. How much would a hotel room cost? Could we find one for the cost of supper and forgo food for the evening? With an inward groan I felt sure that whatever place Susan was expecting someone like me would take someone like her would cost more than two hundred and fifty *pesetas* for the night. What to do?

It was just as I was thinking all this that something horrible happened. I got this really sick feeling in my stomach, and I knew something had unsettled me. I couldn't figure out what it was. There was just this terrible feeling in my stomach. I scanned back and forth at the tourists and the waiters and the little dogs with their owners promenading past to see what it might have been.

Then I went back to the tourists sitting at the tables and picked over them again. There was a group of swanky yanks knocking back beers from the bottle, an English couple with their children (the couple were bickering with each other and then noisily telling their children to be quiet) and then the other tables were taken up by Italians and French and Swiss and every other well-dressed nationality you can think of, and then there, amongst them all, I saw her. It was my wife.

Yes, there was my wife, of all people, sitting bold as brass in the midst of the tables, sipping at a glass of what I assumed, knowing her, was tonic water. My wife had never been a drinker; she preferred to be abstemious so she could keep a clear head for sneering at me, should I get tipsy.

From where I sat, I couldn't see her face clearly. She was turned away at an angle. My beacon was the distinctive way her brown hair curled outwards at the bottom, and the sight of the edge of her blue hairband which was always in position to ensure every strand of her hair was swept tidily back off her face.

Her hand reached out and picked up the glass of tonic. Just from the way she did it, bolt upright, as if she were spiked to the chair, raising the glass to her lips rather than moving her mouth down to her glass (refusing as ever the compromise, the meet you halfway); I knew it was her.

I felt sick to my stomach. How had she found me?

'Roddy, are you listening to me? What is it? Have you seen someone?'

I remembered Susan again. 'What?'

'I said have you seen someone?'

'No, no,' I said in a hurry, and manoeuvred myself so as to put my wife just behind Susan's shoulder. I covered the action up by putting my hand on Susan's thigh at the same time, as if that had been my plan all along. 'It was just a passing dog. I'd been thinking of getting one.'

'Oh, which one?'

'A poodle perhaps.'

Now I could see who was sitting at the table with my wife. It was a man opposite her, scruffily dressed I would say, not her type of person at all, and I realised with a shock that was doubly hideous, that made the fruit of the Sangria come right up to the very top of my oesophagus and threaten to re-emerge, that the man was surely a private detective.

He was leafing through papers, and every so often showing them to my wife. It was no doubt the evidence he had collected of my flight across Europe and of my being on the island. How had he done it? What an expert he must be. How much could my wife be paying him? Or perhaps she wasn't paying him at all. Perhaps it was someone else, someone with an even bigger axe to grind against my neck, and perhaps she was just along for the ride.

'Roddy, what is wrong with you? There is someone, isn't there?'

Susan turned round and looked at the tables, but what could she see other than a sea of tourists? She could never know that amongst them was one for whom love had turned to sour disappointment, who was out for revenge.

'It's nothing,' I said hurriedly. 'I was just thinking I'll tell the builders to put the flooring back down and damn the reconditioning. I can't go on like this.'

Susan smiled in satisfaction. Then she started talking about something, and I let her ramble on and nodded wherever she seemed to want me to. It gave me the perfect cover to watch the other table.

The private detective ordered a drink and cracked a joke of some sort which made the waiter laugh. The drink arrived quickly after that, quicker than our Sangrias had come, and it looked to be a whiskey or a Scotch of some sort. The private dick dropped one ice cube into the tumbler, swirled it around and then took a slug of it. Then he sat and watched my wife reading the documents.

I could see his face clearly, and I could see the cunning in his eyes and his frame, the cunning that had made him so good.

My wife looked up from the papers to the street name attached to the building beside us and then over towards the *Avenida Rey Jaime III* where the *Hotel de la Almudaina* lies. Did the investigator discover I had eaten there? Had he gone in and shown a photograph and given them some line as to why he was looking for me: a long-lost brother, a confused friend returned from the war?

A panic took hold of me. What should I do? Should I wait and follow them and see what they got up to and discover how much they knew? Or should I go home and hide in *Ca'n Mola* until I'd thought of my scheme to make money and be off? Perhaps I should leave the island this very moment.

In any event, right now there was nothing I could do. I couldn't get up or the detective would see me and know that he had his man. I needed to get to the ferry port, that was the thing to do. Get a head start while he was sitting there drinking with my wife.

The private detective got up. He went over towards the bar and disappeared inside. I stood up. Now was my chance. There was a hand round my wrist. It made me jump.

'Roddy, where are you going?'

I looked down at Susan. I saw the concern in her face and I thought what a sweet, lovely girl she was, and how happy she would make a man.

'I'm terribly sorry,' I said. 'I've just remembered I'm supposed to be at ... at a christening.'

'A christening?'

'Yes. My neighbour's child. What an idiot I am. So forgetful.'

'Is it in the evening?'

'Yes, crazy isn't it? That must be why I forgot. I had better hurry over there.'

'Shall I come with you?'

'Well, that's kind, but they're strict Catholics you know and...'

'I see. Don't worry. Gosh, you'd better hurry.'

'Yes.'

I took a moment and kissed her.

'Will you come with me to that party next week?'

'Yes,' I said hurriedly, and kissed her again.

Then I put down twenty *pesetas* and fled to the nearest side passage. I turned and peered back around the corner. My wife was still sitting there, and the detective had not yet returned.

Susan was immediately approached by an Italian who asked if the seat opposite her was free. The man took it and the two started talking.

Then something very strange happened. My wife raised

her index finger. A waiter came hurrying over and then, much to my surprise, and following my wife's instruction, he started pouring gin into the tonic.

He kept pouring, watching and waiting for the tiniest signal from my wife. Finally she made a minute movement with her beautifully manicured finger, and the waiter let the flow of the gin subside, lifting the bottle up with a flourish.

I watched transfixed. My wife lifted the glass, looked into its depths and then raised it to her lips. She tipped her head back and let in a great mouthful, all in one go. Then she started to slowly turn her head around towards me, as someone will when a sixth sense tells them they are being watched.

I was coiled like a spring, ready to leap out of sight, but just then the detective returned from the bar's interior and called her to attention. He bent down and kissed my wife full on the lips. Then he returned to his whiskey and papers while she picked up the menu from the table and glanced down it.

I felt sick to my stomach. I don't know which streets I ran down but I must have made a wide arc through the back streets of the *El Terreno* district, rushing past the American tourists lurching about with their arms about one another, until I came down onto the embankment close to Tito's.

There, I managed to force myself to stop. I bent over, with my backside up against a wall, and tried to catch my breath. I couldn't seem to breathe. People were coming over and speaking to me in all sorts of languages, then the doorman of Tito's was there and all of them were leering and speaking into my face.

Had it been my wife? Had I got it wrong? Not once in twenty years have I seen her touch a drop of alcohol. And kissing her private detective? It wasn't her style. Perhaps it hadn't been my wife at all, but someone who looked very like her. It was six months since I'd seen her, and sometimes when I think of her now I can't remember what she looks like.

Sometimes, if I concentrate hard, her image floats towards me and is crystal clear but, other times, it becomes blurry and bizarrely is replaced by that of my father-in-law with his violet cheeks, and then strangely by a man in a white coat who is asking me questions in a kind voice.

A whistle was sounding and the crowd around me parted to let someone through. He had a hat on his head, and it was that which shook me out of it. It was a *polizia*.

'Are you all right?' he said to me in Spanish.

I nodded quickly and patted my chest. 'It was just an attack of asthma,' I wheezed. 'I'm fine, please don't worry.'

The *polizia* was a young man. He looked closely at me, with concern showing in his youthful face.

Then I saw his eyes narrow and he cocked his head to one side. 'What is your name, Senyor?'

Names went through my head like the ribbon on the typewriter ... Rodriguez, Sebastian, Waddington ... even Gomez was there. Waddington. I was supposed to be Waddington. But I was speaking Spanish, and too well to suddenly become a Waddington.

The *polizia* saw my hesitation and made up his mind.

'It's you!' he shouted, and he lifted his whistle to his lips.

I did the only thing I could. I collapsed. The *polizia* tried to catch me but he was only slight and he struggled to do it. He let me slide onto the pavement.

The pedestrians crowded closer as the *polizia* went over to the road to signal to his colleague further down, blowing on his whistle the whole time. I saw my opportunity, and was on my feet in a flash running back into the lanes behind Tito's. Through them I went like a mad thing, the sound of the whistle always just behind me.

Finally it seemed to die away, and I found my twisting had by chance brought me further west, close to where the Jag was parked. Grasping my sides, I staggered to it and, trying hard not to faint from the exhaustion of my terror, I got in and drove home.

Chapter XV

Had it been her? Had it? The next morning I went over and over it in my head, but I just couldn't figure it out. My wife drinking and openly embracing a man in the street? It surely couldn't have been her. Of course, stress can drive one to drink, but to drive one to drink and out the other side? Impossible. I was feeling guilty, that was all it was. I was feeling guilty about leaving my wife in the mire, so I'd latched onto a woman who looked like her. I never even saw her face for goodness sake. I berated myself, for if I had waited to see, I wouldn't have been in this horrible state of doubt now.

That policeman didn't have any doubts though, I thought, darkly. He'd recognised me all right. He'd looked as if he thought he was going to get a medal or something when he went rushing off blowing that whistle of his.

I should have to keep my head down from now on. No more bars, no more trips to the city, and certainly no more Susan. From now on it would have to be write, write, write, until the book was ready for Salvatore. Because if I didn't get the money from Salvatore, I didn't know how I'd get off the island. Now they'd almost certainly be watching the ports for me, so I'd need to bribe a fisherman to take me over to Alicante or even Morocco. I was trapped like rat in a cage.

With that thought I went straight to the study and buckled down to the necessary task of writing. It was hard because my mind kept wanting to think of Isabella rather than the world of Father Gomez. I kept finding myself in the midst of a scene and realising all I was imagining was what might happen between Isabella and me at my supper party for the girls.

I was certain that either something would happen between us that night, in the romantic courtyard of *Ca'n Mola*, or I would forever be thrown into that bargain basement labelled 'friends'.

All day I was temperate. I so didn't want anything to go wrong. As the evening approached, when my supper was all prepped and ready to go as a professional chef would do, I had a sudden thought that I ought to get some champagne. It couldn't be afforded, but I wanted to impress Isabella. So I hurried out to a village that was as close as I dared, and purchased a bottle and some ice. Then I rushed back to the house and put the champagne with the ice in a bucket on the table.

When the time for Marta and Isabella to arrive came, I was beside myself with nerves. Isabella looked quite lovely in a low-backed blue rayon dress, but it was my attire she was looking at curiously.

'Thomas, *mio caro*, what are you wearing?'

I looked down in surprise at Rodriguez's white suit. Damn it. In my rush, I had entirely forgotten to change.

'Oh, it's an old suit of my father's. Bit old fashioned, I guess.'

'No, no. You look handsome in it. Just different, that's all.'

With that compliment stored up and a resolution to always wear the white suit with Isabella from then on, I settled them down at the table and lit the citron candles to keep the mosquitos away.

Marta looked about her in an approving fashion. 'It really is very charming, Mr Sebastian.'

'See,' said Isabella. 'Didn't I say that it was?'

'And is this the well you spoke of?'

I agreed that it was. Isabella took the empty jug, and she and I went over to it. The bucket went down and came back up with its usual clunking and splashing, but Marta didn't get up to see (I don't know why I had thought that she would). She just called out questions regarding the technical workings of the well which I wasn't in the slightest bit qualified to answer, but I attempted regardless. Isabella brought the jug over to the table and we watched and waited while the calc settled to the bottom. Then she poured us each a glass.

'Splendid, Mr Sebastian, how refreshing it tastes.'

I insisted Marta call me Thomas (though this must have been the tenth time I had done so), and then I went inside to check on the food. While I was there I allowed myself, finally, to take a quick tot of something, and then I went back out and offered the girls a choice of the Bordeaux or the champagne. The Bordeaux (not a great one, but the choice in the cellar was becoming more limited with each day that passed) was already open and breathing and the champagne was there in the ice.

To my surprise, Isabella asked for a glass of the red.

'Are you sure? Did you see the champagne?'

'Sorry, Thomas?'

'Wouldn't you prefer champagne?'

'Well, yes that would be lovely. Let's have champagne.'

'Ah, but I think you'd rather have red.'

Isabella laughed at me. 'I would like champagne over anything, Thomas.'

So I poured her a glass of champagne, being careful not to let it fizz up and waste any over the top of the glass, and sat down again.

Isabella continued to smile. 'And what about Marta?'

I leapt to my feet. 'I'm so sorry. What would you like, Marta? The red or the bubbles?' I poured Marta some of the Bordeaux, and sat down again. 'How was the field trip?' I asked.

Isabella replied it was ok and Marta said it was fascinating at precisely the same moment, and Isabella laughed and Marta gave her what I considered to be quite a patronising smirk.

'Well, the study was a success for Marta,' said Isabella.

Marta turned to me. 'I told her she should go back to the hotel and sit by the pool, but you know how she is, Mr Sebastian. She does hate to be alone.'

I wasn't sure whether to agree with Marta because it seemed a little rude to Isabella, but I saw the truth in it. It cut me to the quick, because I knew Marta was suggesting Isabella only spent time with me out of a desire for company.

'Isn't it nice to be able to sit without a jersey in the evening now?' Isabella said.

We all agreed it was and, after I served the food, we sat in silence for a moment while no one could think of anything to say. I thought how lovely it was to hear the song of the cicadas against the rustling of the palm trees and behind it the faint suggestion of the sea, until Marta ruined it with one of her dull conversational gambits.

'Tell me Thomas, when was *Ca'n Mola* built?'

Well goodness. How on earth was I to know? I made up a date and Marta was completely satisfied by it, so from then on I determined I was going to give her a whole lot of facts and fill her up with them, which is what I did, telling her all sorts of things like the fact that the estate extended right the way to the top of the hills behind us and that all the olive trees between here and there were planted in the year the possession was built; I explained about the different outhouses, the laundry, the chapel, and the building where they pressed the olives. I told her the walls of the press room were smoked black – it was essential since the olive oil was sensitive to light. This she found particularly of interest.

Most of these things were true, since I had found some pamphlets on the production of oil in the house, but I confess I was tempted to embellish if only to stop Marta herself droning on in her usual dull fashion. So I told how, at the turn of century, the owner at the time had tried to modernise the estate by bringing in a new press from the mainland, and how the workers, horrified at the traitorous behaviour of the Senyor, had revolted and killed him and both of his donkeys for good measure. And I told her half a dozen other ridiculous things that couldn't possibly be believed but she was so pompous and dull she couldn't see the joke and believed it all.

While I was making all this nonsense up, I pointed out certain parts of the estate to illustrate. I could see she had half a mind to get up and look, but her laziness got the better of her, so she just squinted out into the darkness.

Isabella, half smiling, was on to me. She frowned with mock disapproval when Marta was looking away, so I stopped and the conversation frittered to nothing again.

'And what about you, Thomas?' Marta suddenly said. 'You're part Venezuelan, if I remember correctly?'

By now the evening had grown quite dark. We were sitting in the bubble of the light cast by the oil lamp, and the garden around us had disappeared into the black. I was feeling pleasantly warm from the wine. 'My father was English and my mother Venezuelan.'

Isabella rested her cheek on her palm. 'Do you remember her much?'

'Not really. Just that she had very dark eyes, like mine.'

Isabella looked into them and I held her gaze, but Marta interrupted the moment.

'But your father was English?'

'As English as they come. Shall I tell you how they met? It's very romantic.'

Both of the girls were keen to hear, so I poured myself another glass of wine and made sure the girls were ok; I took another *Ducado* from the packet Marta offered, lit up, and blew the smoke out into the darkness. Then I began.

'Well it was back in the 'twenties. My father had taken a

threshing machine over to Venezuela. It was to revolutionise harvests no matter the crop – coffee, tobacco, sugar, opium – it would work as well for all.'

'Interesting,' said Marta. 'How did the threshing machine work for the tobacco plant?'

I told her I didn't know, and Isabella told her it wasn't important.

'This was bandit country then, of course,' I said. 'And the machine proved so popular that my father was invited deep into the jungle, past the plantation houses with their flag poles and maids in starched uniforms, past the copper and bauxite mines of the Andes, and to the mountain estate of the local *Caudillo*.'

'What's a *Caudillo*?'

'He's sort of a rich landowner. They usually get involved in some coup or other in the end.'

Marta was frowning. 'Is there copper in the Andes?'

I inhaled slowly on the *Ducado* and counted to five. 'I might have some of the details wrong. I only know what my father told me, and of course I might have forgotten over the years.'

'So he went over the Andes…' Isabella prompted.

'That's right. For ten days he journeyed inland, tied to the back of an open-top jeep, a giant Browning strapped to the front.'

I thought for a moment Marta was going to interrupt again, so I ignored her and directed my story from then on at Isabella. 'When the driver turned to smile at my father, chewing tobacco oozed out of the gaps in his teeth.'

I grinned and showed my teeth which made Isabella clap her hands, delighted. 'My father stayed there with the *Caudillo* for three months and during that time he fell in love with the *Caudillo*'s daughter. But they hid the fact from the *Caudillo* because they knew he would never allow my mother to marry a foreigner.'

I took in a breath of the night time air and I have to say

that I don't think I have ever been so happy as I was in that moment, with Isabella hanging on to my every word and giving me that look.

She begged me to go on and tell them how it ended.

'Well, eventually they eloped,' I said. 'They stole a jeep from a sleeping guard and made for the port at Maracaibo where they found a priest to marry them. Then they fled over to England.'

'What a wonderful story,' said Isabella, but Marta looked puzzled.

'And the machine?'

'I beg your pardon?'

'What happened about the threshing machine?'

At this, Isabella and I couldn't help catching one another's eye and we were doing all that we could not to laugh, but unfortunately we didn't try hard enough for Marta saw it and the damage was done.

'Did I say something funny?' Marta said, coldly.

Isabella lost her smile in an instant. 'No, it was just that...'

'I don't see what's so funny.'

'Well, it's just that the story wasn't about the machine.'

'I know that, Isabella,' Marta continued, slightly too sharply, I thought. 'I was just interested in the machine. Is that so funny?'

There was an awkward moment when neither Isabella nor I knew what to say, and I hated Marta for being so spiteful to Isabella when it had only been a little joke, so I tried to fix it by topping the wine up and asking if anyone would like some *manchego*.

But I will say this about Marta. She didn't hold a temper for long. In a minute or two she was back to her usual self and she made a few flattering comments towards Isabella which I could see were designed to say sorry in a roundabout way, and Isabella took them graciously but was still a little cool in her manner towards Marta after that. I couldn't help but think that the two of them had been living together on the island for far too long. They had started to act like some old couple and I felt quite the gooseberry for a minute.

After the cheese, Isabella suddenly said she had eaten too much and would Marta mind if she and I took a walk over to the cliff path.

Marta had just taken a cigar from her bag and, after offering one to me which I declined, she had lit up and was comfortably leaning back in her chair enjoying it.

'Why didn't you say so a moment ago, before I had lit this?' Marta complained, but then she didn't seem to care; she just waved us off with a frown.

The walk over to the cliff top was such a joy for me. Imagine me here in the moonlight with Isabella, side by side. I could smell her evening perfume and I tried to consider in what way it was different from the one she wore in the daytime.

We went a little way along the path. It went dangerously close to the edge, much closer than the English would have allowed.

'What do you think of Marta?' Isabella asked suddenly.

I wasn't sure what to say, so I spluttered out something about how intelligent her friend seemed and how kind and knowledgeable, and some nonsense in that vein.

And then Isabella turned to me and said, 'And what do you think of me?'

I could see the outline of Isabella's face with the moon shining on her cheek.

I was even more at a loss but I knew this was the invitation I'd been waiting for. The sound of the waves crashing on the rocks below came up to us from bottom of the cliff. I knew that if you were brave and went right to the edge, as close as one could dare, you could see down to where the water turned white and foamy as it became smashed and destroyed.

I came closer to Isabella and our fingertips touched.

Then, to my horror, there was a noise behind us and

Isabella jumped back. I took hold of her arm because I was afraid for her, but she shook my hand off.

A figure loomed in the darkness from the direction of the house.

'Mr Sebastian. I hope you're not taking Isabella too close to the edge.'

That infernal woman. She was like some great heifer trampling about with her grisly hooves everywhere. How I wanted to take my hands and put them around that egregiously fat neck of hers and squeeze and squeeze until every last inch of her boring breath was silenced.

Isabella reassured her that we weren't anywhere near the edge and said she was feeling much better now, and the three of us were obliged to walked back up to *Ca'n Mola*.

We decided that it had grown cooler, so we brought our wine glasses into the house and I made the girls coffee and we settled down in the sitting room. I made a joke of showing off Rodriguez's old-fashioned gramophone.

Isabella leafed through his record collection.

'Nat King Cole, Frank Sinatra ... It's terribly old,' she said. 'You must get more with it, Thomas.'

I could barely think of what she was saying. All I wanted to do was to think of a way of separating her from Marta so that I could once and for all make my move.

Now was the time. The wine had obviously given her the courage to admit her feelings towards me. And I had enough spirit inside me to make such a move, yet not so much I was the wreck I often became over long.

But it seemed impossible. So I took another glass of wine and decided to sit right next to Isabella on the couch, and, when she shuffled away a little, I shuffled along with her.

Marta was looking at me in a pointed manner and I saw that her cheeks were flushed; I suddenly realised what it was all about. Marta was in love with Isabella herself. I wondered if Isabella knew. I didn't have long to ponder on it, because just then Marta came out with a comment that so floored me

I was stumped at what to say in response.

With no preamble or coming to the point, or building up to it as other people would, she just came right out and said, 'Tell me Mr Sebastian, are you a homosexual?'

'I beg your pardon?' I spluttered.

'I asked if you were homosexual, Mr Sebastian. Now don't take offence.'

I still wasn't able to put together a response I was so in shock, and Marta just carried on with her rambling monologue.

'It's just that you live here alone and Isabella says that you often meet up with a friend of yours in the city. We don't mind at all if you are, I was just wanting to get the facts right, seeing as we are close neighbours and friends, you see...'

We don't mind? Was she speaking for Isabella? I looked at Isabella but her face was blank so I couldn't understand what she might be thinking. Then suddenly she got up and went over to Marta.

'What a thing to ask,' she said. 'I think you've had quite enough wine.'

And she took Marta's glass from her (as a wife would to a wayward husband who is making a fool of himself at the end of a dinner party), and replaced it with a cup of coffee. Then she sat down beside Marta.

Marta had a slightly satisfied look upon her face and thoughts started to come to me as to what it all meant.

This was what Isabella must have told Marta in order to keep the woman off her back. I saw at once how it allowed Isabella the freedom to spend her days with me. There were so many facets to this I didn't know where to begin. Isabella must at least have considered it to be the case, or the thought would never have occurred to her to suggest it to Marta.

I looked at Isabella for a clue, but she dropped her eyes to the floor. 'I've told you Marta, Thomas is married and has a wife back in England,' she said, and she took a sip from her own cup.

'Now don't take offence,' Marta said again, brusquely, and she looked across as if to catch Isabella's eye in a, 'See, I told you he wasn't,' kind of way. Urrgh. I felt sick to my core. Then Marta leant over, cleared her throat, and apologised in a very manly way and I have to confess I could hear my father joking in my head that Marta was more of a man than I'd ever be.

'We just misunderstand your English ways,' the awful woman finished. How I hated her with every cell of my body.

'Darling, Thomas,' Isabella said, trying to give a light little laugh. 'Don't mind Marta. It's just a reputation Englishmen have, that's all.'

I wanted to recover my composure and brush it off like Isabella, but I couldn't stop thinking of the times when there had been a certain tension between us, even just then on the cliff, whereas in fact perhaps this was what she had been wondering all along. My hatred for Marta took on a whole new dimension, because, rightly or wrongly, I blamed her for this. I couldn't help that I was a little effete. It was an affliction I'd always suffered from. Over the years I'd tried to butch it up. And it didn't help that my eyelashes are long like a girl's. I've always thought that was a part of it, my eyelashes; they give such a feminine look to my face.

I was bullied at school because of it. And at Oxford I took to wearing a plain suit like the townies because I thought it looked tougher, but still I was approached by a crowd convinced I belonged in their club, and, though I tried politely to brush them off, those approaches only made my cohort all the more convinced. I don't know what I was more afraid of, the approaches themselves or the thought of prison.

It was only when I was married that the feeling of people judging and misunderstanding me finally went away. What a joy it had been to bump into old acquaintances and introduce my wife to them and see their faces alter as if to say, 'Sorry old boy, I had you wrong all this time,' and then they'd invite us to a dinner party or to the theatre as if to make up for all the invitations they should have made in the past but never did.

But then of course no children came along, and all those looks started to return – the looks that linger too long as if people are trying to read from your features what goes on behind closed doors or in darkened alleyways. And my wife was never keen on the whole thing anyway and eventually I got the impression that even she began to have her doubts, which was unfair since it was she who had taken a dislike to the bedroom business in the first place, and I had only followed suit out of kindness and respect for her.

I realised Isabella was biting her bottom lip, and I noticed that my nostrils were flaring out of their own accord and that I'd been silent in an angry way for so long it had ruined the evening. Even though it was Marta who had spoken out of turn it was I who had ruined things by not being sober enough to laugh off such a comment as I should have done. And I'd promised myself I wouldn't drink too much so I wouldn't do or say something stupid, and look, I'd embarrassed Isabella in front of Marta. And after the evening had been going so well and we had just been talking earlier about how we must do it again some time.

But then I looked at Marta and could see that she didn't care one jot.

She sat looking at me as if I were a particularly interesting lizard. Perhaps I looked like one to her, sitting there stock still as I was, with my nostrils flaring rhythmically, and my tongue clamped to the top of my mouth as if it were about to shoot out and catch a fly.

Finally I managed to pull myself together and force out a laugh.

'So that's what you think, is it? Well, I never knew that.'

Marta frowned. 'It was my mistake, Thomas, and for that I apologise.'

'It's quite all right.'

'No, it was rude of me, and I apologise.'

'And I accept your apology and can promise you I am quite the full-blooded male.'

Isabella seemed satisfied by this, Marta less so, but at least our supper party was to some extent restored.

After a few awkward attempts at further conversation and a few false starts, we finally settled back at the topic of the late Senyor Rodriguez. They knew it was something I was interested in, and I suppose it was their way of making amends. Isabella even had some new facts for me, which Marta had found out earlier in the week.

'Apparently he was working on a masterpiece, isn't that right Marta? When being a patron to the arts didn't impress his Russian princess, he decided to become an artist himself.'

'Typical of a man,' said Marta, as if there wasn't one present. 'To think he could just become a talented artist overnight.'

I still felt horrible inside about the whole row and how I had disgraced myself. Isabella got up and went over to take a cigarette from the mantelpiece and I hurriedly got up to light it for her.

'It's actually quite romantic when you think about it, isn't it?' she said.

I agreed with her, but I didn't say so. I thought of Rodriguez's attempts at painting. There were a few watercolours in the *casita* along with an expensive array of paints and easels. The watercolours were all quite dreadful. But then I realised, of course, it was his book, not a painting, that was probably his masterpiece – and I was about to get it published for him. I felt quite public spirited about the whole affair suddenly. What a service I was doing for Rodriguez. If only he were alive to know it.

'It is romantic,' I said. 'And quite sad too.'

'Yes, how sad,' Isabella sighed, and I could see from the way she did, waving her cigarette around in a dramatic fashion, that she had got a little tipsy from the champagne.

'Would you like a little more wine, Isabella?' I said, but

then Marta cut in, and, bore that she was, she told Isabella it was time that they left.

With a heavy heart I walked with them down the hill in the moonlight, with Isabella between Marta and I. I was forced to endure a kiss on the cheek from Marta before I could receive my usual ones from Isabella.

I thought Isabella lingered overly long on it and she held me close while she did so, much closer than usual, and it took me by surprise.

After they had gone into the villa I stood by the car in a dejected state and my feelings towards Marta took a dark turn. I thought of her lying, dead, and stiff as a board. Isabella is in my arms, sobbing, and I am saying to her: 'Isabella – remember what Marta said. You must live for the moment.' And Isabella agrees with me and looks into my eyes. Now we would both want to kiss at that moment, but it wouldn't be appropriate, with the body of Marta lying right beside us, so I would masterfully steer Isabella away and into the other room and then we would fall upon one another and the passion would encompass our every thought and all the parts of our bodies: our limbs, our mouths, our hands, her breasts.

I got into the car. I knew it would be crazy to go back to the city, but the voice of Rodriguez was in my head. 'What harm could it do?' he said to me. 'You can keep in the shadows and to the back street bars.'

Although I couldn't see him I answered and told him he didn't exist, and, even if he did, who was he to come and give me advice?

He was silent at that, but I knew he was giving me that old rogue smile of his, with that twinkle in his eyes that said he had seen and done wilder things in his time than I could even dream of. I knew at once he was insinuating I should not be such a little squirrel of man. 'Come on!' he said, eventually. 'Think of how beautiful the city is at night, with the stonework of the *Seu* bathed in orange, and the lights dotted in a ring around the bay.' I explained very patiently to the man that it would be dangerous and the stupidest thing I could possibly do, but Rodriguez, with all his charm, could be most persuasive. Eventually I caved in.

'Are you sure, Rodriguez? Do you really think it would be the best thing?'

'Thomas, Thomas,' he said to me, and I had a thought of him, sliding his glasses down to the end of his nose, and peering at me over them. 'Man or mouse?'

Chapter XVI

Now it may be considered that I am my own worst enemy and if someone were to say it, I would be the first to agree. Later that night, I ended up at a party. It wasn't down to any deliberate plan, but the one good thing that could be said was that at least I wasn't spending any of my own money while I was there.

It was a long time since I'd been to a party. I try to avoid them at all costs. For parties, by their nature, are pretentious affairs where everyone is determined to have 'fun' and be 'fun', and because of that they are anything but.

I can never decide which is worse. Is it the sort where no one knows each other, and must go about making polite opening gambits such as, 'Was your journey over here terribly hard?' or suffer impertinent questions such as, 'Is your wife with you this evening?'.

Or is it the opposite sort? Where the guests know each so well, it gives one the impression the party has been lurching away for eternity.

The party I arrived at later that night was one such as that. It might have been going on for months, perhaps even years. It resembled the end of an illicit affair, where the same tired people go round and round, eating and drinking their way towards copulation, yet all the time trying to convince themselves that there was some other more meaningful purpose to it all.

How I came to be at the party is something of a comedy of errors and I would never have allowed it to happen if I'd known it was going to.

I'd been keeping, as Rodriguez had suggested I should, to the quiet little bars of the Arab Quarter, but the locals weren't accustomed to seeing tourists there and I hadn't felt entirely welcome. They were gazing over at me and whispering amongst themselves and, although the barman was friendly and polite, the whole thing made me exceedingly unsettled and I have to say, also rather lonely. It's horrible to go somewhere just to be surrounded by people and to have the feeling those people would rather you hadn't come. So I started to become melancholy and then I thought of Susan and her cheery dedication to me, and I thought how silly I was being. Because Isabella would never know, and after the way my supper party had gone that evening, I doubted she would even care.

So I asked the barman if I could have the use of the phone, and I called Susan up. She answered straight away, which took me by surprise, because I was steeled for the usual battle with her landlady. I detected a note of tension in her voice and wondered what it meant.

'Where are you, Rodriguez?' she said.

'In a bar over by *Casa Oleza*.' The line went silent. 'Are you there, Susan?'

'What are you doing in a bar, Roddy?'

'I'm having a drink.'

Again the line went quiet and I wondered if perhaps I should ring off and reconnect, but then she spoke again, and I could tell she was definitely cross about something. I thought perhaps she was upset because of the abrupt way I had left the last time, but then she said, 'And are you coming over?'

'Yes, of course,' I replied. 'I'll come right now,' and I hurried over there as fast as I could.

When I arrived, she came out and kissed me on the

lips and I could tell I was forgiven for my misdemeanour, whatever it was.

She looked very pretty. Her hair was done up in a chignon, and I couldn't help but notice how short her dress was.

'Come on,' she said, briskly. 'We're going to be late.'

'Are we?'

She looked at me with an uncertain look on her face. 'Where did you park?'

'Just off *Rey Jaime*.'

'We'd better hurry, then.'

Now I began to get a little nervous because I didn't have a clue what she was talking about, but I had a sneaking suspicion that perhaps I should and I searched about for a way to find out.

'What time were we supposed to be there?'

'Not any particular time, but still ... we're very late.'

We cut through the back streets down to the centre and I opened the door to let her in the car and then sat for a minute, pretending to fiddle with the choke, while I played for time.

'What do you think would be the best way to go?'

'Out through Santa Maria?'

'Righty ho.'

It was a pleasant enough evening for a drive in any event. Susan stretched her arms above her head and looked around her at the car.

'I've never been in a Jag before.'

I gave her a smile which I thought said everything and soon we were out of the city, heading north.

'Did you speak to your protégé?' she asked suddenly, and it seemed to me that the comment came out of the blue. Why did she have this persistent need to go back to every little thing I'd told her and follow it up, wanting facts and what happened next and so on? I knew I frowned.

'Don't look at me like that,' she said with a wagging finger. 'We've got to help him get out there.'

I acknowledged it was true (which of course it wasn't).

'Now I know you're going to be cross with me, Roddy, but I went back to the gallery again and I spoke to the owner.'

Oh, heaven forfend. What had the girl been doing?

'He'd be happy to display the boy's work.' She glanced across at me looking decidedly pleased with herself. 'He said that if you thought the boy's talent was worth pursuing, it had to be the case.'

At this I was surprised and, despite myself, a little proud.

'Why would he think that?'

'What do you mean?'

'Well, why would he think it was worth it just because I think it's worth it?'

'Rodriguez, darling, you are silly. Mr Ortega knows all about you. He said so.'

Now that was an alarming remark. Exactly who did he know about? The worry made me wonder where our journey was taking us and whether there would be a drink at the end of it.

'Tell me,' I ventured. 'This gathering tonight...'

'Yes?'

'Who will be there? At this ... gathering?'

'Oh, everyone.' Susan took her compact out of her bag and looked into it. 'I can't wait for them all to meet you.'

'But who, specifically?'

'Well, let's see. Geoffrey will be there of course. He's very keen to meet you.'

I waited patiently.

'I expect Chip will be there. He's always everywhere.'

Why would the curator think he knew all about me? Had the private detective and my wife been to see him? I didn't think it likely. Why would they think to visit some gallery owner? So the wretched man must think he knows who Senyor Rodriguez is. Could there be two of them? I hope he didn't think I was the Senyor Rodriguez, the Rodriguez of *Ca'n Mola*; if that was the case, then he mustn't have heard that I'm dead, that is ... I mean ... he must not have heard that the real Senyor Rodriguez was dead. Oh, it was too confusing. It didn't make sense. Susan was still going on. I had forgotten to listen.

'And you must make sure you speak to Zavier and Rufus. They're both here to write books.'

'So it's more of a party than a gathering would you say?'

'Yes, Roddy. It's more of a party than a gathering.'

Susan pointed out the turning and I took the road. As it wound its way up the hill we began to hear the party's music floating down to us. It mingled in with the swishing of the pines each time the Jag's engine died away in a switchback.

The villa was at the top of the hill. We knew we were close when we saw a glimpse of it through the trees. Its lights guided us in like the traction beams of a large, concrete UFO. I parked up between an Alfa Romeo and a Cinquecento.

Susan took my hand in a masterful manner (it was her set of friends after all) and led me into the house. Then she manoeuvred me through the rooms, introducing me to the guests as we passed. It seemed likely to be a disastrous situation, but then I spotted the drinks table with a mixture of excitement and relief and I decided to manoeuvre myself.

They were desperate for fresh blood. I knew this because each one of them hung onto my hand for too long and said things like, 'Do come back and talk to me.'

Of course I sounded interesting. Susan had found a way of mentioning to every single one of them within a moment of meeting them that I was exceedingly rich and a renowned art collector, even though I'd asked her not to.

My earlier liveners seemed to have evaporated on the drive over, leaving me feeling nervously sober. My mouth was quite dry, and I was starting to feel a bit queasy about all the people around me. So I helped myself to a glass of wine, as big as I thought I could get away with, polished it off quickly, and helped myself to another. No one batted an eyelid. With a sudden warm feeling, I decided I was going to like Susan's friends.

Susan herself didn't notice because she was going on and on about my shark-shaped pool, though I kept giving her a look which meant 'Be quiet,' but she took as much notice of that as she did of the bottle of Scotch I had picked up and was carrying around with me.

'Who did it? Was it Pablo?'

'I beg your pardon?'

'Was it Pablo who did the shark-shaped pool?'

'I forget.'

I was introduced to a girl called Carole, who wanted to give me a body massage. 'Perhaps later', I said. Then to Chip, who I suspected was a heroin smuggler (though of course that wasn't how he was announced). He wore a denim jacket and white sneakers and his belly hung over his jeans.

'Come out on the boat with me tomorrow, Rodriguez,' he said, and his deep American drawl rang out strongly in the room despite the music. 'Let's you and me fish for marlin. What d'y' say?' And he tapped me on the chest which I didn't like.

Next I was pulled into another room and somehow introduced to Carole again, who snuck around the back of me as I tried to explain we had already met and who started to massage my shoulders through the linen of Rodriguez's suit.

'So much tension,' she purred in my ear.

The party was spread out across the two rooms. It was Geoffrey's house, I eventually determined, because he kept pointing out items of furniture and art work to me and telling me how much they had cost.

It seemed to me that the party could be divided into two contingents.

On the one side were the likes of Chip, the heroin smuggler; some older ladies who wafted around in garish kaftans (Susan explained to me in a whisper the concept of Pucci); our host the Olde English fruitcake, Geoffrey, whose hair was desperately thinning, but who was making the most of it where he could; a couple of actors (everyone was taking such pains to treat them as if they were normal I could only assume they must be terribly famous); and then finally some young toffs, just out of Harrow, who were deliberately scruffy like that chap from the Rolling Stones. These last two pups said they were taking a break in their careers to get the novel out the way. They said it as if it were a known fact that every decent human being would eventually write a novel – it was just a question of when and where.

In the other corner (figuratively speaking), there were what might be called, if one were being friendly 'the others', and if one were being unfriendly, the 'hangers on'.

Susan, I fear, belonged to this category. As did a beautiful young Italian chap who was friendly with Geoffrey, (and who I could have sworn I recognised, which made me very nervous). There was Carole of course, she of the body massages; two young girls with beads in their hair and a guitar they kept passing between them. They would start a song and then forget it and then the other would take up the guitar and claim that she knew how the song went and would only get so far before she had to stop, and, all the while, the young writers would be roaring the words and the chords at them, and you couldn't hear it anyway over the music of the party and I just didn't know what to say about it all or how to be part of it.

Also among the others was Susan's friend, Maureen.

With a jolt I saw that she was the girl who had been with Susan when we had met at the 23 Club and my palms sweated up. Maureen flashed me a smile, and it all came back: the lines on her face and her blonde hair piled up on her head and how soft her breasts had felt and how she had tasted of absinthe when I had kissed her outside in the moonlight while Susan was off powdering her nose.

Maureen gave me a wink, and I could do nothing but pour myself another measure of Scotch and hope that my face said how lovely it was to see her again and how of course I hadn't forgotten that silly one-off kiss the night we had embraced while the world had spun around me and my Sangrias had threatened to return.

'You remember my friend Maureen, don't you?' Susan said.

'Of course. How lovely to see you again.'

I went to kiss her on the cheek and she whispered something in my ear. I hadn't been prepared for what she said so I reddened, but no one seemed to notice, except for Maureen who pinned me down with a knowing eye.

'Susan tells me you collect art?' said Geoffrey, steering me (as if it were accidental) to stand in front of one of his most impressive pieces.

He balanced up onto his toes as he spoke. It was a nervous habit, and it had the misfortune of causing his head to fall forward so you could see the full extent of his comb-over. 'I have an interest myself, you know,' he said.

I didn't know what to say to this man, but I got the sudden feeling he knew even less than I would pretend to know. So we talked about art, and I dropped a few names I knew would impress him, and he dropped a few others he thought would impress me.

As this exchange was going on, Geoffrey's young man (the one I had recognised) sidled up to us, hooked his arm into Geoffrey's, and was now staring at me intently. It made me very nervous because I knew he was about to come out with something and I didn't know what it was.

'So tell me,' he started snappily with his head cocked off to one side and a cheeky smile on his lips. 'How is the book going?'

At last, too late, I recognised him. He was one of the waiters at Luigi's who had brought profiteroles and sung *For he's a jolly good fellow* while I'd tried to shush them and begged Salvatore in desperation to get them to stop.

I tried the tactic of not answering, but Geoffrey had not missed the question.

'Book? What book?'

'It's nothing. Just a little thing,' I protested.

'Nah!' wailed Geoffrey's friend. 'Senyor Rodriguez is genius. His book is to be published all over the world!'

Again I protested no such thing was true, but Geoffrey said,

'All over the world? My man! How startlingly wonderful. Susan! Susan, get over here. You didn't tell me Rodriguez was a famous writer.'

I tried to tell them that I wasn't a famous writer, and was not even published, but they insisted I was just being modest and, within a very short period of time, the whole crowd of them was gathered around me asking me questions like, 'When do you write? Is it early in the morning or during the day?' or 'Where do you get your inspiration from?' and other such nonsense.

Some of the questions I was forced to answer, and others I tried to swerve, but in the end I was made to fabricate a whole heap of new nonsense about my writing hours and the years I had slaved over my masterpiece and how wonderful it was now to finally get recognition for my talent.

By the end of it they were all swooning from being in love with me, and I thought I could probably have any one of them served to me naked on a plate. Susan could do nothing but stare at me in open-eyed worship, and when I tried a little move on her she jumped back in surprise, as if she had been touched by a giant.

There came a point when I felt it really was time to leave. There's only so much party a man can take, and for some reason I'd lost any interest in the pursuit of Susan. It had all become too much effort and I had to admit it was more dangerous than it was worth what with her endless need to talk about every little thing I told her regardless of whether it was an obviously preposterous lie or not.

So I went out into the garden to lie down on one of the loungers by the pool, with the intention of clearing my head for the drive home.

Have you ever listened to a party from the outside? Listen to it now, with all the chest beating and high-pitched squawking that goes on.

I can hear it there, in the house, but I've turned my back on it. How I like the pool here. It's so blue, so very blue. I thought of my pool in the shape of a shark which didn't exist. Perhaps I would get it lit from underneath like Isabella's and this one. It makes for a very pretty pool. Why would one have a pool in the shape of a shark in any event? Wouldn't a dolphin be better? But perhaps one could sit in a tooth and have a gin, and have Isabella sit in a neighbouring tooth with her own gin and then the two of us could talk about things.

'There you are!'

The voice made me jump. I looked up and a female head loomed over me. It was one of the squealers and hawkers of earlier.

'Susan?'

'It's Maureen, pet.'

Then the head twisted and her body came into view and Maureen sat down beside me so abruptly I was forced to play catch up and make room for her.

'What are you doing out here?'

'I was thinking about my pool. Should I change it to a dolphin?'

Her head loomed large again. 'You can change it into whatever you want, Rodriguez.'

She kissed me on the lips but I didn't respond because I was still thinking about the pool.

Then she was kissing me and touching me, but I was too drunk to care one way or the other, so I let her have free rein. I had a sneaking suspicion Susan would be cross with me if she saw, so I supposed I had better say something as I didn't want a scene. I really was bored of the party. I had just wanted to lie there until I felt well enough to drive home.

'Now, now...' I said, the moment an opportunity arose.

'Now?' she murmured.

'No, I mean, "Now, now..."'

'Now?'

It may be difficult to believe, but honestly it happened before I had a chance to object. I think perhaps rape is a strong word, but sometimes one must call a thing by its name. There was a menacing rustle of silk. I tried to think of the polite thing to say to make it stop, but my words were getting muddled in my head, and in any event it was difficult to get them out because Maureen's tongue kept getting in the way.

Suddenly, a vision of Isabella came to me. She was above me and was wearing a thin negligee which was pulled up to her waist. Her nipples could be seen in the moonlight through the sheer material, just as they bud out on the beach when there is a cold breeze.

'Isabella,' I whispered, and the form above me gasped and groaned.

There was a recognisable dampness and I stumbled out the beginnings of an apology.

Maureen's head lurched closer one final time. 'Don't you worry, pet. I love a quickie, me.' Then she muttered something about getting cleaned up and disappeared back to the house. Unfortunately, not without promising to be back.

I made everything secure down below. Then I thought with a groan that the car keys were in Susan's handbag which I knew for a fact was sitting on a table in the sitting room where most of the guests were gathered playing some ridiculous game involving a cereal box.

It was difficult to know what to do. Before I could formulate a plan, Maureen was back. I heard her creep up behind me and she put her hands over my eyes. It was more than I could take and I decided I had to tell her so.

'That really was very naughty of you,' I started.

'Whatever do you mean?' she replied, and I jumped with

a fright to see that it was Susan rather than Maureen who was behind me.

She came around and laid herself down on top of me.

'I know I've been unsure about us, Roddy,' she said. 'I just wanted to wait until we went to your villa, but I don't think I can wait any longer.'

Somewhere behind me, I heard Maureen coming noisily out of the house.

'Still there, pet? I've brought us a little something.'

I could hear the chinking of glasses against a bottle and then she was standing beside us looking down at Susan and me. She seemed to stand there for an eternity.

'Is everything all right, Maureen?' Susan asked.

I sat up sharply, causing Susan to tumble to the ground. Then, apologising profusely, I helped her to sit back on the lounger and got unsteadily to my feet.

'Would you both excuse me for moment? I just want to get my cigarettes.'

'But I've got some here, Roddy,' said Maureen. 'I thought you might like one.'

'Maureen,' Susan said, sharply. 'Rodriguez and I are busy out here'. Then she caught hold of my hand and tried to stop me leaving. 'Roddy, I've got some *Ducados* if you'd like one.'

'Oh. Thank you.'

I took a cigarette and both Susan and Maureen rushed to offer me a light. I looked at the two little flames glowing in the darkness.

It was not a choice I was in a fit state to make.

'I'm going to have to leave you ladies for a moment. I'll be back.'

It didn't take too long to get from there, into the sitting room, over to Susan's handbag, and out of the front door.

I had to tread softly over the gravel because the driveway was not too far from the pool and by the time I got to the car I was starting to hear those high-pitched voices that women make when they get overly excited about something.

It was then that a rage descended on me out of nowhere. Why must life always be so difficult? It was Isabella I wanted. Why couldn't I take my good bits, my kindness, humility, and sweetness, and add to them Rodriguez's courage when Isabella and I were lying side by side on the beach? Instead I have this ... this revolting nocturnal impersonation of Rodriguez.

'Why?' I shouted. 'Why can't we be us?' And I banged both my hands down on my bonnet so loudly that I fear I left imprints in the metal from the base of my palms.

I got in the car and reversed it noisily over the gravel. In my rear view mirror I saw Susan appear around the corner of the house. The car's engine idled for a second or two, but Susan didn't make an attempt to approach the car. She just stood there, and even through the confines of that little square of silvered glass, I could see her disappointment and dejection. It lurked in every angle of her body. I felt a terrible guilt. But how could I give her what she thought she was looking for? With the tyres scrunching as they slipped over the stones, I drove off. I knew I would never see her again and the thought deeply saddened me.

Of course I wasn't in any fit state to drive. I would just have to concentrate. It was the switchbacks I struggled with most, those and the trees, which seemed intent on trespassing onto the road. I must confess I hit a few of the blighters – one that bashed the front, one that took a swipe at the side, and I even managed to back into one when I accidentally hit reverse in a particularly tight s-bend.

From there it was a straight road down to the coast so I relaxed, thinking I'd be all right, but of course that wasn't how my evening was going. I lost my concentration, just for a moment, and wandered slightly over the line as a car was coming in the other direction.

The other driver was as drunk as me, that was my view, because there wasn't any need for him to take the radical action he did – there was plenty of room. And there was certainly no need to go careering off the road like that.

I've done some terrible things of late, but I'm not a bad chap at heart, so I slowed down and turned to see if the fellow was all right. I was confident he was because he was making an almighty to-do. His front bumper was gnarled against a rock, but that seemed to be the only damage and from the way he was shouting at me to come back and explain myself I could see that he was perfectly all right. He really was making quite a fuss.

So I left him to it and hurried along towards home and, the first opportunity I got, I pulled over in order to sit quietly for a time until I could attempt the rest of the journey. I considered it was the responsible thing to do.

The road had dropped down to the sea, where there was a line of untidy boulders bordering the shore. When I'd driven past before, I'd often seen the locals stop along here to barbecue and swim at the weekends.

I got out of the car and went to sit on a rock. In the night sky a plane came low and banked right to begin its descent into the city. Probably another Super-Constellation or a Caravelle from Manchester or Glasgow. Round and round they go these days – landing, spewing their guts out onto the tarmac, and then sweeping back to collect more.

After a while an urge came upon me to slip into the black waters. They looked cool and refreshing, and I thought a quick bathe might be just the thing to sober me up before the next stretch of more challenging road.

After stripping off my clothes and taking off my shoes, I gingerly approached the edge. The sea was very still and there were barely any waves lapping at the rock on which I stood.

It wasn't easy to see where to step in, or how deep it was, so my method of entry was tentative like a flipped-over crab, with my stomach raised up into the air, and my hands and feet beneath me feeling their way down amongst the roughened edges of the submerged rocks.

I remember it was painful, but I told myself to be a man and went for it anyway. It was a wonderful swim and as I came out I thought what a good idea it had been. I suddenly felt very optimistic about life. They hadn't caught me yet, even if they were hot on my heels, and with Isabella our love just needed a bit more time to find its path. If our falling in love could coincide with the book being published and me receiving a whole new stash of cash, that would be ideal. For then everything could be paid off and sorted out and my wife, I was sure, would be glad to be free of me in a proper manner which wouldn't upset the neighbours. Surely it could work out for me, just this once.

Chapter XVII

The next morning I discovered a terrible gash on the bottom of my foot. It took me several minutes to work out how it might have got there. As I ate my breakfast, I thought of my drunken swim from the rocks, and my foot began throbbing rather maliciously in time with a pounding in my head. I could do nothing but sit and think how wretched I felt and berate myself for being such a fool.

'Because you're drunk,' Isabella had said on that other occasion, and for the umpteenth time I wondered whether this should be considered an encouraging sign. It might imply that when I'm not drunk, she does want to kiss me. I limped into the house, got a stool on which to prop up my foot, and spent the next hour or so going over and over everything. She had liked me in the white suit. She had said so, and it had given me the courage to be a little bolder with her, and that had paid off. I thought of our fingertips touching in the moonlight. Then I thought again of how she had wriggled out of my arms when we had stood by her patio doors the previous time. If only I'd found the right words on that occasion. Rodriguez would have found them; I was certain of that.

None of it was easy to figure it out – particularly when consideration of the Isabella conundrum had to compete with my concern about the money situation, my fear that the writing wasn't coming along as it should, and the terrible pain in my foot. What was to become of me?

And to top it all, when I looked up in joy at the sound of someone down by the gate (thinking it was Isabella come to apologise for Marta's outrageous comment), I saw the retreating back of a postman. He had obviously just posted a letter into the mail box. Hell's bells. Why couldn't that blasted real estate man leave me in peace? I hadn't the time for his nonsense. I had a full day of writing ahead of me; then I had to go into the city and meet Salvatore for supper and I wasn't looking forward to it, that was for certain. He was going to go on and on about deadlines again. I would have to hold him at bay once more and reassure him the writing was going splendidly, even though I didn't have anything to show him.

I limped down and got the letter and then limped back up to the house. There I eyed the envelope nervously. On it were the words 'URGENT AND IMPORTANT' written in red capitals and underlined. Now this just wasn't going to do. I was a writer. An artist. I couldn't let my creative vibes be ruined by this sort of nonsense.

I limped into the house and put the letter on the bureau for later, placing it so that the red, underlined writing was facing the wall. Then I grabbed the brandy bottle (for medicinal purposes because my foot was in such a state) and headed into the study to work.

And I did work hard at it, but the evening came around much quicker than I'd hoped, with only a few pages under my belt. I missed an hour or two in the afternoon because I had to go and lie down when it became too hot. I only woke up when the sun was setting, which meant I was going to be horribly late for Salvatore. In a panic I rushed down the hill (there was no sign of the girls, fortunately), drove like a madman into the city, parked up as far in as I dared, and then limped, in agony, as fast as I could into the centre.

By now the sun had set and, fearful of *polizia*, I kept to the waterside of the embankment and then came creeping into the city via the lanes beside the cathedral. My foot really was very painful by then, and I was truly feeling sorry for myself.

The sound of asthmatic pigeons perched upon the curlicues made me look up at the doors of the cathedral as I passed. Such unnecessarily huge doors they were, as if God were some giant who might visit and need to be accommodated. By the time I reached Luigi's I could barely walk.

Salvatore came out of the kitchen as I arrived.

'Here he is at last! Here is my writer! The suckling pig's the thing to have tonight, Rodriguez,' he said, and he flicked his scarf over his shoulder.

The waiter fussed around both of us showing us first one table, and then deciding it wasn't good enough before we had even said anything, and then showed us to another. I looked nervously at him to see if it was the waiter from Geoffrey's party but fortunately it wasn't.

'Have you hurt your foot?' Salvatore asked, and I was forced to tell him a car had carelessly mounted the pavement and run over it as I was walking over. But then he made such a fuss and insisted the waiter bring some ice for me to strap to my toes that I wished I hadn't been so colourful with my tale.

As soon as we had sat down, and the bag of ice was balanced on my foot, Salvatore pressed me for the final chapters. I assured him they were nearly complete.

'Had you expected me to bring them?' I asked.

'Well, yes,' he spluttered. 'I did. I thought you said you were going to. They are nearly finished, aren't they?'

'Of course they are.'

I could tell he was getting increasingly nervous about the whole situation, but I could also see he was the type who hated anything resembling a scene. I knew he was sitting there telling himself to be trusting – after all, I had arrived out of the blue with the book and would surely do the same again with the ending. But the whole thing (with the lying) was making me nervous myself, so I suggested he order another bottle of wine. The first had gone down very quickly. I waited patiently, with an empty glass, for him to act upon the suggestion.

'And how is that girl of yours?' he asked, all of a sudden.

I hesitated. I couldn't remember telling Salvatore about Isabella.

'Which one?'

'Which one, eh? Ho, ho. Aren't you the rogue. The one in Madrid, of course!'

'Of course! I finished with her.'

'I'm sorry to hear that.' Salvatore put down his knife and looked at me in a respectful and serious way.

This was too much. That he should be upset for a woman who didn't exist. 'Don't be,' I said. 'It had to happen eventually. It turned out she was running around with half of Madrid. And then I discovered the child wasn't even mine.'

'I'm so sorry, my friend.'

'Yes, I'd grown attached to the child,' I said, and I tried to take another glass of wine, even though I knew the bottle was empty. Salvatore called the waiter over and told him to hurry up and fetch another.

'These things make better writers,' he said, trying to console me, and I agreed with him that it was indeed the case.

The waiter eventually arrived with the second bottle. It wasn't the boy who had been at Susan's party to my great relief. It was another lad who might have been his brother; they looked very alike. There was plenty of opportunity to make this observation because the young lad fretted to a ridiculous extent over the wine, insisting I try it, and then asking if it was to my taste, and then making another fuss over pouring it for me. In the end, I had to stare at him until he finally got the hint and left the table and even then he didn't go that far off, but hovered a couple of tables away. There's the rub in what Salvatore had been saying, I thought, that the angst will make me a better writer.

171

Damn it. I had left my wife. I was on the run from the law. There were just a few *pesetas* left in the pot, the wine in the cellar was low, and the woman I loved was playing hard to get. By rights I should have been Tolstoy.

Then I realised Salvatore was saying something that made my heart leap into my mouth. I instantly lost my appetite even though I had been on short rations for several weeks now.

'And I told the man,' Salvatore was saying, 'not to be so ridiculous. Because of course you're not dead, are you?'

'I beg your pardon,' I spluttered.

'I said, of course you're not dead, are you?'

'No. Very much alive, thank you.'

'See!'

There was part of me that didn't want to know, but it had to be out. 'Salvatore, who said I was dead?'

'The barber, of course.'

'Yes, of course, the barber. And why did he say that?'

Salvatore stuffed his mouth with suckling pig and I was forced to endure a minute of silence while he chewed and rolled his eyes at how delicious it was and pointed at his mouth to indicate he would continue once it was freer.

Finally he made progress enough to find room to get the words out. 'I was telling my barber how this new writer of mine was a philanthropist who supported the arts…'

'A philanthropist?'

'Now don't be modest, Rodriguez. I have heard all about you.'

I glanced nervously at the waiter, and saw that what I had taken to be over-attentiveness was actually some sort of obsessive reverence. The young lad was standing there with his buttocks resting on some poor sod's table, and his eyes were clamped to me as if I were the Queen of England herself. Then I looked and saw that all the staff, dotted around the room, had fixed me with a similar look.

'So they have told you, have they?' I said.

Salvatore held his arms wide. 'Don't worry, Rodriguez. Your secret is safe with me. I understand how it is. You want your talents to be recognised without your wealth getting in the way. Is that why you came here, to this little island, to sell the book?'

I pretended it was true. There was little other option open to me.

'But what of the barber?' I prompted.

'Yes. Where was I? I was telling the barber how my new writer was a philanthropist who supported the arts...'

'Yes?'

'And he asked me your name.'

'My name?'

'Yes. And I told him it was Rodriguez. And then do you know what he said?'

I forced myself to swallow a mouthful of pork, and shook my head.

'He said that you were dead!'

I made a noise to show how surprising I thought the suggestion was.

'Exactly! I told him you were well and truly alive and that I'd seen you only last week.'

'Good,' I managed to get out at last.

'And do you know what he said next?'

Again I shook my head.

'He said that it couldn't be true, because you had thrown yourself off the cliffs over in the west, and that the whole village had seen it.'

Well, how Salvatore and I laughed at the suggestion.

'Rodriguez is quite a common name,' I reminded him.

'Yes,' he replied. 'But two Rodriguez on one little island? And both of them philanthropists renowned for supporting young artists? It's a coincidence, isn't it?'

I agreed that it was, and he asked me if I wanted dessert, but my appetite had quite disappeared. It had been as much as I could do to force down the last of the suckling pig.

'Not for me, Salvatore,' I said. 'I have writing to do.'

I wanted to get out of that restaurant as quickly as I could. I stood up abruptly.

'Yes, of course,' Salvatore exclaimed and he also leapt to his feet and threw his napkin down onto his plate. 'Best to get back to the writing.'

As we parted I tapped him up for a bit of cash. Not as much as I'd hoped because he didn't have much on him, but enough to cover provisions for a few days. I suspected that if he hadn't heard I was exceedingly rich he wouldn't have given it to me, but of course everyone will lend to the rich; it's the poor buggers who starve to death, as I know to my cost.

As I limped back to the car I realised that my entire body was shaking and I was afraid that my legs were going to crumble beneath me. There was nothing for it. I would have to stop for a brandy to reinforce me and give me the strength to get back to the car. So I stepped into one of those local places out on the front.

I went straight over to the bar and ordered a brandy. They didn't have one, so I was forced to take glass of sweet wine instead. I can tell you, it wasn't a friendly place. The locals stared at me and muttered amongst themselves.

I tried to ignore them as I nursed my wine, and then I was forced to ignore them for a second time as I had another quick one for the road, and then for a third time as I contemplated what I would say to Isabella. I needed to be more forceful. I had to be a real man, like Rodriguez. And did you notice how she had said I looked handsome in the white suit? And how she had held my hand and moved closer to me in the moonlight out by the cliffs? She really couldn't have been clearer about her intentions. And with that thought I felt ready to continue home.

Chapter XVIII

There were just four bottles of wine left. Each time I took one, I looked with a terrified eye at the dwindling few that remained. They reminded me of friends who abandon you, one by one, in your time of greatest need. The stress, I was certain, was getting to me. I caught things out of the corner of my eye which I knew couldn't really be there, and sometimes I heard voices in the house. When I went into the room to see who it might be, I found there was nobody there. The letter from the agent was sitting like a demon on the bureau. For three days I had tried to ignore it.

The day before I had nearly cracked and opened it, but then I gave myself a stern talking to about creating a space in which I could express myself, away from the commerciality of life. I decided I would do it the next day. What could it matter after that? The final chapters had to be delivered to Salvatore the following evening, so that was to be my last day of writing. I had just two days left to finish the book.

I decided I would go into the orchards and attempt to write in the open air. Perhaps this would make me more productive. I took half a bottle of wine with me and fortified it with some of the last of the brandy from Rodriguez's bureau; I knew it was silly to mix my drinks like that, and that it would only make matters worse.

It was a foolish and stupid thing to do because it caused me to have another vision of Rodriguez – how I hated the way things were going. If only I could get the book finished and get the money in so that this terrible stress would be lifted off my shoulders; I know I'd get back to rights.

The vision of Rodriguez appeared before me between two blinks, and I have to say he looked as real as any man could be, considering he was dead. I felt if I were to reach out and touch him, he would be as solid as the tree against which he was snoozing.

His glasses had fallen askew and were about to drop onto his chest. I couldn't, for the life of me, figure out how to make him vanish, so I just had to accept his presence and muddle along as best I could. To be truthful, even though I knew he couldn't really be there, his presence was comforting. It was terribly hot, and earlier I'd been raving like a loon. The August sun had raised the mercury to levels unheard of in England, and the almond trees were giving scant relief, being so short and spindly.

How pleased I was to see him. I watched him for a moment as he slept, but he must have sensed my eyes were on him because he woke with a grunt and fixed his sleepy gaze upon me.

'How goes it, my friend?' he asked, and I was filled with love for him even though I knew he wasn't real.

I told him it wasn't going well and that I had tried four or five different endings and none of them were right. I said it all in a rush and he held his hand out and nodded gently at me, insinuating I should slow down and take a deep breath.

'They are tricky things, endings,' he said. 'Don't take it so hard when it doesn't come easily.'

He searched in his pocket for his glasses and then finally found them on his nose. Then he reached across and picked up one of the pieces of paper I had earlier thrown down in a temper and started to read.

'I so want Father Gomez to live,' I explained, 'but he's too old to look after the child. It would never work.'

Rodriguez peered at me over the top of his glasses. 'Is it a happy ending you want?'

'I'm thinking of killing him off. What do you think?'

There was a long pause while Rodriguez mulled it over. So long, in fact, that I thought he had forgotten the question and was thinking about something else, but then he answered.

'There has to be hope.'

I pondered on that for a while, and then I took up my pen and started writing.

Then a thought occurred to me. 'Why didn't *you* finish it, Senyor?'

Rodriguez sighed. 'My friend, I was afraid.'

I waited in the hope that he might continue and when he didn't I was forced to prompt him and ask him what he was afraid of.

He looked around us, up at the chopped up sun, and then back at me.

'I was afraid of what terrifies us all.'

'And what is that?' I was brave enough to ask.

'Well, the end, of course.'

I decided then I would drop it, because it didn't seem polite to talk with a dead man about endings, but Rodriguez changed the subject himself.

'How does it go with your lady friend?' he asked, and smiled at me in a friendly way.

I made a few vague but evasive comments that I hoped would satisfy his curiosity. I didn't want to have to admit to him how little progress I had made with Isabella. He, no doubt, would have been far bolder and would have made headway in one direction or another by now.

'I was in love once,' he said suddenly. 'With a Russian princess.'

'So I heard.'

'You heard?' He looked at me in surprise. Then he seemed to resign himself to the fact. 'How they gossip in the village,' he moaned. 'Take my advice, Thomas. Don't go down there. They'll winkle your secrets out of you, just for the joys of spreading them.'

I was bold enough then to ask him of his Russian princess.

'I met her at a ball,' he said. 'I couldn't take my eyes off her. They were drawn to her face whether I wanted it or not.'

'What did she look like?'

'Delicate features, like china, and she moved as a ballerina would.'

He was silent for a while, with a far off look; I didn't like to interrupt him with any more impertinent questions, but he came back to the topic unprompted.

'I was going to impress her with one of the books, but I couldn't seem to finish any of them. You will have to do it for me.'

I promised him I would give it my best attempt, but I had to confess that I, too, was struggling. 'I'm not a writer, like you,' I said. 'I can't even seem to piece a sentence together.'

Rodriguez looked again at the words on the page in his hand. 'Mmm. I see what you mean.'

A sheep came wandering by giving a lonely bleat. Its bell jangled in a way that soothed the panic mounting inside me.

'Will you help me, Rodriguez?'

'I'll try,' he said. 'But I do fade in and out these days. It makes it so hard to concentrate.'

So we tried together for the rest of that afternoon and managed to write a few good pages, but then I must have dozed off, for when I awoke he was gone and the sun was setting. I made my way unsteadily back to *Ca'n Mola* and took myself straight off to bed; it had been a hard day's writing and I was exhausted by it.

The next morning, buoyed up by my excellent day of writing and the visitation of Rodriguez, I decided to tackle the letter from the agent over breakfast. I found, once I opened it, that the situation had taken an interesting turn. I shook my head in disbelief. This is what the letter said:

Dear Mr Waddington

I have to say that I am disappointed to find that payment has still not been received and I am having to find myself in a difficult and complicated position of being forced to explain to the Rodriguez family why there is no rental income from the island estate for the summer.

I have to complain that you put me in an awkward position with this continued delay and that I have made excuses for you. It is my intention to come to the island and collect the rent in person from you as I am intending to show the house to a couple who are interested in a winter rental.

As I'm sure you may have heard, for it is much talked about, the settlement on my client has been delayed following rumours of the late Senyor Rodriguez not being dead but in fact being out and about and going to parties and frequenting the art galleries he used so much to enjoy.

This is throwing things into much confusion and delaying the production of the final Certificate of Presumption of Death and as such my client has been forced to continue to let out Ca'n Mola for a further six months rather than move to immediate sale, as had been his initial desire.

If the couple are finding the property to their liking, you and your wife will need to vacate with immediate effect. I hope you are understanding the reasons why the family would be wishing to have a different tenant and will be gracious and amicable with your vacating of the property.

For this purpose I shall be coming to visit the house with the interested party on the afternoon of the 28th. Please could I be asking you to ensure that the property is clean and tidy and is fit for viewing by the said aforementioned couple, and that you have the funds ready for handing to me when I arrive. I shall also be taking this opportunity to complete the inventory check, which is my duty to the

179

family, in my care of the estate, so I also ask of you that all the items of the house are in the places where they are supposed to be residing.

Yours with warm felicities,
Jose Antonio Gonzalez
Madrid

I scrambled around counting days on my fingers and, after double checking twice, it could only be admitted that today was the 28th.

My breakfast was immediately abandoned. I took a limping run into the house. The place had to be spick and span. As I mopped and cleaned and tidied I reflected on what the agent had said.

So, my careless involvement with Susan had accidentally thrown doubt over whether Rodriguez was truly dead. What a stroke of luck. They couldn't possibly sell *Ca'n Mola* while this was the case. If they were to track down Susan as the person who currently knew the whereabouts of Rodriguez, she'd have them chasing all over the east side of the island looking for a fancy villa with marble flooring and a shark-shaped pool.

They'd never think of coming to look for Rodriguez here at his very own house, for the property agent would gladly tell everyone it had been taken by a good-for-nothing Englishman, who was behind on his rent.

Yes, it was all too perfect. I just needed to somehow keep the merry dance going on for a month or two more until Salvatore gave me the money for the book and Isabella had fallen in love with me. As soon as that happened I would speak to Marta and let her know my intentions were honourable. I would get a speedy divorce from my wife (who I was sure would agree to it if there were funds to pay off the debts and the lawyers' fees and to pay the right people to brush certain things under the carpet), and then Isabella and

I could be married, assuming she wanted me.

It might be difficult to return to England and I wouldn't want Isabella mixed up in all that nastiness – but we could go to Paris, or over to America. She did keep saying she wanted to visit her cousin in New York.

When the house was clean and tidy, I thought with a panic of the cellar, and took my limping run out to the back of the house.

What could be done? Perhaps the remaining bottles could be placed on the front rack in the hope the agent was too lazy to venture in … No, it would never work, there were too few of them left. I would have to seal the door completely.

Once all the cleaning of the house and the locking up of the cellar door was complete, I felt I might collapse in exhaustion. I was desperate for a drink, but the last of the wine was now locked up, so I fetched the nearly empty brandy bottle and went and hid amongst the murderous pinks and greens of the myrtle bushes which had burst into bloom only the day before. And not a moment too soon. I heard voices and then I saw the agent coming up from the gates with a couple of people.

'It isn't on the mains,' the agent was saying, 'But it could be arranged with a little investment.' He was wearing the same cheap beige suit with stains under his armpits he had worn the day I had met him at the start of the summer, back in Madrid.

Of the viewing couple, the husband reminded me of a grasshopper in his green slacks and mustard shirt, all gangly arms and legs. He was sweating profusely and rubbing his handkerchief over his head in a near constant fashion. His wife, on the other hand, was pretty, and flounced about the place in her gingham sun dress. How, I wondered, did a man like that manage to secure a dream of peaches and cream like her?

'What do you think, darling? Will it do?'

'It's wonderful!' she exclaimed. 'I love it.'

The grasshopper smiled, looking pleased with himself. 'I knew you'd like it. It's got lots of potential, hasn't it?'

The man came over and peered down the well, but his wife continued turning circles in the garden and, when she came to a stop, she was looking in the direction of the *casita*. The agent came over to her.

'I would say you knock it down. It would have a good location for a terrace, no?'

He looked up at the windows of the house and around about him. He was obviously wondering where I was and why I had not come out to greet him.

'There is a water deposit at the back. It would be easy to make it into a pool.' He pointed over behind the house. Then he turned and searched about him for the husband (having another discreet look around for me) and, finding the man standing right beside him, he said, 'Shall we go inside?'

They all went through the front door, and I heard the agent calling out for me. I clamped my mouth shut, in case some silly instinct in me answered, and the man's voice receded. Every now and again they passed by the windows, working their way up through the house. When they reached Rodriguez's bedroom, peaches and cream stuck her head out of the window.

'Look at the view!' she exclaimed.

It was then that I saw Rodriguez had materialised again and was standing with me in the myrtle bushes. He looked distraught and was rubbing his stubble with his fat, rough fingers.

'Did you hear them say they would pull the *casita* down?' His voice cracked as he said it.

I put my fingers to my lips in an attempt to shush him, but he was undeterred and started moaning, softly at first but then getting louder by the minute.

'Be quite,' I hissed. 'They mustn't hear us.'

Rodriguez nodded, and he did pipe down, but then he looked as though he might cry and it broke my heart to see it.

So I whispered to him to stay where he was and I crept around the side of the house towards the back door. I was just in time to see the viewing party step out, with the woman coming last.

'Hasn't it been nicely looked after?' she said.

The agent nodded in agreement, but rather begrudgingly I thought.

'Here is what I want to show you. You are going to really like it.' The agent took them over to the cellar door and tried to open it. 'It has a natural cellar for all of your wines, built right into the cliff.'

I held my breath.

'I'm so sorry. Bit … how do you say? Bit sticky…'

The grasshopper was itching to take over. 'Let me try,' he said.

'No … it usually opens easily. It needs only for me to…'

'Don't you want me to try?'

Don't let that man at it, I thought in a panic.

'*Joder*. I cannot understand why the door does not open.'

Then, to my annoyance, the agent stood aside and let the man wrap his fingers around the knob. After a few failed attempts, the giant grasshopper took a wide stance with his great long legs, placed a hand on the frame and pulled with the other for all his might. The door burst open, ripping through the nails that I had tapped into the top and bottom of the frame.

They all went inside. A minute later the agent came out on his own. '*Mierda*,' he said, forcefully. There was fury on his face. He flung up his hands in anger. One of them caught against the broken nail sticking out of the doorframe.

'*Mierda*,' he said again and then stopped to examine the remains of the nail.

The grasshopper came out, followed by his wife.

'Everything all right?'

'Yes, yes. I caught my hand on the door.'

The wife looked at his hand and they all went back into the house so she could clean the cut.

Rodriguez had by now made his way around the side of the house to join me. He stood so close I could smell his sweat and the stale alcohol on his breath.

'What will we do, Thomas?' he said, mournfully.

'Don't worry, Rodriguez,' I said. 'Soon I'll be coming into money, and then everything will be all right.'

As soon as the agent and the couple were gone, I fetched one of our last few friends from the cellar and sat with Rodriguez in the kitchen. Even though I knew he was nothing but a ghost or a vision, the two us took a glass together.

I was careful not to drink too much for I was meeting Salvatore later, and I knew it wasn't going to be a pleasant meeting.

It took a while after that to make myself presentable for company. Things had been running out of hand a little of late on that front.

The cold water from the well over my head helped, and the job of cleaning the white suit, pounding the dirt out of it before hanging it out in the hot afternoon sun to dry, sobered me up. Whenever I went to pick up the car there was always the possibility Isabella and Marta might be there at the front of their villa, so that gave me the incentive I needed to stay out of the bottle for a few hours.

Finally I went upstairs and faced a job I had been putting off for a long time. The sight of what was in the suitcase nearly caused me to start weeping. So much for counting how much was left. There was just a single one hundred *peseta* note.

I picked it up and put it in my pocket. So that was it, the last of the funds from Europe. The blue silk linking was empty; it no longer had a job to fulfil, it was no longer a loving home, a nest for those cuckoo's eggs.

Instead all those *pesetas* were flowing around the island

from bar to bar and pocket to pocket and I doubted I would ever see them again. Perhaps, by a tragic twist of fate, one might pass through my hands one day and I wouldn't recognise it as one of my own, but for all intents and purposes they were gone.

I went down to the study and looked at the random collection of pages I had typed over the last few days. There were some passages amongst them which were good, but the rest couldn't be said to match Rodriguez's quality of prose. Nothing was good enough to bring. So, with a heavy heart and empty hands, I went to face Salvatore.

Chapter XIX

The girls were out on their patio and couldn't help but see me when I stopped to collect the car. I didn't want to be caught creeping past. Isabella was sunbathing on a lounger whilst Marta was sitting at the table beneath a canopy attached to the wall of the villa. As I stood at their little white gate, Isabella was the first to look up.

'Thomas!' she called out. How adorable she looked in her yellow bikini (my favourite), with her sun visor and pearls, and her hair up in a ponytail. She looked to me like summer tennis and meadows with wildflowers. I gave her a great helloing.

'Why are you standing over there? Come over join us.'

'I've got to go to the city,' I said, but to my delight Isabella insisted.

'Surely you've time for a quick drink? I've made Martinis.'

I said that I definitely had the time for a quick one, and I tried to saunter over the flagstones towards them.

'Heh! Are you all right?' Isabella exclaimed, jumping up.

'Yes, yes. Quite all right.'

Isabella pulled the nearest lounger over to be closer to her and I sat down upon it.

'But what happened to your foot?'

'Oh, nothing, really. I cut the bottom of it.'

'Poor you. How did you do it?'

'Oh, it was stupid. I caught it on a nail in the floorboards.'

Marta was most polite then and she got up and shook my hand and said how nice it was to see me again and how sorry she was that my foot was cut. Then she went off into the house to get me a Martini.

Isabella smiled at me and seemed to be looking me up and down with a strange expression on her face.

'You're wearing that suit again. It's very becoming on you. How different you look these days.'

I tugged up my sleeve and held out a tanned arm.

'Only because you taught me to sunbathe.'

Isabella giggled behind her hand. 'And picnic,' she ventured.

I tried to smile good naturedly and when she looked away I sucked in my stomach.

'Yes, you look very well, Mr Sebastian,' Marta said, returning with the drink. 'We can see the Venezuelan in you now.' I thought that was a nice thing to say, but then she had to ruin it.

'Don't let us make you late, Mr Sebastian.' Why wouldn't the blasted woman call me Thomas?'

'Don't worry about me, Marta.'

'And are you doing anything exciting in the city?' Isabella asked.

I took a swig of the Martini, after which half of it was gone. 'Just meeting that friend of mine who has the book.'

I looked at Isabella's pool, which was a dull rectangle, and thought with a smile of my shark-shaped pool.

'What's so funny?'

'Nothing, just a silly thought. So what have you girls been up to the last couple of days?'

The girls glanced at each other as if neither were sure what they were supposed to say and I wondered what the mystery was. Marta spoke first.

'We went on a field trip to the north, but Isabella was bored, so we came home early,' she said, dryly.

Now Isabella would usually have denied a comment like

this, sending the girls into a spat of bickering, but on this occasion she stayed silent and looked off towards the hills and up to *Ca'n Mola*. I looked at it too. How lovely it looked with the low sun bathing the hillside so that the house looked to be made of the sunlight itself. Everything was so clearly defined, one felt one could see every individual branch and each single leaf on the trees around the house.

'So what have you been doing instead?' I asked.

Again, it was Marta who answered. 'Sitting around and doing nothing, Mr Sebastian.'

'Oh, do call him Thomas,' Isabella said, brusquely, which surprised me. There was an awkward moment and then she turned to me.

'I'm so unspeakably bored. Won't you teach me to swim, Thomas?'

I looked at the pool. It was littered with lots of little white petals which had fallen from a palm by the gate. I looked up and saw there were many more up there, waiting to fall, as if Isabella had been given a lifetime supply of confetti. I knew she didn't mean it – about the swimming that was.

'I haven't got my togs.'

'You could go and get them.'

'If you want I will…'

But Isabella yawned. 'Don't bother. I didn't mean it. I just can't believe how hot it is and look, it's after six o'clock.'

The sun's evening rays seemed to burn into the patio and turn it into a giant barbeque. The white walls of the villa threw everything back at us so we had the heat twice. Even the sea was silenced this evening, as if it too was filled with exhaustion from the ferocious onslaught of Spanish sun. I thought about being in the pool amongst the confetti with Isabella floating into my arms, but then Marta called to Isabella from where she sat under the canopy. I was surprised to hear her speak, because I had forgotten she was there with us.

'Isabella, come out of the sun. Your nose is burning.'

With a sulky look Isabella did as she was told, and we both moved to join Marta at the table.

'One should be vigilant, isn't that right?' Marta said to me. 'Even at this time of day.' But neither Isabella nor I answered. Isabella laid her head down on her arms and looked into her glass.

'Say, Thomas. I spoke to my cousin this morning.'

'Ah. And what is the news from New York?'

'I'm not entirely sure. I could barely hear him.'

'I don't know why you don't write instead,' said Marta. 'It costs a fortune to ring and you can't hear what he says in any event.'

Isabella sat up in a disgruntled way. 'It doesn't. I reversed the charges.' Then she turned to me. 'He was trying to tell me about the festival.'

'Your festival? The one in America?'

'Yes.'

'Is it soon?' I tried to keep the anxiety from my voice.

Isabella ran a finger down her glass and then put the wet tip in her mouth. 'No, I missed it. It was ages ago, remember?'

I have to confess I had forgotten and only yesterday I'd been fretting about when it might be. So I felt a great relief to hear again that it was gone, because if she had gone to America she would never have come back.

Isabella groaned. 'I should have gone. It's a wonderful thing to see, Thomas. You must go one year. Everyone comes from all over and they're all there for one purpose, the same thing, and it's the music. But then it's not just the music, it's about more than that. It's about a feeling. I feel alive when I'm there, as if I'm part of everything and part of the world, like I have a place and a purpose and a point to being here – do you know what I mean?'

I didn't really, but I nodded and said that I did.

'And there's also a feeling that none of the bad stuff that's happening over there matters,' she went on. 'The missiles and the Bay of Pigs and what happened to Kennedy. None of it matters because we are all humanity and we can sort it out if only we listen, and listen to each other. Not just listen, but really hear. Then we'll come through and persevere and sanity will prevail. It has to prevail, doesn't it? Otherwise where will we be? And no one wants that.'

There was a moment when no one said anything, and I realised Isabella was close to tears, and I hadn't a clue what was going on. But I knew what she meant by that last part. After their Kennedy was shot, it had seemed as if it had all gone to pot and there was no hope for any of us. I was just surprised Isabella could feel that way, when she was so young.

I tried to think of something to say to make it all right, but before I could Isabella said again, 'I wish I had gone. I should have gone, you know.'

And then suddenly Marta got up and went into the kitchen, and I realised at last that the two of them must have had a row.

'I'm sorry,' I said. I wasn't sure what I was sorry about, and I felt an intense anger towards Marta.

'Thomas,' Isabella exclaimed, making a very obvious effort to look cheery, 'Why don't you stop by for a drink later, when you're done with your friend?'

But Marta hadn't been far away because she came straight back out of the house and said sharply, 'I thought we were going to invite the professors over?'

'So?' said Isabella, and I could see that whatever had happened between them during their argument had shifted some of the power over to Isabella.

She looked across at Marta. 'You don't mind if my friend, Thomas, drops in for a drink later, do you?'

'Of course not,' said Marta, and she smiled at me, but I could see it was a fake smile. It was only her mouth that smiled whilst her eyes stared at me coldly.

So I promised I would stop in later, professors or no professors, and then I was forced to leave because Isabella started to fret that I would be late for the supper with my 'friend'. Again she said the word in her usual half-joking and half-pointed way, but I ignored it because I didn't want to get into all that again.

As I got in the car and drove off, a notion came to me. It was imperative I made my move, and the sooner, the better. Isabella was bored; the girls weren't getting on. The pair of them could up sticks and leave the island at any time. Tonight was my chance and this was my plan: I'd hurry through my meeting with Salvatore and get back to the girls as quickly as I could. I would be so charming and elegant that Isabella would realise what a catch I'd become, now I was worldly wise after reading Rodriguez's books and handsome in my suit and with my tan.

She would want it, I was sure. Maybe not as a permanent arrangement, but she'd consider a little fling; an older man who was experienced and would be sensitive to her needs what with everything she had been through; perhaps she'd see it as something to set her up properly with the world, before she went off to the States. And then of course once we were together she may change her mind and find she didn't want to leave me.

I parked the car up by the harbour again and took my circuitous walk to Salvatore's office. Although I didn't really want to, I stopped into a few bars on the way, just to fortify myself, and by the time I got there I have to confess I was in a state of nervousness, for I knew the deadline was passed and I hadn't anything to give him and I didn't know how angry he was going to be.

As soon as I came into the office and saw the look in Salvatore's eyes I knew he had reached a point of fury, but I could also see he was so relieved to see me he couldn't carry through with his anger. 'Rogriguez! Tell me it's good news.'

'It's very good news, Salvatore.'

His eyes went to my empty hands. 'Don't you have the chapters?'

'Very nearly.'

'Well, look, Rodriguez. This won't do. I've been fending them off – I got a week's extension and then another. If it's not in Barcelona by tomorrow the whole thing's off.'

I sat down in the chair, but Salvatore remained standing. He didn't even notice his scarf had fallen down. It lay dejectedly on his chest.

'What is it? Is it writer's block?'

I couldn't think what to say, so I was forced to succumb to the truth. 'I just have so many endings I can't decide which to use.'

Salvatore looked panicked.

'They're all typed up,' I hurried on to say. 'It's just a question of picking one.'

'Well, what are they?' Salvatore said. His tone was a little brusque for my liking. There was so much frustration being held at bay in his angular frame that the heat of it radiated from him. I had the feeling that at any moment he might launch himself across the room, and put his bony hands around my neck and throttle me.

I wondered if I should say that I couldn't share my ideas at this delicate time, but I knew for a fact it would make him madder and might even cause him to explode.

I felt queasy and realised the backs of my knees were sweating. It was then that I noticed a small kitten in the corner of the room. How pathetic and adorable it looked.

What an earth was Salvatore doing with a kitten in his room? Did he even know it was there? Its mewing was so pitiful. Was it Salvatore who had put that sweet little pink bow around its neck? Why does he ignore it? Perhaps it's not there.

'Rodriguez. Are you listening to me? You do have a terrible habit of letting your mind wander off. My career is on the line here, you know.'

I wanted to suggest that the island was already the terminus of his career, but instead I explained how I had been embroiled thinking about how to best finish with Father Gomez.

'It goes over and over in my head,' I said. 'Until sometimes I start to think like Father Gomez.'

'Well, Father Gomez, how do you end it?'

'I probably don't. Why would I?'

'Then have that as the ending. Just say "and so Father Gomez carried on with his life. The End".'

'I think you have it there, Salvatore. That's exactly what I'll do.'

'Good. Now go home and type it up and bring it back to me tomorrow.'

'Yes, Salvatore. That's what I'm going to do.'

Salvatore looked down at me with fierce eyes. 'The very latest is the day after tomorrow. If it comes to that I shall have to take the four o'clock ferry to Barcelona and deliver the manuscript myself.'

'I shall be back long before that.'

'Be sure that you are. Or never darken my door again.'

I glanced into the corner, but the kitten had disappeared. I imagined it had run under the desk, and I had a quick look, but I couldn't find it there either.

'What's the matter? What are you doing?'

There was no point mentioning the kitten at that point, as Salvatore looked fiercer than ever. So I ignored his question and left the room as quickly as I could.

Now the important thing was to hurry home and type what we had agreed. Just any old words, so that we had a finished manuscript. Since I had barely a peseta to my name there was little other choice in any event.

I had even less by the time I had stopped into a couple of bars on the way back to the car. I needed to think, you see. I needed to figure out how I was going to get those last chapters written. If only I could visualise them in my head.

Afterwards even I could see that my driving was erratic and dangerous. But there wasn't any time to waste. Salvatore had been right on that score. I was hooted at on several occasions and one gentleman even stopped his car in order to poke his head out of the window and shout at me as I sped away. I could tell I was hitting the kerb a lot, but to be fair I was in a real hurry and I was so worried about what would happen if I didn't get those words typed up and get back to Salvatore with the last chapters.

I had nothing; little in the larder, nothing in the suitcase, and now nothing in my wallet. If I didn't get those chapters to him I would have to go back to my wife and face the music. The thought of it sat like a troll in a room, all warty and impossible to ignore.

I imagined my wife's surprise when she heard my key in the lock. She probably wouldn't recognise the sound at first, but then I expect old Henry would start barking in a way she'd recognise, and she'd know I'd come back. She'd probably wonder, as she went over to the door, whether I was returning with my tail between my legs or whether I was returning a hero. She'd probably know the minute she saw my head hanging low, not even able to meet her eyes. I expect she would tut and tell me to wipe my feet, and then go into a different room as I took my suitcase upstairs to empty it. She wouldn't follow me up the stairs asking me where I'd been and what I'd been doing, she'd just take on a steely silence which would tell me she couldn't care two hoots about me anymore, and that I could stay in the house for all she cared, because we married for better for worse, but that she too had a new life now, and I wouldn't be able to stop her in that.

But that wasn't going to happen, I told myself. Firstly, because I was going to work through the night and finish the novel and secondly, because Isabella was going to tell me she was in love with me any day now, and she wouldn't want me to go back to my wife.

At the thought of Isabella and Marta my stomach lurched. What if they'd been having a row again this evening? What if they'd agreed to call an end to their island holiday and were at that very moment packing their bags?

I suddenly realised how essential it was that I should go to Isabella without a moment's delay and tell her how I felt. 'It's time for the dance to end, Isabella,' I said to the wind. 'You were meant for me and I am meant for you.'

I parked outside their villa and tripped over the kerb as I tried to get out of the car. Blasted kerb. Always in the way.

The house was lit up and the sound of voices, quite a few of them, came from the upper terrace.

Isabella was having a party. How splendid. And I was wearing my suit. I would sweep in and impress everyone just as I did at that place over in the hills.

Chapter XX

'Both sides have discovered that if you are going to land on the moon, the most important thing is to know where it is.'

'Fascinating,' said the Dutch professor who, in the darkness of Isabella's sitting room, could only be distinguished from the rest because his knitted woollen tie was a different colour. 'And the Russians know where it is better than the Americans?'

I paused before answering, and it caused the professors to hold their breath and move a fraction closer. 'Indeed, but…' I indicated they should come closer still. 'Don't repeat it to anyone, but I understand the Russian programme is stuck on cryogenic ullage.'

'Cryogenic ullage?'

'Yes. They can't understand how to keep the cryogenic tank insulated. So they've been forced to set up a honey trap.'

'A honey trap? Is that a reverse thruster?'

'Of course not, you idiot,' interrupted the professor who wore a cardigan beneath his jacket and who held a pipe in his hand, which I never once saw him smoke.

I smiled at them indulgently, and then I continued. 'Let's just say this. There's a Bulgarian go-go dancer in Houston who knows an awful lot more about free surface micro-gravity propulsion than one would expect based upon appearance.'

'I still don't understand,' said the knitted tie. 'Is she an intern?'

'No. She's the honey trap, you idiot!' his colleague snapped at him.

I surveyed the professors gathered round me. We were crowded into a corner of the room, where they had gravitated towards me over the last hour or so. They were a pleasant enough bunch once you got to know them. A trifle slow on the uptake what with their enormous brains.

It was then I saw Isabella watching me from across the room. She was trapped between Marta and an old woman who appeared to be impersonating a Red Indian. As the woman swayed up and down, ululating and waving her arms above her head, Marta watched her transfixed, but Isabella was watching me.

My chest swelled with pride and I gave her a little smile.

'But tell me, Rodriguez. How do you know all this?'

'I beg your pardon?'

'How do you know about the honey trap?'

I leant towards them and placed a finger discreetly on my nose. 'I don't like to take sides, but I spent a bit of time in Kamchatka. I really can't talk about it.'

The knitted-tied professor looked even more confused. 'Whatever does he mean?' he asked his colleagues, but he was quickly hushed as a man approached who had previously been introduced as a visiting professor from MIT.

Then it occurred to me that one of the professors had called me Rodriguez and I stopped with a slight panic when I realised this must have been how I'd introduced myself.

When I'd first arrived at the party – it was actually more of a gathering – it looked to be at the chaotic stage a party can often reach before it comes to a close. No one was really making sense and those who had drawn the driving straws were fed up of pacing themselves and even more fed up of having to repeat themselves to those who hadn't. I felt as if I fitted right in, from the moment I arrived.

Isabella had cooked a spaghetti vongole (the abandoned plates could still be seen through the glass doors out on the terrace), and the professors claimed it to be the most exceptional thing they had ever tasted. Marta had bought the clams that morning from the fishermen down in the village, which apparently had an enormous amount to do with why it was so tasty. Then they'd all had a series of pancakes that the visiting professor from Cambridge (Massachusetts) had cooked up.

Isabella had introduced me to everyone by declaring: 'Darlings, look! My neighbour is here! He's come to complain about the noise.'

And they all laughed and cranked the music up louder and started doing some crazy dance one of them had been taught by a student. I watched from the side at first, but then Isabella laughed like a drain when I launched myself right into the centre of them. She clapped her hands, delighted, when she saw that I could already do the dance and how expert I was at it. The poor professors – they thought they were on to something new, but the dance was at least a year old and I knew (and I'm pretty sure Isabella must have also known) that the kids had already moved on to something else. But who cared; I mashed those potatoes with gusto and was declared a marvellous dancer by all.

After that, the professors treated me as one of their own. They crowded round me with questions, but I couldn't for the life of me think when I had introduced myself as 'Rodriguez'. To give me the time to think, I mentioned what a wonderful cook Isabella was, and for a full minute they all took turns to agree.

Then the tallest one asked, 'Do *you* ever venture down to the village for fish?' and I made up some nonsense about how I had been down there a couple of times and that once a fisherman had insisted I come out with him on his boat.

'I was as sick as a dog,' I said, 'and the boat was forced to turn around and come home early – they'd never seen anyone taken so badly with sea-sickness.' I told the professor I'd had to dip into my own pockets to make the fishermen good for their empty nets.

Marta came across the room at this point, so I was forced to abruptly change the subject because she would have known it wasn't true, and instead I asked the professors exactly what they were professors of. One was a professor of marine biology, two were zoologists like Marta, and the fourth was a professor of psychology. He was a very thick-set man, dressed entirely in black. I thought he might break out into mime at any moment.

'What do you think of Schrodinger's latest?' I asked, 'That the world is merely a construct of our sensations?' I made lots of hand movements as I spoke, just in case, but he was perfectly capable of both hearing and speaking.

'I'm a rationalist in these matters,' the man said, and I watched in disappointment as his arms stayed resolutely by his sides.

Then they asked me about *Ca'n Mola* because, when they were having their dinner earlier that evening, they had looked up at the *finca*, and it seemed that Marta had filled them in on all the ridiculous things I had told her about the place.

'Did they really flog all of the workers when the goats caught Syrian Flu?'

I said it was true.

'What exactly is Syrian Flu?' the psychologist asked, and to my delight both the zoologists claimed to be completely familiar with the disease and started comparing notes of their own.

'It can spread very quickly through droppings,' said one.

'Yes, there was a terrible disaster in the eighteen fifties when perhaps a fifth of the Asian goat population was wiped out.'

Everyone agreed how terrible that must have been, and I agreed the loudest.

It was then that the visiting professor from Massachusetts came up to me.

'Are you Rodriguez?' he hissed, and he tried to annex me with a tug of my arm into the corner as Marta looked at me, confused.

'Of the *house* of Rodriguez,' I said quickly and as loudly as I could, then I allowed myself to be dragged across the room and over to the drinks trolley, which of course suited me fine.

'Tell me, Rodriguez, is it true?'

I could see that the man had taken far too much drink on board. He was swaying in an unnerving way, such that I was afraid he might knock the drinks trolley over. I put a hand on it to keep it steady, just in case. 'It's true,' I said, trying to think back to what he might be referring to.

'And when will it start?'

'Not for ages,' I replied. 'You've plenty of time.'

'Months? Do I have months?'

'Most definitely, perhaps even a year,' I reassured him, and he looked horribly relieved and I was pleased to be able to give him some comfort even though he was obviously quite mad.

At that point one of the zoology professors came and put an arm around his shoulder. 'Come on, then,' the man said. 'It's probably about time we took you home.' Then another came over and the two of them marched the visiting professor over to Marta to thank her for the supper and then over to Isabella.

I watched jealously as Isabella kissed them each on the cheek and then I was forced to endure the whole pack of them deciding it was time to go and lining up to kiss her.

I had the impression the marine biologist was lingering at the end of the line, so I went over to Isabella, slipped my arm around her waist, and grabbed the man's hand and shook it.

'Finally,' said Isabella as soon as they were gone, and she flopped herself down on the sofa next to me and put her feet on my lap just as an enormous hiccup came out of my mouth. Both Isabella and I giggled, but Marta looked stony faced.

'Are you a bit tight again, Thomas?' Isabella asked, and, now that the bustle of the party was gone, I realised that she too was a little tight.

'Isn't it wonderful when a party is over?' she said, waving her arms about her in a dramatic fashion. 'You spend all evening fretting over what to cook and where to sit everyone, and then you panic there's too much food and no one will turn up, and then they all do, except someone's bound to bring along a friend, and then you start to panic that there's not enough, but somehow it all works out in the end, doesn't it?'

Marta went over to the trolley and poured two drinks and brought one over to Isabella. I tried to ignore her rudeness in excluding me, but since I had a full drink in my hand it was easy. I had to concentrate hard on not spilling it, because I had filled it a little too close to the brim. I didn't want to drink any because my wrist was beneath Isabella's ankle. I didn't want to do anything that might cause her to change her mind and rest her feet elsewhere.

'Did someone call you Rodriguez?' Isabella asked me suddenly.

'No, I don't think so.'

'I could have sworn they did,' she said, shaking her head.

'Not that I heard.'

'They certainly did call you Rodriguez,' said Marta. Isabella giggled, and Marta continued, 'Professor Johnstone was convinced it was your name. I tried to tell him it wasn't, but he kept tapping his nose and telling me "of course, of course". He'd drunk far too much.'

'Well, I can't be held accountable for your clever professors after they've had too much wine,' I protested.

'Perhaps,' Marta said, 'But you might want to be careful with that sort of confusion. There are some very odd rumours floating around in the village about Rodriguez these days.'

To cover my confusion I worked with Isabella to extract my drinks hand from under her leg.

'Oh?' I said, trying to sound disinterested. 'How strange.'

'Yes,' continued Marta, 'There are reports of him going about the city at night.' She was trying to draw us into conversation, but I certainly wasn't going to pick up on that topic, and Isabella was plain ignoring her. It could not have been more apparent that the two of us wanted Marta to make herself scarce.

Marta sat in silence after that with a look of thunder on her face, and glared at us. I knew exactly what her problem was. She wanted Isabella for herself, but that was never going to happen. This was my moment and I wasn't going to let her ruin it.

'Are you all right, Marta?' I said. 'You look a bit tired.'

The woman ignored me and turned to Isabella. 'It's been a very late party, Isabella. I think it's time Mr Sebastian left, don't you?'

At this, Isabella swirled the ice in her drink and laughed, and then she looked up at me with those eyes. 'I don't feel in the slightest bit tired, do you Thomas?'

I assured her that I didn't, and still the wretched woman wouldn't leave.

After a very long silence, which seemed to stretch into eons, Marta said, 'Mr Sebastian, did you tell Professor Boerman that you had once lived in Kamchatka?'

'I don't remember. If you say that I did, then I'm sure I did.'

'And have you ever lived in Kamchatka?'

'Of course. Why would I say it, if it wasn't true?'

'Tell me about the place, Mr Sebastian.'

I frowned at the woman. 'I shall do no such thing. If you'd like to know what Kamchatka is about, you shall have to go there yourself.'

Marta looked triumphantly at Isabella and it made me furious to see it. I knew what her game was, trying to keep

Isabella and I apart, and I knew why – it was for her own selfish reasons, and I suddenly took it into my head that it stood to Isabella's friends to tell the truth and put an end to it.

'There is nothing wrong with travelling the world, Marta. It expands one's understanding of life. It's a damn shame Isabella didn't make it over to her festival in America.'

'And what do you mean by that?'

'I think you know perfectly well what I mean. Isabella should have been encouraged to go.'

'I don't see that has anything to do with you, Mr Sebastian.'

'It has everything to do with me.'

I started to feel the blood rush into my ears. 'It's selfish of someone to keep a person somewhere specific against their will, just to keep themselves company.'

At this Isabella tried to interrupt with some distracting words, but neither Marta nor I had any interest for them.

'And to whom are you referring with that statement?' Marta bristled.

'You know perfectly well,' I said, defiantly.

'So you think it's selfish of me, is that what you're saying?'

At this point I knew I was heading down a path I hadn't intended to take, but sometimes in the heat of the moment a thing appears right, even though a little voice is screaming at you to back-pedal.

'I'm just saying Isabella would do better to take advice from people who have her interests at heart rather than their own.'

At this Marta went bright red. I saw the flush of it sprout up her neck. 'Better to take advice from me than an old drunk,' she said.

How dare she, I thought. How dare she? 'A drunk?' I spat out. 'Better to get advice from someone with a little life inside them, rather than a dried up old maid. Really. You should keep a host of cats by your side, not Isabella.'

Once more Isabella tried to interrupt, but Marta spoke

louder than ever until Isabella's husky voice was lost beneath it.

'It was Isabella's choice to come to the island. After her suicide attempt, she was the first to admit she wasn't ready for New York.'

I couldn't believe that Marta would refer to such a thing so openly, and it threw me into confusion.

'Ha!' Marta continued in triumph, taking her chance where she could. Her face was ugly with anger. 'I don't suppose she told you that, did she, Mr Sebastian?'

'Of course she'd want to hide away,' I stormed. 'After what happened, it's only to be expected. But she can't hide forever. A true friend would encourage her to get back into the world, unless...'

And here a terrible (and terribly mistaken) thought occurred to me. 'Are you blackmailing her?'

I turned to Isabella. 'Is she blackmailing you about the baby in order to keep you here, is that what it is?'

It was only when I saw Isabella's face that I realised how badly off track I was.

Isabella leapt to her feet. My glass was knocked to the floor and the drink spilled onto the tiles.

'*Basta, basta*! Enough! Be quiet, the pair of you. As if either of you want what's best for me. You are both as bad as each other.'

Then she turned to Marta and I listened in satisfaction as she said, 'You know perfectly well at least part of what he says is true. Now go to bed and I'll show Thomas out.'

And suddenly Marta was the weaker of the two. Looking deflated as if she had thought she had won but now realised she had lost, the woman left the room without once looking back.

I was such an idiot. It was going through my head that Isabella would be pleased with how I'd defended her, and, as I followed her down the stairs and through the dark house to the patio, I was thinking she would turn at any moment to kiss me.

The notion was chased out of my head when we got outside and she put a hand on her hip, just like my wife used to when she was angry with me. So I started to grovel and apologise instead.

'Stop all that,' Isabella said sharply. 'Marta is right. You have drunk too much. And you were telling a lot of silly nonsense to everyone.'

I told her I was sorry and that it had just been for fun, and then, for some particularly stupid reason, I told her I was in love with her; such a stupid thing to say when she was so mad at me.

Isabella heaved a great sigh and I watched her anger soften to pity and sadness. It was a horrible thing to watch. Pity and sadness was not how I had envisaged she would react to me when I finally confessed my feelings. I had been over this in my head a dozen times, and not once had I envisaged it panning out this way. I felt such a fool.

'Thomas, darling, are you sure?' she said to me. 'It's just that...' I waited, hanging on her every word. 'It's just that I think your being in love with me is something you're trying on. Like your act with the professors. Like all those clever books you read to try to better yourself. Like this white suit you've taken to wearing of late.'

I shook my head. 'No, it's true, Isabella. I'm certain this is real. Don't you feel it too?'

She didn't answer and I could see from her face that the answer was 'no'.

'Not ever? Didn't you ever want me? Even a little?'

A breeze took up from the sea and caused the palm tree beside the pool to rustle. A new batch of white petals came tumbling down onto the water.

'Perhaps a little at first,' she said. 'But then you didn't do anything, and the feeling faded. You see it's so hard to feel anything now, but when I'm with you I feel ... well, I feel lighter about everything. You're wonderful to be with, but not in that way. I'm sorry, Thomas. I do care for you, but I'm just dead to all that at the moment.' She bent down and put her finger on one of the petals and pulled it through the water, so as not to look at me as she was speaking. 'I don't know. I just feel as though I'm at a dead end, so there wouldn't be any point to it anyway.'

'What do you mean?' I said.

'I mean ... I've taken all these turnings, and all of them seemed sensible and the right thing to do, but they've just led me to a dead end. I can't go back and I can't go forwards, and it isn't anyone's fault – not my parents' or Marta's – they were all trying to do what they thought was best. It's just how it is, you see.'

I gently put my hand on her head. 'It's not a dead end, Isabella. It's a safe little prison. And it won't help you to get better. If anything it's the worst of all. Here, you keep going over and over it, and dwelling on what happened. You've got to move on. I know there's some little person growing up somewhere who isn't part of your world, but he's there all the same, and who knows what the future might hold? You've got to do whatever it takes to make you happy again, so that you can get well. I think that's got to be going over to America to see your cousin. Go over there and go out every night and picnic every day in the park, and go to your music festivals and parades and marches and my guess is you'll fall head over heels in love with some great chap who'll fall head over heels in love with you. And I can promise you, that's the best thing in the world – to love someone and to have them love you back. Go to America, Isabella, and fall in love with someone.'

She looked up at me, 'Do you really think I should?'

'Of course you should. You need to be with young people again and start over.'

'But I'm scared,' replied Isabella, and stood up and took my hand and kissed it. 'But what about you? I don't know how to help you,' she said.

'What do you mean?' I stuttered. 'I don't need any help.'

'Yes, you do. You think I don't know that you sit there, in that house of yours, moping and drinking?'

I felt ashamed when she said that, but she wasn't done.

'Do you think I haven't seen you go off into the city when you're in no fit state to drive there, let alone back? I'm scared for you, Thomas. And that car of yours! Do you know the police came a few days ago? They said it was stolen.'

We both glanced at the car and those scratches and scrapes stood out in accusation in the villa's lamplight.

'The police were looking for you because they said you were behind on your rent. And when they couldn't find you they got interested in the car. They came onto the terrace to ask about it.'

'What did you say to them?'

'I said I knew nothing about it.'

'And what did they say to that?'

'They're going to come back with a truck, tomorrow, to take it to the station.'

I really didn't want to hear any more, but Isabella continued on regardless. 'The police say it was reported stolen from the Rodriguez family estate in Barcelona, along with a whole heap of cash. They can't understand how it could have ended up here.'

I started to protest it was all a mistake, but Isabella didn't want me to. Instead she kissed my hand again.

'Thomas, darling. Don't you think it's time you went home to your wife? She must miss you terribly, and I have a feeling you need her help.'

Then, as if she was suddenly exhausted by it all, she turned to go back into the house.

'But I can't go back,' I said in a small voice. 'I haven't finished my adventure yet.' But Isabella shook her head and told me it was time to go home.

Chapter XXI

When I got back to the villa after the party I couldn't face entering the house. I felt as if I didn't deserve to and in any event the night was so hot there really wasn't any need. So I lay down on the ground and curled into a ball and started to cry, and somewhere amongst the night I must have slipped into a miserable unconsciousness. All I could think of was that Isabella didn't want me and I knew that she never would.

I woke with the sun in my eyes at dawn. I was still prostrate on the chalky ground and at first I wasn't sure where I was. There was water on my cheeks and on my collar, and I saw there were some stone bricks rising up beside me. It took me a minute to realise I was in the courtyard of *Ca'n Mola* and that it was the well beside me. My forehead was pressed against it and my feet were tangled in a jasmine bush. I don't know how long I had lain there, sleeping and sobbing, but I felt drained – as if my life force had been squeezed out of me; that it had sunk into the earth and was feeding the waters down in the well.

I decided that since everything had come to an end, I just would lie there until nature took its course. There was dirt on my hands and on the side of my face, and also on the white suit, which distressed me, but there was little I could do. I hadn't the will to get up and get on with the cleaning of it and with all the living and being and carrying on that would entail. I felt as if the process of death and decomposition had started already and the earth was taking me into its bosom.

My wife's face seemed a solid thing in my memory that day. Her brown hair was swept tidily back as ever behind her hairband and for once I could see a kindness in her face I had long since forgotten could exist. She was saying something, but it was too distant to hear. Her lips were moving – not in an angry way as they did at the end, but how they did before we were married. She thought I was the cleverest, funniest man alive, so it must have been at our wedding day – it couldn't have been after. I have her now, she is in her white dress, and the words she is mouthing are 'take thee, Thomas Sebastian'; her father is bursting out of his morning suit behind her, not with pride, but with too many golf club suppers. Then, later, in her going-away suit of pastel pink, with white gloves like an air hostess, there was a flash of disappointment when she saw the car I had rented to take us down to Cornwall. It cut me to the quick. It said I had failed in this one simple task, and I could see in my wife's eyes the fear she had made a mistake. That look came back over and over the following years, until it became the only face I knew, and the one of tender love was long forgotten. How lovely it was to be able to see it again now. As I lay in the dust, I clung to the memory of my wife's face as she married me.

Then I thought of the dust on my trousers and of all the microscopic spores within. The beginnings of ferns and myrtle bushes and mushrooms. How long until they germinated? How long until they set forth shoots?

How confused they would be to find the soft white linen beneath them rather than the chalky earth. But nature will out, I thought with satisfaction. I needed only to lie here and let the process of living and dying occur as it has so many times in the past and will do so many times again in the future when we are all long gone and not here to see it.

The microscopic root ends of those tiny spores would

delve between the warp and weft. They'd find skin and think at first that they were thwarted. But in time the skin would swell and crack, offering up black, inviting chasms between banks of festering flesh. And the little seedlings would dig down and find worms and maggots and know they were home. They'd bury further, down to the earth itself and the process would be complete. Nature and I would become one.

I thought then of a doctor I had once known. He was a kindly man, with intelligent eyes, and a considered approach. I can't remember where his clinic was. The memory escapes me. He asked so many questions and in the end he said there was nothing he could do for me, and he would be lying if he said that he could.

My stomach rumbled. It was taking an infernally long time to die like this. A little bird I had never seen before flew overhead. I thought of Rodriguez's nature books and knew immediately which one I should look in to identify the bird.

My stomach growled for a second time and I realised how thirsty I was. I could perhaps take some water from the well and then lie back down again, perhaps over in the shade rather than here in the open sun, which was starting to make my head hurt. From where I lay I could see the bougainvillea draped up and along the side of the house. I realised its riot of purple flowers was gone. Every one of them, the entire wall of colour, had turned as if to paper.

How infernally irritating life can be. How horribly difficult to dispose of. And how useless I am; I can't seem to even do the simple task of lying still until I am dead.

Try harder, I told myself. Apply yourself, Thomas. So, to pass the time, I made up a little poem and called it out to the sparrows, competing against the attention-seeking buzz of the cicadas.

This weary life is done,
yet still this turgid grey
completes its pointless up and down

and round and through my veins.
Would that I could take back time
and never see The One
who made my blood
choke up with ash…

But it was no good. I was a terrible poet and even I couldn't bear my verse. Also a desperate desire to drink the water from the well had taken over me. What a thirst crying can give one. Reconciled to the fact I must live for at least another morning, I got up and dusted myself down.

I pulled some water up from the well and drank greedily from the bucket. Then I washed the dirt from my face and hands and tried to wipe some of the dust off my suit, but I shouldn't have done it, because all that happened was the dirt became muddy stains against the white instead. Resigning myself to it all, I went over to *Ca'n Mola* and the house welcomed me in, like a long-lost friend.

The rest of that day I spent hoping Isabella might visit, and I washed the suit and put myself into an orderly state just in case. Then I took down the book of sea birds and went and sat at the table in front of *Ca'n Mola*, looking up at the sound of every twig breaking and every little patter that the chickens made. Finally, she did come.

She came slowly up the path from the cliff and didn't speak until she was right beside me.

'Are we still friends?' she asked.

I closed my book and put it on the table. 'Of course we are. We shall always be friends.'

We talked then for a while of silly unimportant things, until finally Isabella told me she was going to go to New York.

'When will you go?'

'I think the day after tomorrow.'

It was so soon. I hadn't meant for her to go so soon.

'I know it's sudden, but I've been thinking about what you said, and you're completely right. Now I can't see the point in hanging around any longer, other than I'll miss you, of course.'

'What about Marta?'

'Oh, she'll be all right. She's got her professors. She's very sorry, you know.'

'About you leaving?'

'No. She knew that would happen eventually. She's just very sorry she was rude to you.'

I felt ashamed at that, for there was as much fault on my side, and I remembered her walking without a word off to her bedroom and how upset she must have been. 'I feel terrible about it as well. Will you please tell her I'm sorry too?'

'Certainly.'

'And what will Marta do?' I asked.

'Nothing, what can she do? I'm above the age of consent. She might write to my parents and tell them she doesn't agree, but I can go where I choose.'

That hadn't been what I meant, but I let the misunderstanding stand.

'I rang my parents up, you see, and told them I was bored but fully recovered.'

'That's good, Isabella.'

She reached out and put her hand on mine. 'I told them I'd made some wonderful friends here who had really cheered me up and helped me get better.'

We smiled at each other. So that was that.

'Do we have time to go to the beach again?'

Isabella looked upset. 'I'm sorry, Thomas…'

'What is it?'

'They towed away your car this morning. I tried to stop them.'

I was careful to keep a neutral face. 'What a pain. I suppose

I shall have to go into the city and straighten it out.'

'How will you get there? Marta could take you on the scooter if you like?'

'I'll figure it out, don't worry. I'll do it in a day or two.'

'Anyway, I shall be running around packing and organising flights tomorrow. There's so much to do. Tony wants me there by Friday for some big party he's organised.'

'Of course, there must be lots to arrange.'

'But why don't Marta and I come up here for supper in the evening? It's your turn to host, isn't it?'

'Marta wouldn't mind?'

'Of course not. She feels horrible about the row. She wants to be nice and make it up to us both.'

We were silent for a while and then she said, 'You will be all right, won't you?'

I reassured her that I would.

'What will you do?'

'I'm going to go home to my wife, just like you said.'

Isabella looked relieved to hear it. 'Once you've patched things up, the two of you must come and visit me in New York.'

I told her it was a splendid idea, and I went into the house for some notepaper, and she wrote her cousin's address down and gave it to me.

Then she gave me her usual Italian kisses and we parted as the best of friends.

Chapter XXII

That night I dreamt in my mother tongue; everything from the names of the objects in the room and the names of the stars twinkling through the window, to the words of the lullaby my mother was softly singing, even the voice that came from my mouth. As soon as I woke I got up and went to the study, and the words poured from me and onto the page.

It was as if Father Gomez was there in the flesh. I saw him outlined in such great detail, I knew the very thoughts in his head. I knew the words he would say, how he would say them, and what emotions would bubble up in his soul as he said them. He was a holy man, lit up by his love for God, yet torn apart with secrets and torments. He had regrets, of course, and times when he wished he'd been stronger, but he needed to realise that decisions can only be judged in the moment. The deciding is part of the judging and the judgement is the decision.

I would sooner kill myself, I realised, than put on that black cap and call an end to Father Gomez.

So I typed him a happy ending, a lived-happily-ever-after ending, and he grew old and understood how decisions could only be judged in the moment and he forgave himself. And, as soon as he forgave himself, he began to live again, despite the fact that he was old.

And it all came out, flowing into that mechanical box.

Even the machine agreed to the process; the keys no longer became wedged together, but they splattered smoothly onto the pages like raindrops on hot tarmac.

All day I typed. Then I stacked the pages on the table and made sure all the edges were neat; then I tied up the bundle with a ribbon from Rodriguez's bureau. How satisfying it was to see. There were chores to be done after that.

I fetched the white suit from the laundry, and hung it in Rodriguez's wardrobe. Next I pulled my suitcase out from under the bed. How forlorn the shiny blue lining looked without any *pesetas* to care for, so I quickly filled it with the clothes with which I had arrived on the island. I was very careful not to accidentally take anything that belonged to Rodriguez. Then I took the case and put it downstairs by the front door, hidden behind a chest so that the girls wouldn't see it.

Afterwards, I went to the larder and pulled out all the last bits of cheese and ham. I made fresh mayonnaise from the last of the eggs and added wild garlic from the garden. There was one loaf of bread left and two bottles of wine, which I fetched from the cellar. I had just laid the usual red cloth down upon the table in front of the house, and placed this feast upon it, when the sound of Isabella and Marta's chatter came from the direction of the cliff path. It sounded as though the girls were rising up from the very sea itself.

When they arrived, they found me scrubbed and cheery and the best host anyone could imagine. Isabella had brought with her a record that had arrived in the post that very morning from her cousin. It was a recording from the festival she had missed, with Bob Dylan and Jonny Cash, and she said with great joy how it made her feel as if she was nearly back there already. She said she was so excited she couldn't wait, although she was going to miss us both terribly.

'Put it on, Thomas, and let's dance.'

So I went into the house and cranked the volume up and

Isabella and I danced to *Big River* amongst the wildflowers while Marta watched on, nodding her head in time with the music.

Afterwards, Marta and I danced. Though it was awkward and didn't last for long, there was peace between us and I forced myself to smile at her and she forced herself to smile back at me, and though I knew we wouldn't ever be friends, at least we would never now be enemies. After all, we had both lost Isabella.

Then I danced with Isabella again for an age, and I held her and we laughed and I spun her round. It was like that first day when we went to the beach, and she had laughed at the heap of stuff I was carrying, when we were both at the start of our time here on the island, when everything had been new and in front of us. And it felt like that again – that everything was in front of us and about to happen. Not to us together, I don't mean that, but separately in our own individual ways.

When they left, I kissed Isabella goodbye, first on the cheek and then on the hand. I held her hand, and held it, and wouldn't let go, until she laughed and tugged it away. Then she turned and blew me a kiss and then she was gone.

I didn't sleep that night. I sat in the sweltering heat, under the stars, and listened to the ocean until the sun rose over the top of the palms at the bottom of the garden. A breeze took up and made their blackened leaves clatter as they knocked together, and the whole place was filled with the heavy scent of jasmine.

Eventually I got up and tidied the house; then I fed the remains of the food to the sea birds out on the cliff. The sea looked particularly beautiful that day, with the sun catching the edges of the waves making the white horses sparkle as if they had been gifted diamond bridles. I looked up at a plane in the sky and wondered if Isabella might be on it.

I spent much of the day like that, brushing up the dead leaves of the bougainvillea, making sure the garden chairs were back where they should be in the *casita*, and all the things I had picked up and carried from one room to another were back were they had been when I'd first arrived.

When the sun was once more touching the tops of the trees, I went up to Rodriguez's bedroom and opened his closet. There was the suit, with its white linen, so soft and beloved, an old man with a stoop.

I sat on the bed and waited until it became properly dark. Then I stripped naked and lay down under the sheet. I must have dozed off, because when I awoke it was to the sound of Rodriguez, gently calling to me from downstairs.

'Come down,' he whispered.

I knew he wanted to show me something but I wasn't ready to see it. Soon I would need to take my case and say goodbye to *Ca'n Mola*. I would have to find some way back to England and fall upon the mercy of my wife. How her father would make me pay, over and over.

But I knew that wasn't what Rodriguez had in mind. He didn't want me to return to that failure of a life; to the smog (more dependable than I), to the greys, to London Bridge, and to the rows of gardens and sheds and lawnmowers and ice-cream vans.

'Come down, Thomas,' Rodriguez called out, more crossly this time. Then he tempered himself, like an adult who realises it does no good to lose one's patience with a child, and he continued again more gently by saying, 'Come down, Thomas. There *is* another way.'

But I was reluctant to go to him. I didn't want to hear about his other way. I had a suspicion I knew what it was.

'You don't exist,' I called to him, pitifully, and I leant over and peered around the corner of the door. But there he was, looking up at me, as real as any man could be. His face had an expression that showed his fatherly concern.

'Come down,' he replied.

I knew there was nothing for it. Even if I got under the bed, and hid there forever, he would wait just as long.

So reluctantly I got to my feet and wrapped the sheet around me. I went down the stairs and followed him through the house. He stopped by one particular door and indicated I should go in.

'Go on,' he said and pointed at the study.

I held back.

'Do as I say,' he said, and now that he had me there he finally allowed himself to lose his temper, and he pushed me through the door. I knew what it was he wanted me to look at.

I glanced at the bundle of pages I'd finished typing the day before. The blue ribbon tied around it partly obscured the manuscript's title, *The Tale of Father Gomez*. But I knew that wasn't it.

Rodriguez raised a hand and pointed at the shelf.

I didn't want to do as Rodriguez directed and tried to back out of the study, but he blocked the door. 'Let me out,' I whined, but he wouldn't. 'Get out of my way, Rodriguez!' I shouted.

Then he took me roughly by the arms and wrists and he forced me forward over towards the shelf. He couldn't care less that my legs had collapsed beneath me and that now he was forcibly dragging me forward.

'Please,' I said, even more pitifully. 'Don't do it, Rodriguez.'

Rodriguez used his knees to pin me in place and prevent me from escaping, his hand slipping on the white sheet that was still wrapped round me so that my chest was bared. His strength surprised me. Then he reached up and took a manuscript from the shelf and forced it into my hands. By now I was crying and begging him to let me go but Rodriguez didn't care.

Through my tears I turned the manuscript over and smoothed out its crumpled edges and wiped off the dust that clung to it. I read the title and looked up at Rodriguez, but now he was silent.

The title of the manuscript was made up of five words. They were printed clearly and correctly on the front sheet. There had obviously been no difficulty for Rodriguez with this one. It was *The Tale of Thomas Sebastian*.

'What does it mean?' I asked, but still he didn't answer. He just stood back to give me a little more room and waited, and I knew what I was supposed to do.

I placed the manuscript on the floor and turned to the first page. It read,

> *My name is Thomas Sebastian. I am an Englishman, well-bred but not overly so. My father sold machine parts across the Americas. I have his nervous temperament and thick, clumsy fingers. Mother died when I was young. There is little of her left in me — just my unnaturally dark eyes, too dark for an Englishman, and the hint of a Latin tongue which I can't seem to shake off.*

I looked at Senyor Rodriguez, but his placid face gave no brook to my confusion and fear.

'Why did you write about me, Rodriguez?'

My eyes were drawn back to the manuscript, though it made me sick to continue.

> *My parents met in Venezuela where my father had taken across a new threshing machine for sale. It was to revolutionise harvests no matter the crop — coffee, tobacco, sugar, opium — it would work as well for all.*

The next time I looked up, Rodriguez was gone. I threw the papers onto the floor and ran into the hall.

'Rodriguez!' I shouted. 'Where are you?'

There was no answer, so, clutching the sheet to my chest, I took a limping run through the rooms and shouted at him to come out. Then I raced up to the bedroom and searched for him there.

'Why have you written my story?' I demanded, but he wasn't there either, so I limped back down and over to the back of the house. Then I went out and into the empty cellar.

'Tell me!' I stormed. 'How have you done it?'

But I couldn't find him anywhere. So I went back to the hall to wait for him. I lay down on the floor with my head under the bureau.

Had Rodriguez written his book before he had met me? It was impossible – yet my fingers were thick with the dust from it, and I knew in my heart they had trailed across that manuscript before, yet somehow failed to pull it out from the shelf.

Rodriguez had written about me – before we had met. He had written of my parents, of my wife and my life in England. He had written everything – even that preposterous story of how my father and my mother had met, and of how my mother had died – and then, after all of that, Rodriguez had killed himself.

I didn't know if he was still around.

'Rodriguez, are you there?' I said in a whisper. And, as I whispered to him, I looked across the floorboards at what I saw in the foot of the looking glass fixed to the wall of the hall. How round my face had become. The jowls of one side of it were squashed up against the floor.

I saw my stubble of a beard, and my scraggy long hair spilling out onto the floorboards, and I looked at my swarthy skin. How I had come to look like Rodriguez, I thought, now that my island life had fattened me up, and the sun had stripped me of that wan skin and those hollow cheeks.

And then I thought of how I stood like Rodriguez these days, up square, with my hands in my pockets and the jacket of the white linen tucked behind, with that confidence of his. Not like Thomas at all, with his uncertainty and affected politeness.

I called out to Rodriguez and asked him the question I'd

been afraid to ask for so long.

'Rodriguez, am I you?'

There was no reply. I knew he was gone. He was gone, but still he was here, beneath the bureau.

As I lay there, the notion of being Rodriguez fell over me in much the same way as the sheet. It crumpled and clung and was cold, yet comforting.

I looked up from where I lay, to the unstained grain of the wood on the bottom of the bureau, then over to the barometer on the wall, to the light fitting and the lintel above the door of the sitting room. And I knew they were all mine. They belonged to me.

Indeed they belonged to me along with a thousand other things that flooded into my brain – cars, fountain pens, bedrooms, ornaments, contracts of employment for housekeepers and gardeners, watches and paintings. I thought of each of them, and it was as if I could see all those things in my head at once, down to the smallest details; the smooth dark blue of my favourite Mont Blanc in a house in Gstaad, the mix of brown and white pebbles in a gravel driveway, the way the maid's curls swept down to tickle her nose when she polished the bronzes lined out in a hallway the length of a yacht.

For a second I felt the joy in all of those possessions; the pride that I should own them, that I had chosen each and every one of them, with my taste and excellent eye. But that second was followed in an instant by another, which is always the way. And the weight of all of those things fell upon me, with a smothering, cloying grasp, demanding attention and praise and reassurance.

How lucky Thomas Sebastian had been, to have been a failure; to have lost everything he had ever owned, to have gambled and risked it all away in one disastrous venture after another. How I'd envied him. From the moment I'd first laid pen to paper and began to tell his tale, I'd envied him.

And I'd loved him too – such a ridiculous man, so pompous

yet unsure of himself; so desperate to please, yet so happy to fail.

I wasn't sure what to do. So I remembered instead. There was the fall from the cliffs. The way the water had punched me like an angry friend, hard on the jaw. It had made my head snap back and my skull become filled with a white hissing.

I remembered the cold blues at the bottom of the sea; I remembered drifting up to the sun, floating in its warmth; I remembered the fishermen who dragged and pulled at me and hoisted me out, while I moaned and begged them to give me back to the sea. I thought of their voices, their kindly and confused tones.

And later – was it Rodriguez or Thomas who had peeped through the windows of a palace and saw the fountain pens and paperweights, so tasteful and expensive? Who knew where the safe was? Who crept in and filled his pockets with cash?

'Thomas,' I cried out. 'Come back to me, Thomas,' and I swore out loud in my agony – he was gone. But he wouldn't come back. He was trapped once more in the pages that were thrown onto the floor of the study. Dead little letters, frozen flat to the page. And I mourned him.

I pulled my head out from under the bureau and hoisted myself up to a sitting position. My legs were numb from the hardwood floor, so it was a struggle to stand. I had to lean against the door frame as I stumbled out into the garden, into the hot night air. My sheet trailed on the ground and caught on the wild flowers, so I wrapped it tight around me. What was I to do?

Some instinct drew me down to the front of the estate, down to those old gates that were hung open and rusted, where the moon could be seen shining onto the sea. It was a thinner moon than when I had stood with Isabella, when her hand had slipped into mine.

I ignored the gap between the gate posts, and instead

worked my way into the bushes to one side of them. I had to scramble up the bank and fight my way through the brambles until I stood on the top of the mound, my feet catching at old rock and previously undisturbed soil. Twigs and leaves restrained me, their messy confusion snared at my sheet and stopped me from falling down onto the path.

It would be the work of little effort to launch myself forward, to come falling out, perhaps even to let my momentum carry me forward, stumbling and tumbling over to the cliff edge, my arms flailing in thin air.

I stood there for what seemed an eternity. I don't know how long. My mind was blank. I hadn't a framework by which to measure the passage of time and my conscious thoughts were elsewhere, flitting between names and worlds and people and other ways of thinking.

There were parties and people I had loved; some who had loved me and some who had not loved me; those who had cared for me, and those who had not; some who had cared for my money, even some who had not.

Eventually I heard the sound of singing and drums. It was just a suggestion on the breeze at first, floating in and out, as faraway sounds will. Then the beat of the drums became all and my heart and stomach pounded in time with them.

Next I saw the people themselves, coming up from the village. The hooded figures came first. They held things aloft. A Jesus and two of his mothers came floating by. I gazed at them through the branches as they passed with their lilting sway.

Next came the men of the church in a sombre march, stepping in time with the beat of the drums.

When they were safely past I fought my way out and down from the bushes and stepped onto the cliff path. I watched the procession from behind as it went slowly up the hill. Then I put the sheet over my head and pulled it tight under my chin so that I would look like the churchmen at the front of the queue. The head of Jesus could still be seen

223

swaying above them all.

But they had not all passed. There were straggling children. They moved about me and around me. At first they went by without taking any notice, chattering amongst themselves, but then one turned back and took a look at me, and then another, and then they all stopped and started to whisper and tug at one another's sleeves. But I continued forward, and they scattered like pebbles under my feet.

'Look out!' they shouted, crying for their mamas as they went, 'The ghost of Rodriguez is coming!'

But no one listened to them, and their cries mingled in with the singing and the drums, and they were shushed and told not to be naughty. So I continued on until I was right in amongst them all. I stood with them where the path ends and plunges down the cliff and into the sea.

So many things filled my mind at that moment: the duty and greed and the selfishness of others. I remembered being tired, so tired of it all. I remembered retreat – first to an island, but it wasn't enough. So I went further and remembered my retreat to a man.

And Thomas Sebastian, what a man you were. So polite and diffident. So ready to fall in love and so wanting to be filled by life. I'm so glad you saw the city at night, with its walls of stone bathed in the orange street light. How I loved you.

How I regret you never saw the city at dawn, when it was waking.

What a sight that is. To see the lofty green shutters pop open, propelled by disembodied hands as the sunlight stalks into the alleyways and falls upon the windows one by one; to see the old women unbolting the cross gates of their shops and throwing water on the pavement, or the menfolk sent out with tiny dogs for the first morning pee; or the bearded fathers in their black robes and black overcoats who come to the chocolatiers, *Ca'n Joan de S'Aigo*, for coffee early in the morning before the tourists fall upon it like a pestilence.

I want to see all those things again. But I want to see them with fresh eyes so I can understand their beauty once more. Such a rush of blood and passion and joy it brings me to think of it.

Father Gomez is an early riser. He wanders the city at dawn when the sun is fresh and barely ripe, still orange and red. He is a kind and holy man. He nods, I nod, at the shopkeepers, at the old men with their dogs. As he stands by those great doors of the cathedral, he smiles at the congregation, at the lectors, the catechists, and the dismissal leaders who are gathered to sing and pray. The coachmen nod respectfully back at him as they set up their carriages for the day and find themselves a favourite spot in which to wait for the tourists.

'Bon dia, Pare,' they call out to me, and I nod back in a way that lets them know they are blessed and worthy of God's love. I place my hands behind my back, and tuck my fingers into the cloth of my black robe.

I feel the sun on my face as I walk onto the quay in front of the Seu. The walls of the cathedral rise up behind me, protecting me and proclaiming the power of my meekness. The congregation are singing. Their voices are all around me. How they gasp with delight to see that I am with them and amongst them again. What a cry they take up, full of love and fear and respect, all mixed together.

I am Father Gomez, a priest of the city. I will fall and let the waters take me. I will swim to the shore and be born again on the white beaches.

Down, down I go. As I dive, my robes fly out around me. I am Father Gomez. Let me tell you my tale.

ACKNOWLEDGEMENTS

With thanks to Ruth, Dave, Kathy, Lee, Andrew, Tamsin, Megan, Debra, Wendy, Geoff, Ian, Swithun, Zie and Aliya for their unwavering support, encouragement and assistance.

Thanks also to Emma Davis for providing so much inspiration, and to the team at Fine Books on Calle Morey for so enthusiastically finding me a 1963 guidebook to Majorca amongst their treasures.

And thanks to Johnnie and, in memory, Rene, in much appreciation for their unsurpassed and unfailing hospitality at Son Boronat, which inspired *Ca'n Mola* in many ways.

With additional thanks to Anna Davis, Emma Herdman and Lesley Jones.

ALSO AVAILABLE FROM FAIRLIGHT BOOKS

The Madonna of the Pool
Stories

by HELEN STANCEY

The Madonna of the Pool is a moving collection of short stories which explore the triumphs, compromises and quiet disappointments of everyday life. Drawing on a wide array of characters, Helen Stancey shows how small events, insignificant to some, can resonate deeply in the lives of others.

Richly poetic and entirely engaging, these short stories demonstrate an exquisite understanding of human adaptation, endurance and, most of all, optimism.

Author of *Words* and *Common Ground*, Helen Stancey's writing has been greeted with great critical acclaim:

'In the poised assurance of its writing,… one has a sense of a writer gifted with an instinctive sense of how to tell a story.'
– SPECTATOR

'writing so accomplished…' – TABLET

'palpable excellence' – LITERARY REVIEW